or Captive Trail

Fans of the Old West will welcome another tale with classic elements—a beautiful captive, her rescuer, and her pursuer. Susan Page Davis knows how to immerse her readers in the frontier setting. A compelling read, reminiscent of Louis L'Amour.

—LYN COTE, author, Texas Star of Destiny series

Susan Page Davis's *Captive Trail* stands up to Conrad Richter's classic *The Light in the Forest* as a novel of substance that will endure. Texan Taabe Waipu, like Richter's young Pennsylvanian captive hero, is conflicted over her identity. She escapes a forced Comanche marriage, and her plight tugs at the reader's heart to draw him into a real page-turner of a Western frontier tale.

—ERIC WIGGIN, author of *The Hills of God* and the Hannah's Island series.

*Captive Trai*l blends a powerful plot, rich historical details, and remarkable characters into a story I won't soon forget. Susan Page Davis wove a compelling tale that drove me to set aside everything else to discover what happened—truly a unique and enjoyable read!

—MIRALEE FERRELL, author of *Love Finds You in Sundance, Wyoming*

With *Captive Trail,* Susan Page Davis really captures the essence of Texas in the middle 1850s—the diverse people, the clashing cultures, the setting. I've actually lived near Fort Phantom Hill and recognized the authenticity of her depiction. And

her story captured my heart. This is one of the best books I've read this year. I highly recommend it.

—LENA NELSON DOOLEY, award-winning author of the McKenna's Daughters series and *Love Finds You in Golden, New Mexico*

Susan Page Davis's *Captive Trail* is a wonderfully descriptive tale that will lure you in on page 1 and not let go until you've read The End. Escape and freedom, courage and faith, and the sometimes fearsome beauty of the wild Texas landscape combine for a fast-paced, spirit-filled read. Make space on your keepers shelf for this one!

—LOREE LOUGH, bestselling author of more than 80 award-winning novels, including *From Ashes to Honor*

Captive Trail (along with many other titles by Susan Page Davis—who is high on my list of favorite authors) earns a place on my overcrowded book shelves. Action, authenticity, and compelling characters combine with masterful writing to make it a real page-turner . . . one I would be proud to have written!

—COLLEEN L. REECE, author of more than 140 titles (totaling over six million copies sold)

TEXAS
TRAILS

CAPTIVE TRAIL

SUSAN PAGE DAVIS

A
MORGAN FAMILY
SERIES

MOODY PUBLISHERS
CHICAGO

Edited by Andy Scheer
Interior design: Ragont Design
Cover design: Gearbox
Cover images: 123rf, istockphoto, jupiterimages and Veer
Author photo: Marion Sprague of Elm City Photo

Library of Congress Cataloging-in-Publication Data

Davis, Susan Page.
Captive trail / by Susan Page Davis.
p. cm. -- (Texas trails: a Morgan Family series)
ISBN 978-0-8024-0584-5 (alk. paper)
1. Families—History—Fiction. 2. Texas—History—19th century—Fiction. I. Title.

PS3604.A976C37 2011
813'.6—dc22

2011022407

We hope you enjoy this book from River North Fiction by Moody Publishers. Our goal is to provide high-quality, thought-provoking books and products that connect truth to your real needs and challenges. For more information on other books and products written and produced from a biblical perspective, go to www.moodypublishers.com or write to:

River North Fiction
Division of Moody Publishers
820 N. LaSalle Boulevard
Chicago, IL 60610

1 3 5 7 9 10 8 6 4 2

Printed in the United States of America

To my husband, Jim,
who has been through so much with me.

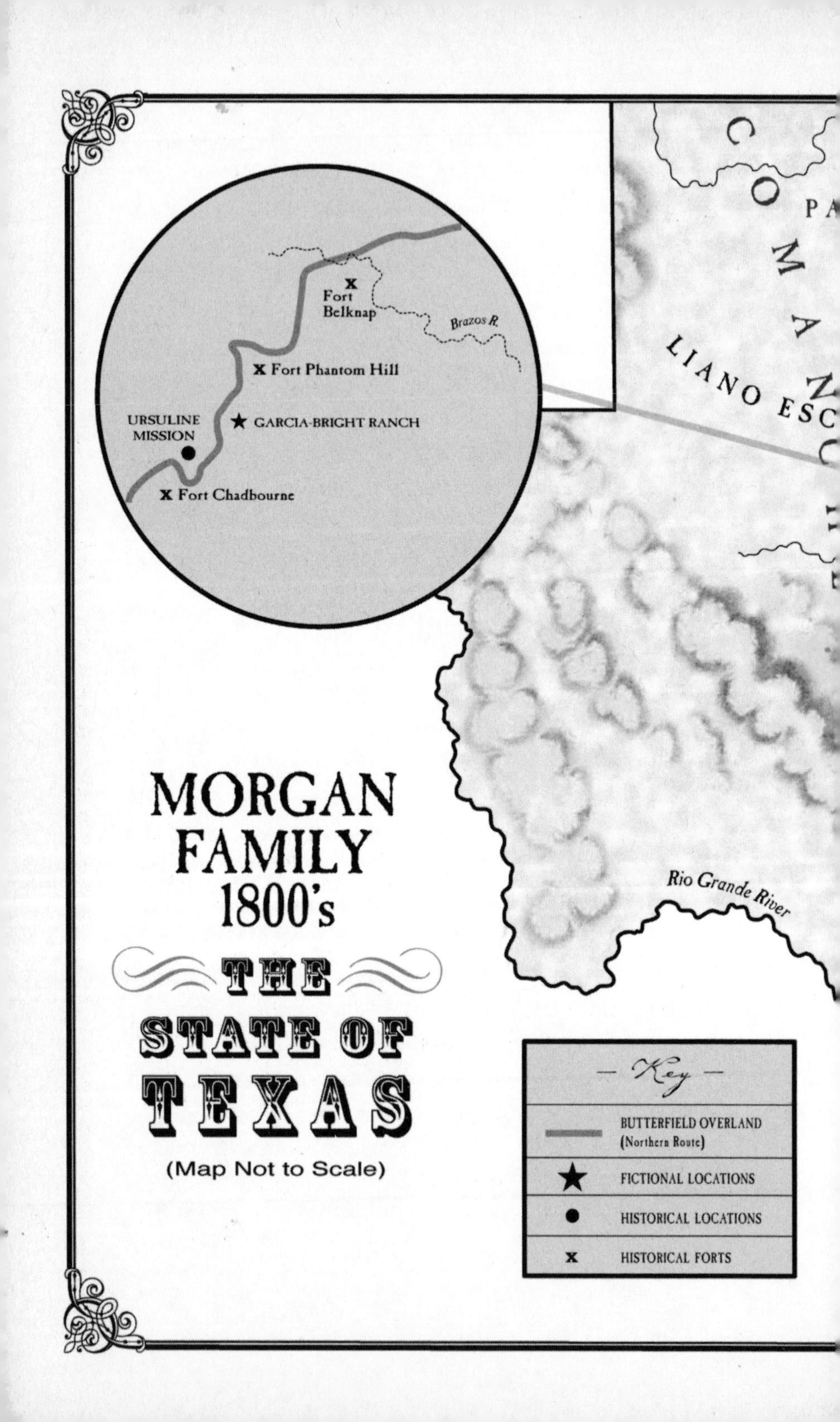

MORGAN FAMILY 1800's
THE STATE OF TEXAS
(Map Not to Scale)
Fort Belknap
Brazos R.
Fort Phantom Hill
URSULINE MISSION
GARCIA-BRIGHT RANCH
Fort Chadbourne
LIANO ESC
Rio Grande River
Key
BUTTERFIELD OVERLAND (Northern Route)
FICTIONAL LOCATIONS
HISTORICAL LOCATIONS
HISTORICAL FORTS

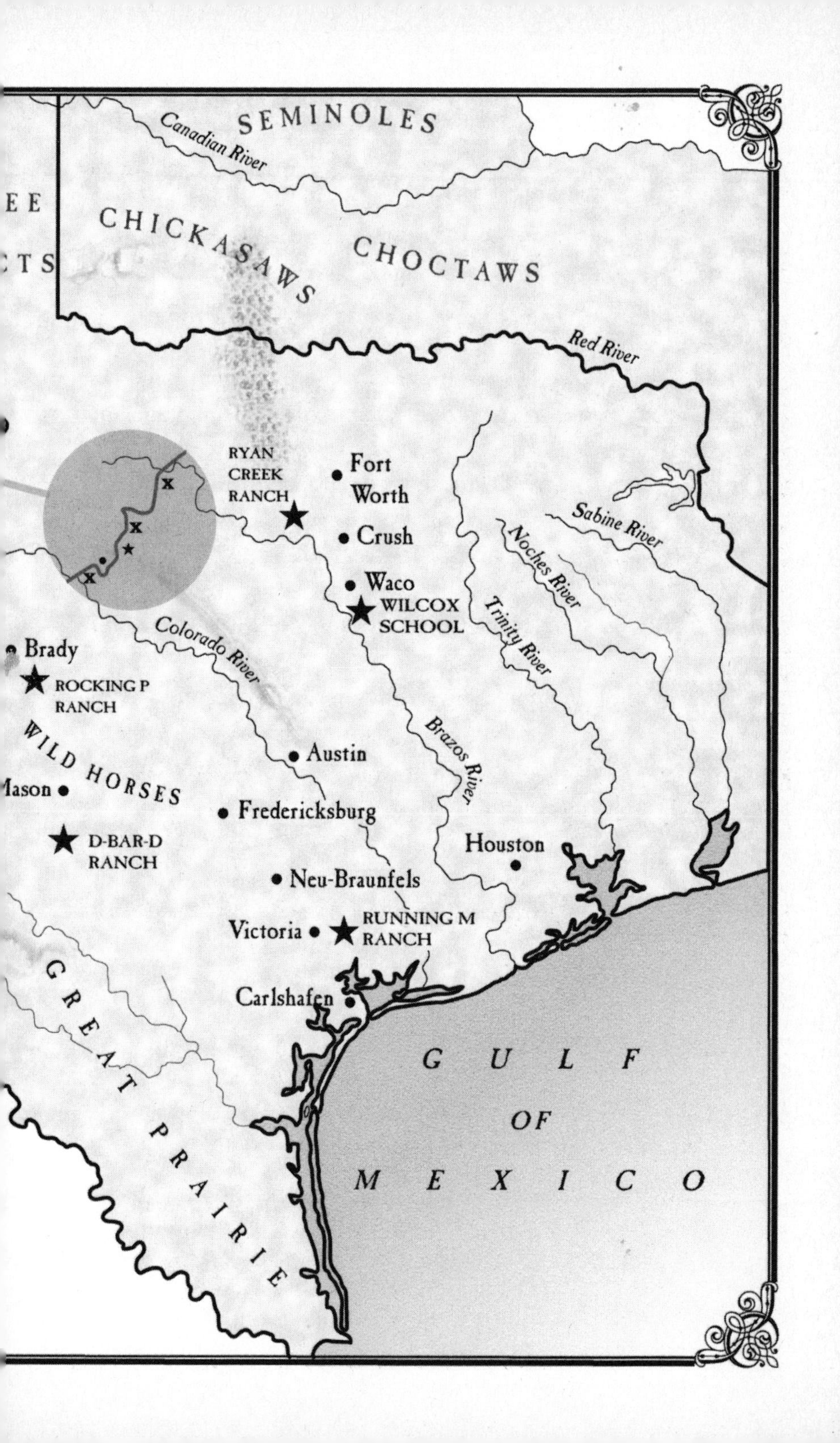

SEMINOLES
Canadian River
EE
CHICKASAWS
CHOCTAWS
TS
Red River
RYAN
CREEK
RANCH
Fort
Worth
Crush
Waco
WILCOX
SCHOOL
Sabine River
Noches River
Trinity River
Colorado River
Brady
ROCKING P
RANCH
WILD HORSES
Brazos River
Austin
Mason
Fredericksburg
D-BAR-D
RANCH
Houston
Neu-Braunfels
Victoria
RUNNING M
RANCH
Carlshafen
GREAT PRAIRIE
GULF
OF
MEXICO

PROLOGUE

1845

Taabe Waipu huddled against the outside wall of the tepee and wept. The wind swept over the plains, and she shivered uncontrollably. After a long time, the stars came out and shone coldly on her. Where her tears had fallen, her dress was wet and clammy.

At last her sobs subsided. The girl called Pia came out of the lodge. She stood before Taabe and scowled down at her.

Taabe hugged herself and peered up at Pia. "Why did she slap me?"

Pia shook her head and let out a stream of words in the Comanche language. Taabe had been with them several weeks, but she caught only a few words. The one Pia spat out most vehemently was "English."

"English? She hit me because I am English?"

Pia shook her head and said in the Comanche's tongue, "You are Numinu now. No English."

Taabe's stomach tightened. "But I'm hungry."

Pia again shook her head. "You talk English. Talk Numinu."

So much Taabe understood. She sniffed. "Can I come in now?"

"No," Pia said in Comanche.

"Why?"

Pia stroked her fingers down her cheeks, saying another word in Comanche.

Taabe stared at her. They would starve her and make her stay outside in winter because she had cried. What kind of people were these? Tears flooded her eyes again. Horrified, she rubbed them away.

"Please." She bit her lip. How could she talk in their language when she didn't know the words?

She rubbed her belly, then cupped her hand and raised it to her mouth.

Pia stared at her with hard eyes. She couldn't be more than seven or eight years old, but she seemed to have mastered the art of disdain.

She spoke again, and this time she moved her hands as she talked in the strange language. Taabe watched and listened. The impression she got was, "Wait."

Taabe repeated the Comanche words.

Pia nodded.

Taabe leaned back against the buffalo-hide wall and hugged herself, rubbing her arms through the leather dress they'd given her.

Pia nodded and spoke. She made the "wait" motion and repeated the word, then made a "walking" sign with her fingers. Wait. Then walk. She ducked inside the tepee and closed the flap.

Taabe shivered. Her breath came in short gasps. She would not cry. She would not. She wiped her cheeks, hoping to remove all sign of tears. How long must she wait? Her teeth chattered. *It is enough*, she thought. *I will not cry. I will not ask for food. I will not speak at all. Especially not English. English is bad. I must forget English.*

She looked to the sky. "Jesus, help me learn their language. And help me not to cry." She thought of her mother praying at her bedside when she tucked her in at night. What was Ma doing now? Maybe Ma was crying too.

Stop it, Taabe told herself. Until they come for you, you must live the way the Comanche do. No, the Numinu. They call themselves Numinu. For now, that is what you are. You are Taabe Waipu, and you will not speak English. You will learn to speak Numinu, so you can eat and stay strong.

She hauled in a deep breath and rose. She tiptoed to the lodge entrance and lifted the edge of the flap. Inside she could see the glowing embers of the fire. The air was smoky, but it smelled good, like cooked food. She opened the flap just enough to let herself squeeze through. She crouched at the wall, as far from Pia's mother as she could. The tepee was blessedly warm. If they didn't give her food, she would just curl up and sleep. Since she had come here, she had often gone to bed hungry.

Pia didn't look at her. Pia's mother didn't look at her. Taabe lay down with her cheek on the cool grass. After a while it would feel warm.

She woke sometime later, shivering. Pia and her mother were rolled in their bedding on the other side of the fire pit. The coals still glowed faintly. Taabe sat up. Someone had dropped a buffalo robe beside her. She pulled it about her. No cooking pot remained near the fire. No food had been left for her.

At least she had the robe. She curled up in it and closed her eyes, trying to think of the Comanche words for "thank you." She wasn't sure there were any. But she would not say it in English. Ever.

CHAPTER ONE

PLAINS OF NORTH CENTRAL TEXAS, 1857

Faster. Taabe Waipu had to go faster, or she would never get down from the high plains, down to the hill country and beyond. South, ever south and east.

Clinging to the horse, she let him run. The land looked flat all around, though it was riddled with ravines and folds. She could no longer see any familiar landmarks. The moon and stars had guided her for two nights, and now the rising sun told her which way to go on her second day of flight. She'd snatched only brief periods of rest. At her urging the horse galloped on, down and up the dips and hollows of the land.

Taabe didn't know where the next water supply lay. The only thing she knew was that she must outrun the Numinu—*Comanche*, their enemies called them. No one traveled these plains without their permission. Those who tried didn't make it out again. She glanced over her shoulder in the gray dawn. As far as she could see, no one followed, but she couldn't stop. They were back there, somewhere. She urged the horse on toward the southeast.

South to the rolling grasslands where the white men had their ranches. Where Peca and the other men often went to raid. Where Taabe was born.

The compact paint stallion ran smoothly beneath her, but as the sun rose and cast her shadow long over the Llano Estacado, his breath became labored, his stride shorter. Where her legs hugged his sleek sides, her leggings dampened with his sweat. He was a good horse, this wiry paint that Peca had left outside her sister's tepee. Without him she wouldn't have gotten this far. But no horse could run forever.

Taabe slowed him to a trot but didn't dare rest. Not yet.

Another look behind.

No one.

Would she recognize the house she'd once lived in? She didn't think so, but she imagined a big earthen lodge, not a tepee. Or was it a cabin made of logs? That life was a shadow world in her mind now. Fences. The warriors talked about the fences built by the white men, around their gardens and their houses. She thought she recalled climbing a fence made of long poles and sitting on the top. When she saw fences, she would know she was close.

At last she came to a shallow stream, sliding between rocks and fallen trees. It burbled languidly where it split around a boulder. She let the horse wade in and bend down to drink.

Taabe stayed on his back while he drank in long, eager gulps, keeping watch over the way they'd come. She needed to find a sheltered place where the horse could graze and rest. Did she dare stop for a while? She studied the trail behind her then took her near-empty water skin from around her neck.

Leaning over the paint's side, she dangled it by its thong in the water on the horse's upstream side. She wouldn't dismount to fill it properly, but she could stay in the saddle and scoop up a little. She straightened and checked the trail again. The horse took a step and continued to drink.

She stroked his withers, warm and smooth. With a wry smile, she remembered the bride price Peca had left. Six horses staked out before the tepee. A stallion and five mares—pretty mares. Healthy, strong mounts. But only six.

The stallion raised his head at last and waded across the stream without her urging. They settled into a steady trot. Tomorrow or the next day or the next, she would come to a land with many trees and rivers. And many houses of the whites.

Would she have stayed if Peca had left twenty horses? Fifty?

Not for a thousand horses would she have stayed in the village and married Peca—or any other warrior. Staying would make it impossible for her ever to go back to that other world—the world to the south.

Eagerness filled her, squeezing out her fear. She dug her heels into the stallion's ribs. Whatever awaited her, she rushed to meet it.

The paint lunged forward and down. His right front hoof sank, and he didn't stop falling. Taabe tried to brace herself, too late. The horse's body continued to fly up and around. She hurtled off to the side and tucked her head.

"Today's the day, Ned."

"Yup." Ned Bright coiled his long driver's whip and grinned at his partner in the stagecoach business, Patrillo Garza. He and "Tree" had scraped up every penny and peso they could to outfit their ranch as a stage stop, in hopes of impressing the Butterfield Overland Mail Company's division agent. Their efforts had paid off. Tree was now the station agent at the Bright-Garza Station, and Ned would earn his keep as driver between the ranch and Fort Chadbourne. "Never thought everything would go through and we'd be carrying the mail."

"Well, it did, and as of today we're delivering," Tree said. "Now, remember—the mail is important, but not at the passengers' expense."

"Sure." Ned took his hat from a peg on the wall and fitted it onto his head with the brim at precisely the angle he liked. "But if we lose the mail on our first run, we're not apt to keep the contract, are we?"

Tree scowled. "We ain't gonna lose the mail, ya hear me?"

"I hear you."

"Right. We've made this run hundreds of times."

It was true. The two had hauled freight and passengers to the forts for several years. They'd scraped by. But the contract with the Butterfield Overland would mean steady pay and good equipment. Reimbursement if they were robbed.

"Oh, and you've got some passengers," Tree said, offhand.

"Great. That's where we make a profit, right?"

"Well . . ." Tree seemed unable to meet his gaze. "There were nuns, see, and—"

"None? I thought you said there were some."

"Nuns, Ned. Catholic nuns. Sisters."

Ned's jaw dropped. "You're joshing."

Tree shook his head. "Nope. There's a pack of 'em at the old Wisher place, out near Fort Chadbourne. Came out from Galveston a month ago to start a mission."

"A mission? What kind of mission?"

"A Catholic one, what do you think? They're going to start a school, like the one in Galveston."

Ned eyed him suspiciously. "You're making this up."

"Nope. Somebody gave them the land, and the convent in Galveston sent them out here. I'm surprised you didn't know." Tree ran a hand through his glossy dark hair. "That's right—they came while you were off buying mules. Seriously, they intend to start a school for girls. I'm thinking of sending Quinta to them."

Ned stared at him. What would the station be like without Quinta? The nine-year-old followed her brothers around and alternately helped and got in the way. She swam like a water moccasin, rode like a Comanche, and yapped like a hungry pup. Since Quinta's mother died, Tree had pretty much given up trying to feminize her, and he let her run around in overalls and a shirt outgrown by Diego—the next child up the stairsteps.

"And I'm taking them to the fort?"

"Can't see any harm in dropping them at their place. It's right beside the road. Two of 'em caught a ride here to pick up some supplies that were donated to their cause, and I told them that if there was enough space, we could haul their stuff out to the mission without them paying extra for it."

"But freight is—"

Tree raised a hand as he turned away. "Don't start, Ned."

Esteban, Tree's third son, charged into the ranch house spouting in Spanish, "Papa, the stage is coming."

In the distance, a bugle sounded.

Tree laughed, his teeth flashing white. "Who needs a horn when you've got kids?" He tousled Esteban's hair. "You got the team ready?"

"Si."

"I'll be out in a minute." Tree hurried into the next room.

Ned stared after him. Only one way to find out if his partner was exaggerating. He strode for the door. Outside in the baking heat, Benito and Marcos, the two oldest boys, had brought the team out of the barn into the dusty yard and stood holding the leaders' heads.

To the right, waiting under the overhang of the eaves, stood two women in long, black dresses. Robes. Habits. Some sort of head shawl—black again, with white showing over their foreheads—covered their hair. Ned glowered at no one in particular.

To his left, Brownie Fale, Ned's shotgun rider, leaned against an adobe wall of the station. He nodded at Ned and spit a stream of tobacco juice into the dust. They'd ridden hundreds, maybe thousands of miles together, hauling tons of freight. No need to talk now.

The stage barreled into the yard in a cloud of dust and pulled up short. Ned looked over the high, curved body of the coach and pulled in a deep breath. Mighty fine rig. Driving it would be a pleasure, if it wasn't too top heavy. Putting some passengers and freight inside would help.

"Howdy, boys," he called to the two men on the box. He stepped forward and opened the coach door. No one was inside, but three sacks of mail lay on the floor between the front and middle benches.

The driver and shotgun rider jumped down.

"How do, Ned," said Sam Tunney. He and the shotgun rider headed out back to the privy while Tree's boys began to change out the teams. Benito held the incoming mules' heads, Diego and Esteban scrambled to unhitch them from the eveners, and Marcos stood by with the fresh team.

Ned turned and went back inside. Tree sauntered toward him carrying a bulging sack on his shoulder. On the side was stenciled "U.S. Mail."

"There's three sacks already in the stage," Ned said.

"*Bueno.* This'll make four." Tree pushed past him, out into the unrelenting sun. Ned followed. The nuns hadn't moved. Tree plunked the sack of mail into the coach then leaned in and set it over, arranging it just so with the other three. He straightened and nodded. "All right, passengers can load." He looked at the nuns. "All aboard, Sisters."

His second-oldest son, Marcos, waved from the rear of the coach's roof and hopped down.

As the nuns stepped forward, Tree said, "We've put your stuff in the boot. When you get to your place, the shotgun messenger will unload it for you."

"Thank you, Señor Garza," said the nearer of the two.

The women glided forward and, with a hand from Tree, mounted the step and disappeared inside the coach. Even with the mail sacks, they'd have plenty of room. Brownie sauntered over and climbed onto the driver's box.

"What do I call them?" Ned whispered as Tree turned back toward the station.

"What you mean? You don't have to call them anything."

Ned stepped into the shade of the eaves with him. "If we have an emergency or something."

"You won't."

Ned felt like slugging him. He'd never seen a nun before. Just knowing they would be sitting back there in the coach made him nervous. "I'm just saying, Tree."

The station agent sighed. "Call them sisters, then."

Ned shook his head. "I can't."

"You can't?"

"They're not—I mean—I'm not—"

"You're not Catholic."

Ned nodded.

"So call them ma'am, or ladies. Whatever polite names you'd call any woman in that situation."

"Right."

Tree nodded. "You know the place? It's about five miles this side of the fort. No one's lived there since Wisher left last fall. You've got no other passengers. If you make good time, you can swing in and set their boxes down for them. Won't take you five minutes."

"But we don't—"

"Ned. They're women." Tree shook his head and walked away.

Ned gulped and strode to the front of the stage. He swung up into the driver's seat and smiled. This was something. Much better than a freight wagon, even if he was driving mules. He'd hoped for horses, but the Butterfield had invested heavily in mules. He'd take it.

He gathered the reins of the four-in-hand team, released the brake, and nodded to Benito. The young man let go of the leaders' heads and stepped to the side. Ned gave his whip three pops, and the mules surged forward.

The team settled into a steady road trot. Ned glanced over at the shotgun messenger.

Brownie grinned. "Feels different from a wagon, don't it?"

"Sure does."

"Not too hot today, neither." Brownie cradled his shotgun in his arms.

Ned started to disagree, but held his tongue. Up here, they caught a pleasant breeze. With his hat and the wind of their speed, it wasn't bad. He held the reins and enjoyed the gentle swaying of the stage, the creak of the leathers, and the *clop* of shod hooves on the packed trail. The only thing that could make it better would be horses in the harness—and paying passengers.

CHAPTER TWO

Taabe opened her eyes. She lay on the ground between two clumps of buffalo grass, staring into the blue sky. The sun hung off to one side. She tried to sit up and moaned. Her head hurt and her arms ached.

The stallion. His fall came back to her. He must have stepped in a hole. She'd flown off to the side, and that was all she remembered. She forced herself to a sitting position. Sharp pains stabbed her right ankle.

She looked around, expecting to see the paint horse thrashing in the dirt, but she couldn't spot him. How far away could he be? She tried to stand and sank back with a grimace. Bruises she could deal with, but the ankle was bad. Had the bones broken? She didn't think so, but they might as well have. She was just as helpless.

She listened, hearing nothing but the wind over the plain.

Holding her right foot up behind her and using her knee and her left foot to push against the slippery grass, Taabe tried to rise. If the horse had survived the fall, maybe he was grazing nearby. But if not . . . She would have to leave as quickly as possible. If the horse lay dead or dying, Peca would soon see the vultures. And if the paint had headed back toward the Comanche village, the warriors would find him even quicker and swoop down on her.

She got a quick look around then fell back to earth and lay panting, fending off nausea from the pain. She'd seen no sign of the horse. He was a good horse, doing everything she'd asked—until she'd fallen off and left him to run free.

Taking stock of her possessions, so few now, she patted her torso. Her water skin still hung about her neck, but it had ruptured in the fall. Taabe pulled it off over her head. Her forearms stung where she'd smacked the ground. They bore red marks, but that was nothing. As she probed the skin beneath her right eye, she winced. The tissue was swollen and sore, but no blood came away on her fingertips. Her only serious injury seemed to be her ankle. Crushed for an instant as the horse fell and rolled? If that had happened, she ought to see him lying nearby. But he seemed to have gone on without her.

She untied the thong from the useless water skin and tucked it into her parfleche—the soft deerskin bag she'd made to hold her few personal items. The split water skin, fashioned from a buffalo's bladder, she dropped on the ground. It would do her no good.

After a second's thought, she grabbed it again. If Peca found it, he'd know she was nearby and desperate. She reached inside the parfleche, thankful she still had it, and felt the items, one by one. She hadn't brought much. Miraculously, her small wooden flute was still in one piece.

Only a handful of parched corn and a small bundle of pemmican remained. Enough for a day in ordinary times. It would have to last until she found another source of food. As to water, Taabe wouldn't need as much without the horse to care for. But she would need some. The rest of her burden consisted of a knife, a small pouch of beads her adopted sister had given her, a piece of paper too wilted and worn to crackle any more, and an extra pair of moccasins. She debated whether to drop any of it and decided to keep everything. If Peca got to this spot and hadn't found her horse, he would find no other clues to her desperation.

She looked at the sun and squinted against the pain brought on by its brightness, trying to orient herself. On the horse's back she'd sometimes seen distant landmarks—undulations in the land, small ponds where water collected, rock formations. Down here in the grass, her view was restricted. She needed to keep going southeast.

The sun was still climbing in the sky. She must have been unconscious only a short while. With clenched teeth, she rose on her knees and looked toward the north, the way she'd come, but couldn't see enough. With great effort, she stood on her left foot, holding the right at an angle, the way horses rested one foot while they stood.

The grass was bent where the paint had run through it, and she could see his trail. A few yards away, scuff marks revealed where he had fallen. She hopped a little closer. There was the hole her stallion had stepped in. There was where he'd hit the ground. She looked long in every direction, but he was gone.

Taabe turned her back to the place where they'd fallen. A stick would help support her weight. That seemed her only option—she couldn't crawl the rest of the way to the white man's land.

Several hundred yards to the southeast lay a line of treetops. It represented her best chance of finding both a walking stick and water. She hobbled toward it, gasping with each hitch of a step. After she'd gone ten yards, she lost her balance and toppled in the long grass. Once more she lay panting, gazing up at the sun. Her throbbing ankle almost made her forget the pain slicing through her head. For a moment she closed her eyes. Getting up was too hard. But if she stayed here, everything she'd done so far would be meaningless.

Taabe rolled to her knees, gritted her teeth, and pushed herself up.

"Did you know about this school the nuns are starting?" Ned asked as the stage started up a long, gradual hill.

Brownie nodded, his eyes scanning the prairie. "I heard something about it. Saw the sisters once when I was going to the fort."

"How many are there?"

"Four, I think."

Ned let that simmer as he guided the mules at a slow trot. Didn't seem right, four women living alone on the frontier. And they expected people to let them educate their children. Girls, no less. Didn't they know how many kids the roaming Apache and Comanche had snatched in the last few years? Out away from the forts, raids had become commonplace. Even the forts were no guarantee of safety. Still, the settlers kept coming and moving onto what had been Indian land. "They don't have a priest or anyone like that living there?"

"Nope," Brownie said. "Just sisters."

They crested the hill, and Ned let the mules set their own pace down the other side. Being mules, that was barely quicker than they'd gone up the hill under his urging, but that was all right. Mules were steady. Tough and steady.

The nuns' mission house should be a mile or so ahead, around a sharp bend near the stream. Ned thought he knew the place—a large adobe with a small pole barn and a shed. A corn crib, maybe. He'd seen that it stood empty and wondered why no one was squatting there. It wasn't a bad spot for a ranch. Wisher had run cattle on it and raised corn. If the nuns worked hard, they might make a go of it—especially if the parents paid well for their daughters' schooling. But it was still too dangerous for a pack of women to live out here without any men to protect them.

The off leader lagged a little, and Ned popped his whip. The mules picked up their pace. Ahead, something dark lay in the dusty road. Ned squinted at it but couldn't make it out.

"What is that?" he asked Brownie, who was scanning the range to the other side.

"What?" Brownie looked forward. "Oh. Can't tell."

"Dead deer, maybe?" Ned leaned forward, letting the mules clop toward it.

"It's a man," Brownie said.

"Whoa." Ned pulled on the reins. The mules stopped and stood swishing their tails. Ned eyed the dark form in the dirt ahead. It did look human. Someone wearing clothing darker than the road's packed earth, with a lighter blob at one end—a hat? Hair? The more he looked, the more certain he was that it was human.

It could be a trap. Someone planning to hold up the stage on its first mail run. "What do you think?"

Brownie spat over the side. "Don't know. Robbers usually stop you at a narrow place or a bridge. Go a little closer."

Ned searched the sides of the road. There wasn't a lot of cover, but Mescalero could hide in the grass or behind a rock no bigger than a bucket. He could whip up the mules and approach at full speed—or maybe take the stage off the road across the open ground. "I'm not losing the mail." He gathered the reins.

"Excuse me! Driver?"

Ned flinched. One of the nuns had spoken. They'd been

so quiet on the four-hour ride, he'd almost forgotten about them, except when they'd stopped at a swing station to change teams.

"Yes, ma'am?"

"Is there a problem?"

He craned his neck, leaned over the side, and looked down at her. She'd stuck her head out the window and was staring up at him.

"Yes, ma'am. It looks like someone's lying in the road up ahead. We—"

Before he could finish, the stagecoach door opened. The nun climbed down in a swirl of black skirts.

"Ma'am, don't—"

Too late. She moved faster than a jackrabbit. Already she was past the wheelers.

"Ma'am, wait. You'd best stay in the coach and let us look into it."

She looked back at him, her brown eyes sharp. "Then do it. That person could be in dire straits."

"Yes, ma'am. Or could be waiting to ambush us." She was just an ordinary woman, Ned told himself. The nun had faint wrinkles around her mouth and eyes, but other than that, her skin was white and smooth. She might be his Aunt Alla, in dress-up clothes—they showed the same tendency for practical bossiness.

She scowled and turned once more toward the distant figure, walking with deliberate strides.

"No, wait!" Ned handed the reins to Brownie and hopped down. He caught up with the sister just in front of the lead mules. "You stay back, ma'am. I'll go check what's going on."

She hesitated, then gave him a quick nod.

Ned pulled his Colt from his holster and pointed it toward the form on the ground. It was definitely a body, but whether dead or alive, he couldn't tell. As he approached, he realized the face-down figure wore buckskins. Long, light brown hair spread over the shoulders and dragged in the dirt.

His heart thudded. Could be a Comanche, though the hair seemed too light, and their men usually braided their hair. A white Indian? He'd heard of captive children becoming fiercer warriors than their captors. Ned looked around, more suspicious than ever. Were a dozen more braves lurking nearby?

He stopped six feet away and held his aim steady. "Get up."

The body didn't stir. He swallowed hard and stepped close enough to nudge it with his foot. A soft moan floated up to him.

"That's a woman!"

The fact that the nun now stood at his elbow startled Ned more than her words. He gave her a quick glance then looked back at the body. Could she be right? He let his gaze travel over the figure, taking in the thin frame beneath the tattered buckskins. The shirt was longer than the men usually wore. One hand was flung out near the head. The fingers were slender and, yes, feminine, but the nails were broken and bloody. And a line of red paint flakes showed faintly at the parting of the hair. A woman, all right.

Ned swallowed. "You want to turn her over? I'll step back and cover you, in case it's a trick."

"It can't be a trick." The nun pushed forward and knelt beside the body. She grasped one shoulder.

Ned wouldn't have been surprised if the prone person grabbed the nun and put a knife to her throat. Instead, the sister rolled the body easily into a face-up position. Another low moan sounded.

Ned stepped forward slowly. Purple bruises puffed out the right side of the woman's face. Her hands and forearms bore scratches and bruises. Slowly, she opened her eyes. Ned leaned closer and looked into her face.

The young woman gazed back at him with fearful blue eyes.

Taabe blinked. Even that hurt. Her head throbbed, and her heart raced.

She didn't move. Two white people stooped over her. She had been found.

What would they do to her? The Numinu told many stories of Indians being mistreated by the whites. She didn't want to believe those stories, but finding herself so near them and utterly defenseless made her quiver.

She closed her eyes again and pulled in a deep breath. One of the faces was stark white—had they painted their skin?

The man said something, sharp and wary. The other answered in soft, gentle tones. A woman. Taabe tried to open her eyes to see the white woman, but it was too hard. The swelling made it difficult to see from that eye anyway. She wanted to tell them her ankle was hurt and she couldn't walk. That her lips were parched from lack of water.

Peca.

She remembered and struggled to sit up.

The woman in a black dress patted her arm and said something. Her voice was almost hypnotic. She spoke to the man, a firm command.

The man bent beside her and spoke. Taabe tried to understand, but it made no sense. Was her first language completely gone?

He touched her, and she shrank back.

Again the woman touched her and spoke. The words were meaningless to Taabe, but gentle. She raised Taabe's shoulders.

The man slid an arm behind her. When he put his other

arm beneath her knees to lift her, the pain was too great. Taabe let her eyes fall shut and lost herself to the pain.

Ned carried the young woman to the stagecoach. The nun hiked her black robe up six inches and ran ahead, black shoes and a bit of black stocking evident beneath her hem.

Brownie stood on the driver's box, alternately staring at Ned and looking down the road and off to the sides, his shotgun ready.

"Sister Adele," the nun shouted. "Help us!"

The stagecoach door opened and the second nun emerged. By the time Ned reached the lead mules, the women were tugging and shoving at the mail sacks.

"Whatcha got?" Brownie called.

"A woman. She opened her eyes for a second. She's white."

"In Comanche getup?"

"That's right." Ned walked to the door of the coach.

"Can you get her onto the seat if we help?" the first nun asked.

"Yes, ma'am, I think I can."

"I'm Sister Natalie."

"Ma'am."

The second nun was younger, with wide eyes making a quick appraisal of his burden. She lifted her skirt slightly and scrambled back into the stage. "Let me take her shoulders, sir." Her words lilted with an accent Ned couldn't place.

The three of them got the injured woman into the stage. Ned stood outside at the open door while the two nuns arranged the unconscious woman on the padded back seat.

"Think she'll be all right until the fort?" Ned asked. He was supposed to let the nuns off in a mile. The unconscious woman might fall off the seat.

"The fort?" Sister Natalie frowned. "You'll leave her with us, young man."

"But if she's a captive—"

"No buts. She's in no condition to travel. We'll take care of her at the mission house. If someone official from the fort wants to see her, he can interview her there."

Ned glanced at the other nun, but she was opening a canteen and raising the young woman's head to put it to her lips. No help at all to his position.

"Ma'am—"

"Sister Natalie, if you please."

"Yes, ma'am. If I go to the fort and tell them we found this woman, but I have no idea who she is, and I left her off with a bunch of defenseless women, I'll probably get in all kinds of hot water."

Sister Natalie looked him up and down. "Probably it will be the first bath you've had in some time. Now I suggest you get up there and drive."

Ned didn't dare open his mouth again. Weren't nuns supposed to be meek and humble? This woman reminded him more and more of Aunt Alla.

What if the injured woman regained consciousness and tried to get away? She might hurt the nuns if she tried to escape from the coach.

He started to speak, but Sister Natalie's glare made him think better of it. If the stage hadn't been spanking new, he'd have slammed the door. He closed it firmly and hoisted himself to the driver's box.

"What do you make of it?" Brownie asked.

Ned unwrapped the reins from the brake handle.

"White woman in Comanche regalia, and it's not sudden. She smells like an Indian."

Brownie laughed. "Is she sick?"

"I don't know. She looks beat up."

"Maybe her tribe doesn't want her anymore if she's sick." Brownie raised his chin, looking far out over the grassy plain.

"More likely she escaped."

"Nah." Brownie shook his head. "They don't escape. Not if they've been in captivity very long."

CHAPTER THREE

The stagecoach rolled up to the home station at Fort Chadbourne an hour later.

"We should have brought her here," Ned said to Brownie as the tenders came out to hold the mules' heads.

"Sister Natalie is right—they'll take better care of her. They're good at nursing."

"How do you know?"

Brownie shrugged. "That's the kind of thing they do."

Ned climbed down and stalked toward the commander's office, leaving Brownie to stand guard while two men unloaded the mail.

Captain Tapley's office, in a stone building facing the parade ground, held two desks, two chairs, a potbellied stove, and a few shelves. Maps and notices papered the walls. He'd been commander of the fort for about six months. The sergeant who assisted with the regiment's paperwork rose when Ned entered.

"May I help you, sir?"

Ned pulled his hat off and looked to where Tapley sat, hunched over his desk. "I came to report to Captain Tapley that we found a woman lying on the road about six miles east of here. She's sick—exhausted, maybe, and she had some bruises. We took her in the stagecoach and left her at the nuns' mission house."

Tapley stood and walked toward Ned, his face showing concern. "Who is she? Do you know?"

Ned shook his head. "She's white, but she was all got up like a Comanche. Her hair's quite light—might be blond when all the tallow's washed out of it. And her eyes are bluer than yours, sir."

"She was unconscious?"

"Out cold when I left her with the sisters. She opened her eyes for a few seconds when we found her, but didn't say anything. Two of the nuns were riding with me, and they said they'd nurse her to health." Ned watched the captain's face for signs of displeasure but saw none. "Otherwise I'd have carried her here, sir."

"No, that's all right," Tapley said. "I'm sure the Ursulines will give her good care. Will you pass back that way?"

"Tomorrow. And we'll come back westbound on Friday."

Tapley nodded. "If the sisters think she needs medical treatment, I can ask our surgeon to ride out there. And send me word if the woman's ready for questioning."

"Yes, sir, I'll do that."

"I'll ask around in the meantime and see if anyone has a clue who she is."

"Well, sir, I've been thinking on it for the last hour, and I believe it might be wise not to let it be known where she is. Those nuns don't have any protection out there, and until you know that woman's story . . ."

"Good thinking. The Indians show up at the most inconvenient times. Your name is Bright, isn't it?"

"Yes, sir. Ned Bright."

"You're Patrillo Garza's partner?"

"That's right."

"Do you think this woman's been living among the Comanche?"

"Sure looked like it. She had on their type of clothes, and her hair was loose, with the part painted red, the way their women do. And she didn't seem to have a horse. Looked as if she'd walked across the range alone."

Tapley frowned. "Curious. If you can check on the sisters and their guest when you pass, it will relieve my mind. I'll try to get out there in a few days and take a look at her myself. If she's able to talk, maybe we'll get some answers."

Ned hesitated. "I'm told they usually can't speak English if they've been long in captivity."

"We'll have to see, won't we? Meanwhile, I'll send out a message along the line and to all the forts, reporting that a captive woman has been found. How old do you think she is?"

"Hard to say, with her face all purple and swelled up. But I don't think she's too old."

Tapley drummed his fingers on his desk. "Well, thirteen or thirty?"

"Somewhere in between, I'd guess. Nearer twenty than thirty."

"Blue eyes, you said." Tapley went behind the desk, sat down, and scribbled in the margin of a paper. "Any other identifying marks?"

"Not that I could tell. Maybe the nuns will know more tomorrow."

"Yes. Perhaps the woman will have told them who she is. I understand several children were captured in this area over the last few years."

"That's true. Too many."

Tapley nodded. "I haven't been here long, but my men have had several brushes with raiding parties. Perhaps I'd better send a detachment out to the mission tomorrow or the next day, just to check on things."

Ned stepped toward the door. "Thank you, Captain. I'll be over at the home station. The stage crew will be sleeping there regularly."

When he reached the yard, the stage still waited before the station with the fresh team in harness. Several passengers were handing their luggage to one of the tenders before they boarded.

Ned went into the station and found Brownie eating a belated dinner or an early supper—a plate of beans, bacon, and cornbread.

"Wash out back, or Miz Stein won't feed you," Brownie said between bites.

Ned ambled out to the back of the house. He'd eaten here before, on their freighting trips, and he should have remembered. The station agent's wife was particular about the cleanliness of her establishment and those who patronized it.

He washed his hands in a tin basin that sat on top of a flour barrel, then splashed a little of the water on his face and dried off with a damp towel hanging on a hook nearby. The second time he entered the dining room, Brownie had a half-eaten slice of pie before him.

Ned hung up his hat and his coiled whip. He had barely sat down before the plump German lady came toward him carrying a heaped plate and a mug of coffee.

"*Guten tag, Herr* Bright."

"And good day to you, Mrs. Stein." Ned grinned at her. "That looks edible. Thank you, ma'am."

"Bitte." She smiled and bobbed her head before retreating

to the lean-to where she reigned over her step-top cookstove. The day Ned and Patrillo had hauled it in on a wagon drawn by eight mules had been one of celebration at Fort Chadbourne. Other than days when she put the blacking to it, that stove never cooled off. In the summer the kitchen would get so hot, no one but Mrs. Stein would venture in there.

Mrs. Stein's food was plain but plentiful and well seasoned, which was more than Ned could bank on at the army mess. He'd eaten there several times before the Steins came and opened their stop for travelers. In Ned's opinion, Mrs. Stein's provender outshone the army's anytime. With Fort Chadbourne now on the coast-to-coast overland mail route, the Steins' place had been the obvious choice for a home station.

Once his belly was full, he wandered out to the corrals. Brownie and the tenders lounged against the fence, debating the merits of the mules that browsed their hay inside, and the difficulty of keeping them secure.

"Can't put 'em out to pasture," said Sonny, a skinny boy of seventeen. "Too much Indian activity."

Brownie adjusted his hat and nodded. "That's right. Leave them in the open, and they'd be gone in the morning."

The second tender, Dutch, was older than Sonny. He'd recently been hired by the stage line's division agent and assigned to the Steins' station. He let out a sigh. "We have to stay up all night guarding them. At least Herr Stein takes a turn."

Brownie glanced at Ned. "I was tellin' 'em about the woman we found."

Ned nodded.

"Did you bring her to the fort?" Sonny asked.

"She's being looked after," Ned said quickly. He gave Brownie a look he hoped the shotgun messenger would understand. "The captain's putting the word out. We don't know who she is, but folks who've lost a girl over the last—I don't know, ten years or so—can inquire at his office."

Dutch shrugged. "I knew a family back in Mason County that lost a couple of kids. Hard thing."

"Yup." Brownie turned away from the fence. "I'm heading over to the barracks. Coming, Ned?"

Ned shook his head. Brownie knew he wouldn't go—Ned never went with him to find a card game. "I'll be in the house."

He went around the back to the little room given over to the stage crews. Mrs. Stein had made up the beds with clean sheets and homemade quilts, and she'd left a pitcher of water and a plate covered with a dish towel. There were even a couple of books on the shelf over the washstand. That surprised Ned. One was a small German book of some kind. The other was in English—*The Scarlet Letter*. Ned laid it on the bottom bunk.

He lifted the corner of the towel over the plate. Doughnuts. He smiled as he took one and covered the rest to keep the bugs off. This was some pumpkins!

Taabe Waipu awoke slowly. The first thing she saw was a white wall. She caught her breath and tried to sit up. Pain ran through her head like stampeding horses, and she clapped a hand to her brow. She was lying on a bed built up off the floor.

Carefully she moved her legs, hoping to swing them from between the coverings and over the side. Immediate pain in her right ankle stopped her. She lay still for a minute, sucking air between clenched teeth.

Finally she felt ready to try again. She lifted the top blanket and slowly slid her foot to the edge. When it hung over the side, she pushed herself up with her arms and sat on the edge of the bed, shaking. Pain throbbed in her skull and her cheek. She put her fingertips cautiously to her face and gritted her teeth. The right side was painful and puffy.

Her injured ankle was bound with strips of cloth, but she could see it was swollen to twice its normal size. She touched her foot experimentally to the floor. Pain made her wince and lift it. She ran her hands over the white garment she wore. Its softness surprised her. And why would anyone wear white? More mysterious—how did they make it so white?

She looked around. Two of the walls were made of dried clay, the other two of boards. All were whitewashed. One of the adobe walls held a narrow aperture about a foot high and four inches wide. It looked as though the walls were at least eight inches thick. The opening seemed more of a slit to shoot arrows through than a window. No man could fit through it.

On the wall over her bed hung a small carving of a man on a torture rack. She studied it for a long time but couldn't guess why it was there. Next to the bed was a wooden stand, and on it a white pottery bowl with a gracefully shaped jug sitting in it. The white jug had a handle, and lifelike flowers were painted on the bulging side. Taabe touched the pitcher. The pottery felt cool and smooth, almost slippery. She peered inside. The jug held water.

She lifted it and was about to put the curved edge to her lips when she spied a metal cup. Holding the heavy jug and pouring the water was difficult while sitting on the bed, and she splashed a little on herself. New pain shot up her leg as she tensed. She set the jug back in the bowl with a clunk and raised the cup to her mouth. The cool, sweet water must have been placed there recently. She drained the cup and set it beside the big, white bowl. Exhausted, she lay back on the bed and closed her eyes. From far away, she heard a faint sound. Music, but not like the songs of the Numinu. Gentle voices singing words she could not distinguish.

The creaking of the door's hinges startled her. She jerked her eyes open and turned her head toward the sound. Her feet pushed instinctively on the bed, and she gasped at the fresh pain in her ankle.

A figure stood in the doorway—a form in a long black robe. The face was thin and as white as a skull. Taabe held back a scream. The eyes bored into her—eyes an odd, light brown, lighter than any Indian's.

The face smiled. Then Taabe realized a woman wore the robe. A woman with a band of snow-white cloth around her face and a black head cloth on top. In her pale hands she held a board with dishes on it. The smell of food hit Taabe, and her stomach lurched. She couldn't remember ever being so hungry.

The eastbound stage was due at Fort Chadbourne at ten the next morning. Ned was up early and ate a huge breakfast under Mrs. Stein's beaming approval. He moseyed out to the stable and helped Sonny and Dutch tend to the livestock. Dutch yawned several times, and he looked a little bleary-eyed.

Brownie wandered out from the dining room an hour later and helped them groom the team of four big mules they'd take on their eastbound trip. They'd stop twice to change teams before they reached Tree and Ned's ranch, sixty miles away. There another driver and shotgun rider would take over for the run past the ruins of Fort Phantom Hill and on toward Fort Belknap. Ned and Brownie would stay at the ranch until the next westbound stage arrived.

"I'm not sure about this twice-a-week schedule," Ned said to Brownie as they lolled against the wall, watching the tenders hitch up the team.

"We'll see how it goes this first week," Brownie said. "We're westbound Tuesday and Friday, and eastbound Wednesday and Sunday. If we need to, we can ride home from here on a Friday night and come back Sunday morning."

"We'll work it out." Ned frowned, thinking about the convent between Fort Chadbourne and the ranch he and Patrillo owned. "Do we have any passengers this morning? I want to stop and get a report on the woman we left with the sisters." *Sisters.* It came out easily now, though the concept was still foreign.

"Yeah, there's two men wanting to ride to Fort Belknap. Herr Stein just sold them tickets. And there may be more on the inbound stage."

Ned nodded. "Well, the captain asked me specifically to stop and look in at the mission. Maybe we can leave a couple of minutes early, if everyone's ready to go."

Brownie straightened. "I'll go check on the mail."

They walked toward the home station. From the fort's grounds, a uniformed trooper strode toward them.

"Mr. Bright!"

Ned stopped walking. "You go on," he told Brownie. He and the trooper met beside the house.

"The captain said to find you if you hadn't left yet. There's a couple over to his office who want to know about the captive woman you found."

Ned looked back toward the stagecoach. "I've only got a few minutes."

"Then let's go." The trooper led him at a fast walk across the parade ground between the barracks and officers' quarters and left him outside Tapley's office.

Ned rapped on the door and opened it.

"Come right in, Mr. Bright," Captain Tapley called out.

Ned stepped into the dim room. The captain and his sergeant had given up their chairs for a man and a woman, who sprang to their feet on Ned's entrance.

"You're the one who found a white woman in Comanche dress?" the man asked.

"Yes."

"Mr. Bright, these are the Cunninghams," Tapley said. "They have a place a few miles south of here."

"We came to the fort to do a little trading this morning and heard the news." The man extended his hand to Ned.

"We lost our daughter," his wife said, her voice choking. "Please, can you tell us about this young woman?"

"Well, she's . . . When was your daughter taken? And how old would she be?"

"Two years ago, when the Indians stole the mail." Mr. Cunningham glanced at his wife.

Ned nodded. "I remember." Before the nationwide contract was assigned, the soldiers received sacks of local mail and helped deliver it to settlers in the area. "The raiders came into the fort to trade a few days later, and they had some of the cavalrymen's things on them."

"That's right," Mrs. Cunningham said. "The same day they ambushed the soldiers and stole the mail, our girl disappeared out of our yard. We never found a trace, except hoofprints and—and Sally's—" She sobbed.

Her husband eyed Ned apologetically. "They threw her clothes on the ground." He put his arm around his wife.

"I'm sorry," Ned said. "That doesn't mean they abused her. Seems they like to put their captives in their own type of clothing right away." *Or some have reported they were made to ride naked for days. But then they gave them buckskins to wear.* Ned didn't voice his thoughts.

Mrs. Cunningham sobbed louder, and her husband drew her close.

"She was ten," Captain Tapley said. "From what you've

told me, this young woman you found is probably not Sally Cunningham."

Ned shook his head. "I strongly doubt it. Not if your Sally would be twelve now. This woman is older than that."

"We need to see her," Mrs. Cunningham said.

Her husband looked to Ned. "If we see her, we'll know, one way or the other. If we don't, we might keep wondering. And if she's not Sally, well, it's possible she might know something about her."

Ned nodded. "All right. The stage is about to leave. Can you come along now?"

"Yes," they said together.

Ned glanced at the captain. "The thing is, we won't come back through until Friday. But the mission is only a few miles from here . . ."

"I'll send a detachment with a wagon," Tapley said. "Better to see them safely back here today."

"All right, then," Ned said. "You can come on the stage now, and Captain Tapley's men can follow to bring you back to the fort."

Mr. Cunningham nodded and reached for his hat. "Thank you. Come along, my dear. You must be strong for Sally's sake."

CHAPTER FOUR

The door's creak wakened Taabe Waipu. She caught her breath. Two of the black-garbed women entered, carrying items in their pale hands. One held a wooden tray with dishes. The other brought a roll of white cloth and a tool. Taabe had seen such a tool—two knife blades fastened in the middle, with handles that made cutting easy—but she couldn't remember what it was called.

She raised herself on her elbows and shrank toward the wall. The woman carrying the tray set it on the table beside the bed. The other sat on the edge of the bed. Taabe winced as the shifting of the bedding caused a stab of pain in her ankle.

The sitting woman smiled and spoke softly in a flowing language Taabe couldn't understand. She raised her own foot and touched her ankle then rubbed it, talking all the while. Taabe guessed she wanted to examine her injury.

The woman stood and lifted the edge of the blanket, raising her eyebrows as if seeking permission. Taabe inched her bandaged foot toward the edge. The woman bent and peered at the ankle, then touched the skin with fingertips so gentle, Taabe barely felt it at first. A slash of pain seized her, and she gasped. The woman raised her hands as though to say, "I won't touch it again." She put a hand beneath Taabe's calf, raised her leg a bit, and slid it carefully away from the edge of the bed. She settled the blanket back over Taabe and smiled at her, uttering more soft words.

The second woman spoke louder and gestured toward the tray, a clear offer of food. Taabe nodded. That woman, who seemed older than the one who had looked at her ankle, turned away for a moment and returned with a soft bundle covered with cloth as white as summer clouds. Both robed women put their hands under Taabe's shoulders and lifted her. She gritted her teeth as the pain washed over her. The older one slipped the white bundle behind her head and neck. A pillow—softer than anything Taabe could remember resting her head upon.

She sank back into its deepness and closed her eyes. Her heart drummed, and her breath came in short hitches. The two women spoke in low tones. Finally they grew silent. Taabe opened her eyes a crack. They still stood there.

The older one spoke to the other and picked up a gleaming white pottery bowl. The younger one left the room and returned with a stool. Taabe eyed it with interest. The three-legged stool looked very sturdy and useful, but it would never do for people who moved about. The Comanche never carried furniture.

The older woman sat on it and dipped a metal spoon into the bowl. She leaned close and held the spoon to Taabe's mouth. Taabe opened her lips and let the woman deposit a spoonful of lukewarm broth in her mouth. It tasted good, but the spoon clacked against her teeth and Taabe winced.

The woman waited until she opened her mouth again. Why couldn't they make spoons of wood or horn? The younger woman left the room, but the older one stayed to feed her. Several spoonfuls of broth were followed by small pieces of a bread that tasted of corn and salt and something else. Taabe wished she could feed herself, but sitting upright would cause excruciating pain, so she allowed the indignity of being fed like an infant.

When she had finished eating, the woman in black touched her chest. "Natalie," she said. "Natalie."

"Nah-ta-lee," Taabe said slowly.

The woman's face lit with a smile. "Yes. Natalie." She pointed to Taabe. "You?"

Taabe touched the front of her soft white gown. "Taabe Waipu."

Natalie frowned. She touched herself again. "Natalie. You?"

Taabe repeated her name.

"Tah-bay-wy-poo."

Taabe nodded.

Natalie's face beamed at this small progress. She spoke again, smoothing the blanket and saying Taabe's name at the end of her words. She rose and moved the stool aside, picked up the tray, and left the room silently, closing the door behind her. Taabe lay back in the dim, cool room and felt her stomach relax as it welcomed the food.

She exhaled and stared at the ceiling that seemed too close. She longed to get outside this box of a room. She thought of her Indian family. Did her sister miss her? Her adoptive parents were dead, as were others she had loved, but for the past two years she had lived with and loved her Comanche sister's family. She'd rejoiced in the birth of her sister's baby girl and taken great pleasure in helping care for the little one.

Where was Peca, she wondered. If she had stayed, she would

be his wife now. Had he given up the chase? And who were these kind women who had taken her in? She'd seen white women's clothing before—things the warriors had brought back from raids. But she had never seen anything like the long, flowing black dresses these women wore. Perhaps they belonged to a strange tribe. And where were their men? She'd seen a man with them when they found her. The men must be out hunting or raiding, she decided as her eyes drifted shut.

She woke to the door's creaking. Closed in as she was, she couldn't tell the time of day, but light still streamed through the narrow slit in the wall.

The younger woman who had examined her ankle entered, carrying a lamp. She peered at Taabe and smiled. The words she spoke meant nothing to Taabe.

The woman tried to get something across to her, using hand motions, but the signs weren't intelligible. Taabe stared at her blankly. The woman placed the lamp on the table, held up a finger, and backed toward the doorway. She went out, leaving the door open. Taabe wanted to rise, but knew she couldn't.

She waited, her heart pounding. Something had happened. What was the woman trying to tell her? Would she have smiled like that if Peca had appeared at the door?

A moment later, she heard footsteps and low voices. One was that of a man. Taabe grasped the edge of the blanket and pulled it up to her chin, over her soft white gown, and peered over the flimsy shield.

The woman appeared in the doorway, with a tall white man behind her. She stepped inside, extending her hands and speaking rapidly. Taabe blinked, uncomprehending, and looked into the man's face. Maybe he was the head of the family. She thought she might have seen him before, but she didn't know where. Was he the one who had found her?

⟵ ★ ⟶

Ned looked helplessly at the injured woman. The right side of her face was a mass of bruises, ranging from deep purple to yellow. Her matted hair hung about her shoulders, and her blue eyes radiated terror.

"You don't understand a word I'm saying, do you?" He turned to the nun. "Has she said anything, ma'am?"

"I am Sister Adele. Mostly she has slept, but Sister Natalie coaxed her this morning, and we believe we have her name. Tah-bay-wy-poo."

The injured woman frowned at the words, her gaze darting between them.

"We've fed her and bandaged her ankle," the nun said. "I was going to look at it again this morning, but it pained her so much, I left it alone. We don't know if she has other injuries. We thought it best not to disturb her too much, so long as she seemed peaceful."

"I don't know what to tell those people out there." Ned sighed and turned his hat around and around in his hands. "We can't ask her questions."

The nun nodded. "It is too soon. Perhaps if they came back later . . ."

Ned shook his head. "They want to get a look at her today. They think they'll know if she's their daughter, and maybe they will. I wish we could tell her what it's about, though, so she wouldn't be frightened."

He took a step toward the bed, and the young woman cringed away from him, toward the wall. She grimaced and closed her eyes.

"She's in pain," Ned said. "This isn't the time to bring strangers in to ogle her."

"No," the sister said. "But if she is their child, they have a right to know."

"You don't speak any Comanche, I suppose?"

"None at all. Do you?"

He shook his head. "All right, I'll go get Mr. and Mrs. Cunningham."

He went out into the mission entrance. The couple waited in the sitting room just inside the door.

"She's awake. If you folks want to come with me, I'll take you to her. Just don't expect too much. She doesn't understand English, and she's in a lot of pain."

Mrs. Cunningham rose. "How badly is she injured?"

"The nuns aren't sure. Her face is bruised. That and her ankle seem to be the worst of it. She'll have to stay off that foot for several weeks."

The couple followed him silently along a narrow hallway, from which several curtained doorways opened. The final opening on the right had a wooden door. Ned paused before it. "They've cleaned her up some, but not completely. They wanted to let her rest."

"All right," Mr. Cunningham said.

Ned stood aside, and they entered the small chamber. Sister Adele was leaning over the bed, holding a cup of water to the injured woman's lips.

"Oh my." Mrs. Cunningham put a hand to her mouth.

Sister Adele turned and said softly, "We have washed her once, but we haven't washed her hair. She needs to rest and heal. Tomorrow, if possible, we will bathe her."

While she spoke, the Cunninghams stared at the woman on the bed, and she cowered against the wall, clutching the quilt to her breast.

Mr. Cunningham turned away. "She's not our Sally."

"Are you sure?" Ned asked.

"She's much too old." Mrs. Cunningham's voice caught. "The poor creature." Tears streamed down her cheeks, and she sobbed.

The patient's gaze roved from Mrs. Cunningham's face to her faded calico dress, then to Ned. In her blue eyes, panic warred with fascination. Ned wanted only to protect her—in that moment and the future. The young woman clenched her teeth and crumpled the edge of the quilt in her hands. Her breathing became shallow as her glance bounced from one of them to another and settled, pleading, on the nun.

"We don't need to stand here gawking at her," Ned said. "Thank you, ma'am."

"You are welcome," Sister Adele said.

Ned walked out to the entry with the Cunninghams. Sister Natalie waited near the door, her hands clasped before her.

"Thank you, Sister," Ned said. "These folks say she's not their girl."

Sister Natalie nodded. "I suppose there will be others coming to try to identify her."

"Will that inconvenience you?" Ned wondered who would care for the injured girl—she looked hardly more than a girl now that she'd regained consciousness and had her face washed—if she was transported to the fort. Mrs. Stein, perhaps.

"The Lord placed us here to serve." Sister Natalie gazed at the floor.

"That's . . . kind of you," Ned said. "I've asked the captain not to spread it around where she's staying. We don't know who might be looking for her. Of course, we all want to see her reunited with her family, but if the Indians are looking for her . . ." It was only fair to warn the nuns. "They say Comanche don't like to give up their captives. If they come here, you would probably do better to give her up than to resist."

Sister Natalie met his gaze. "The Lord will show us what to do."

Ned nodded, but her attitude left him uneasy. He looked at the Cunninghams. "I'll make the same request of you folks. If you hear of anyone else wanting to see that poor girl, tell them she's being cared for, and to contact the captain. Don't let on that she's here at the mission."

"All right," Mr. Cunningham said.

His wife moved toward the door. "We'll wait outside for the soldiers."

"We would be happy to bring you some coffee or tea," Sister Natalie said.

Mr. Cunningham looked hopeful, but his wife shook her head. "No, thank you. We do appreciate your hospitality for that woman."

Ned walked outside with them. Brownie waited for him near the stagecoach. He looked their way, and Ned shook his head.

"Good-bye, folks." Ned held out his hand to Mr. Cunningham. "I'm sorry it didn't turn out well for you."

"Thank you for bringing us." Cunningham glanced at his wife, who dabbed at her eyes with a handkerchief. "If you get someone in here who speaks her lingo, can they ask her about other captives? Maybe she's seen our Sally."

"I'm sure the captain will question her along those lines when she's had a few days to recover."

Taabe slept fitfully, but each time she awoke, the window slit was dark. Once one of the women came in with a candle and a cup filled with a warm drink. Taabe sipped it and recognized the taste of steeped willow bark, a common remedy for pain. She drank the entire cupful and lay back on the soft pillow, thankful for the women's care.

When she woke again, one of the women—the young one with fewest creases on her face—entered carrying an armful of clothing. She spoke to Taabe and smiled. She held up one of the long, black robes they all wore, spoke some more, and laid it on the foot of the bed.

Then she held up Taabe's Comanche dress and leggings. They looked fresh, as though she had cleaned the soft buckskins. The woman nodded to them, then pointed to the robe and raised her eyebrows as though asking which Taabe preferred.

The choice was obvious. Taabe pointed to her own clothing. Though she wanted to leave the Comanche life, the flowing black dresses frightened her. She wished they offered a dress like the woman who'd visited yesterday had worn. That looked right to Taabe—more normal for a woman from the world of the whites. Though the cloth was a drab brown, the skirt had nipped in at the woman's waist. The top fastened in the front, with a row of small, round buttons. The costume wouldn't give her the freedom of her leggings and loose buckskin dress, but something inside her longed to wear a similar outfit. Was that what she had worn when she was little?

The robed woman pointed to Taabe and spoke her name, then pointed to herself. "Adele. Sister Adele."

Taabe frowned. "Ah-dell."

Her visitor smiled and nodded. She beckoned with her hand then helped Taabe rise. The pain made her hold her breath. Adele pulled her close, indicating that Taabe should lean on her. They hobbled across a dim hallway, to another room where a tub of hot water waited. Taabe's heart raced. Were they going to cook her? She drew back, almost falling when the pain in her ankle stabbed her.

Adele caught her and spoke softly, with words like a gently rippling stream. She pointed to the tub and made a scrubbing motion on her face.

So it was for washing. Taabe nodded cautiously. Why so much water? It must have taken a great deal of effort to carry and heat so much.

Adele pretended to scrub her own arms. Taabe nodded again. Her companion leaned over and mimed scrubbing her legs. She drew Taabe a step toward the tub and reached down, skimming her hand through the water. She smiled at Taabe and jerked her head toward the tub.

Slowly, Taabe stooped and touched the water with her fingertips. It was warm, but not so hot that it burned. Adele tugged at the skirt of Taabe's gown, then mimed removing the robe. She pointed to the tub. Taabe paused then nodded. Perhaps they wanted her to wash her garment after she'd washed herself.

Adele pointed to some folded cloths and a lump of something white—it looked like tallow—on a small wooden table near the tub and spoke again.

Taabe frowned. As nearly as she could tell, she was to scrub herself all over and wash her white dress. She balanced herself on her uninjured leg, pulled the dress over her head, and dropped it in the tub.

Adele's mouth opened wide. She stared at the dress floating in the water, then at Taabe.

Taabe's stomach roiled. What had she done wrong?

Adele clapped a hand to her mouth.

The older woman, Natalie, pushed aside the curtain in the doorway, peered in, and spoke. Adele answered and pointed to the tub. Natalie came closer and peered into the water. She and Adele looked at each other and began to laugh.

CHAPTER FIVE

Ned was glad to be back home. He and Brownie sat in the dining room at the ranch, having coffee with Patrillo and neighboring rancher Reece Jones. Ned had told the others about the woman they'd found and the events that followed.

"Papa." Benito stood in the doorway between the kitchen and the large dining and living room of their ranch.

"What is it?" Patrillo asked his oldest son.

"Quinta is supposed to help cook tonight, and she's at the corral watching Marcos ride that colt of his."

Patrillo stood and went to the front door. He shouted in Spanish, "Quinta! It's your turn to help prepare supper. Get around to the kitchen and help your brother. Now!" After a moment he turned and sauntered back to the table where the men were enjoying their coffee.

Reece, who had been shooting the breeze with Patrillo and his boys when the stage arrived, had moved to Texas from Arkansas twenty years ago—and managed to keep his scalp and run a motley herd of cattle. He also helped out occasionally when Patrillo had a large freighting contract and needed an extra driver.

"So, the first mail run turned out to be an adventure," Reece said as Tree resumed his seat.

"That's right," Brownie said.

Ned took a swallow from his coffee and set the mug down. "I sure wish we knew where she came from."

"Doesn't matter where she came from," Patrillo said. "What you need to know is who she is."

"Yup," Brownie said. "If we knew that, maybe we'd know where she was heading."

"She sure was stove up," Ned said.

"Makes me wonder if she'd been beaten." Brownie drained his mug and reached for the coffeepot.

Ned shook his head. "Someone might have blacked her eye, but I doubt they broke her ankle."

"Could be her horse threw her." Reece scratched his chin through his flowing beard. "Hard to imagine a Comanche woman going far without a horse."

"That's true." Ned thought about it as he sipped his coffee. "Reece, you know a little of their lingo, don't you?"

"Not much. Whatcha got?"

"Tah-bay-wy-poo," Ned said carefully.

"*Waipu* is woman." Reece's bushy eyebrows drew together. "*Taabe.* I've heard that before. Sun, maybe?"

"Sun woman?" That didn't make a lot of sense to Ned.

Reece shrugged. "Ask somebody else. It's been a long time since I had any dealings with the Comanche—and I'm not sorry about that. Hey, I remember a couple of years back, a girl was stolen not far from here."

Ned nodded. "Sally Cunningham. Her parents went to take a look at the girl today. She's not Sally."

"Too bad."

Patrillo frowned as though trying to pry an elusive nugget from his memory. "There were some kids taken near Fort Belknap years ago . . ."

"Boys," Brownie said.

"Wasn't there a girl too?"

Brownie shrugged. "Maybe."

Patrillo picked up his mug. "There's always Cynthia Ann Parker."

"No, she'd be too old." Since he arrived in Texas, Ned had heard the stories about one of the state's earliest and certainly the most famous captive. The girl's family had searched for her for nearly two decades now. "She'd be nearly thirty, wouldn't she?"

"I suppose," Patrillo said. "But you say this woman was bruised up, so maybe she's that old and you couldn't tell."

"No." Ned thought of Taabe Waipu's face and his impression of youth—and fear. "She's a girl, but in her teens at least."

"I put her between fifteen and twenty-five," Brownie said.

While Ned was grateful for his support, Brownie had seen her only from his perch on the driver's box, while she was unconscious. Today he'd waited outside with the stagecoach while Ned went into the mission with the Cunninghams.

"Probably twenty or younger," Ned said.

"Ah." Patrillo spread his hands. "Maybe you should send inquiries. Who takes charge of searching for these captives?"

"The governor, maybe?" Ned said. "I suppose the captain will send some letters."

Reece shoved back his chair. "I'd best be getting home before dark. Say, I recall there was a little girl taken ten years or so ago down around Victoria."

"We should make a list," Ned said. "We got any paper?"

Patrillo stood. "I'll find something. Maybe if we get some

names, you can ask her the next time you go by there. She might recognize one of them."

"I'll go check on the livestock," Brownie said. "See you at supper." He and Reece ambled out the front door together.

Quinta came in from the kitchen, scowling and carrying a stack of thick ironstone plates. "Papa, Benito says I have to do the dishes all by myself tonight."

"Why is that?" Patrillo asked.

"He says I should have come sooner to help him cook. I only waited a minute, Papa."

Patrillo tweaked one of her long, dark braids. "I'll see about it. Do a good job on the table, now."

She set out plates for her father, Ned, her four brothers, herself, and Brownie. Flatware and cups followed. She looked at her father for approval, and he nodded.

When she had gone back into the kitchen, Patrillo asked, "Did the nuns say anything about opening a school?"

"Not to me. We had other things to think about."

"Some days I think Quinta needs a female influence."

Ned laughed. "Well, Tree, you could get married again."

"Who would marry a man with five so rambunctious children?" Patrillo laughed but then grew sober. "She can read, but not too well. Her mother taught all the boys, but I haven't done so well."

"You haven't done so badly."

"Ha! She follows her brothers about all day, she dresses like a boy, and she risks her neck to prove she's worthy to be with them." Patrillo shook his head. "I've spoken to the boys about it many times. They assure me they don't egg her on to do these things, but still she persists. She must ride a half-grown steer, or walk a fence rail, or try to throw a calf as big as she is."

Ned rose and patted him on the shoulder as he headed for the door. "Quinta's a fine little señorita. Some day she'll start wanting to act like a lady. Don't fret about that one."

"What do you know? You have no children. Maybe the nuns would be a calming influence."

"I can't—"

Ned broke off as Quinta burst through the kitchen door, screaming in Spanish. She spoke so rapidly, he couldn't quite follow, but he caught the word "school" and the refrain she repeated after each few phrases in her ranting—"How could you, Papa?"

Ned ducked out the door and retreated to his small room at the back of the ranch house.

Taabe sat on the edge of the chair, afraid to move. She watched the four women for cues as to what they expected. Three of them, including Natalie and Adele, sat at the table too. The fourth, whom they called Sister Marie, arranged dishes of hot food.

They all were called "sister." Adele had gotten this across to Taabe after her traumatic bath, while she combed out Taabe's wild nest of hair. "Sister" appeared to be some sort of title. Or perhaps it simply meant "woman," but they didn't call her "Sister Taabe."

She was glad they had let her have her own clothing back, though the leggings seemed stiff, and she wondered if they had washed them. It would take her many hours to work them soft again. Her foot was too swollen to fit into her tall moccasins, and Adele had brought her some loose, knitted stockings to pull on over the bandages.

Sister Adele, the youngest, sat beside her and sent her frequent smiles of encouragement. When Sister Marie had sat down, all the sisters clasped their hands, lowered their chins, and closed their eyes. All but Adele. She smiled at

Taabe and held up her clasped hands.

Taabe put her hands together as Adele was doing. The sister smiled and nodded. Then she bowed her head and closed her eyes, then peeked at Taabe as if to see if she was copying her.

Taabe looked around. Sister Natalie, at the end of the table, was watching through slits of eyes. The other two waited like statues, hands clasped, eyes shut.

Cautiously, Taabe lowered her head and closed her eyes. Were they waiting for something?

Sister Natalie began to speak. Taabe's eyelids flew open, and she gazed at her. The others sat motionless. After Sister Natalie had spoken for a short time, they all said "amen"—at the same moment. How did they know when to speak?

The four women in black were all looking at her. Marie laughed and said something to the one whose name Taabe didn't know. They both smiled and reached for the food dishes. Taabe wished she understood. Maybe they were making fun of her.

She watched as they scooped portions of food onto their plates. Adele held out a dish of cooked beans to her. Taabe pointed to the food and spoke the Comanche word for beans.

Adele's eyebrows rose. The other sisters fell silent and stared at them.

Was it wrong for her to speak?

No, Adele's eyes held an eager spark.

Taabe repeated the word and pointed to the dish.

"Beans," Adele said. "These are beans."

"Beans," Taabe said softly.

Adele smiled at her. "Yes. Would you care for some beans, Taabe Waipu?" She nodded toward the spoon handle protruding from the dish. Taabe took it and carefully spooned a portion of beans onto her plate.

By the time the meal was over, she had learned the words for water and bread, or at least she believed she had. The word Adele spoke when she indicated the crumbly yellow bread might be corn, or some word for that type of bread. But it was a name, and Taabe could ask for the yellow bread now if she wished.

Adele and Marie helped her back to her room. She hopped along, holding them both by the shoulders. They wanted to carry her, but Taabe insisted on supplying some of the power. She wanted to regain her strength quickly—ironic, since the effort made her fall exhausted onto the narrow bed.

Adele tucked her in, then reached down and removed something from beneath the bed. Taabe stared and reached out for it. Her parfleche. She opened it and felt inside. All her things were there, even the split water skin.

She smiled at Adele and nodded. Adele smiled and went out, closing the door behind her.

Taabe lay in the dim room with her hand inside the bag, touching the soft doeskin pouch of beads her sister, Pia, had given her. The odd, muffled sound she had heard once before reached her. The sisters were singing. She wrapped her fingers around the little flute in her parfleche. When she was stronger, perhaps she could sit up and play it.

How long would she be here with these women? They were kind to her. Once her ankle healed, would they help her find her true people?

She closed her eyes and listened to the cadence of their song.

A man wanted to see her. That much Taabe understood. Was it the man who had come before, bringing the woman who cried and her husband? She hoped it was him—the tall, handsome man for whom she felt a connection. She had no way to ask the sisters.

Perhaps it would be another white man looking to see if she belonged to his family. She understood that now—the couple who had come a few days ago hoped she was the daughter they'd lost to the Numinu. More people might come—the Numinu kept numerous Texans and Mexicans among their bands. Some were slaves and treated as such. Others were accepted as family members, as she had been. After some time, when they had proven they would not run away, these were given the same privileges and freedoms as native members of the people.

Taabe curled her lip at the thought. For many seasons, many years, she had stayed with the Numinu—stayed until she remembered little of her other life. Only fading glimpses came to her now. But always she had kept in her heart the knowledge that she didn't truly belong with the Numinu. The crumpled paper in her parfleche was a thread that bound her to the world of the whites. She'd hidden it for a long time, afraid one of her captors would take it from her. The markings on it had meaning, but she could not remember what. Long ago . . . as a child, she had been able to look at it and tell what it meant. And it was important. She knew that as surely as she knew the sun would rise again. But why it was important—that she had forgotten.

The other children in the band told her she would hate it if she went back. White children were made to work hard and to stay inside where you could not feel the wind on your face. They were forced to wear constrictive clothing and eat foods not fit for man.

She had been waiting what seemed a long time. Perhaps the visitor was not a white man. But no—if it were Peca or someone else from the Numinu, the sisters would be alarmed. And they would not know in advance.

She sat on her bed and leaned against the wall, waiting. Sister Marie had combed her hair that morning. She hadn't gone out to the eating room, as she was still weak and feverish. Sister Adele had brought her breakfast on a tray and wiped her face with cool water. The food the sisters served was plain, but they seemed to have plenty of it. For most meals here she got more than she would have in the Numinu village. After she had eaten and rested, Sister Adele returned and helped her put on her Comanche dress and told her a man was coming soon.

The door opened and Taabe jumped. She sat up straighter and peered toward the opening.

Sister Adele entered, smiling, and lit the lamp that now stayed on the small table by the pottery bowl and pitcher. Taabe loved the lamp, with its brightness and warmth. She understood the sisters' mimed admonitions to be careful with it and never, ever, knock it over.

But now she gave no thought to the lamp, except that its flame allowed her to see the tall man who entered behind Sister Adele.

She caught her breath and clenched her hands into fists. She shouldn't fear this man—she had returned to the world of the whites by her own will. Yet it was hard to ignore the reaction that had been drilled into her.

The Numinu were courageous people. But if there was one thing they feared, it was the uniform of the long knives.

CHAPTER SIX

Ned circled the stagecoach and stopped the team heading outward. He set the brake and looked over at Brownie.

"I won't be long."

"Better not be. The passengers are in a hurry."

Ned reached into the driver's boot where he and Brownie kept their personal belongings—right next to the currently empty treasure box—and grabbed the bundle Patrillo had put together for the nuns. He climbed down, hurried to the door of the mission, and pulled the cord that rang a bell somewhere inside the adobe walls.

Sister Natalie opened the door. She looked up at him with a restrained smile. "Mr. Bright. How nice to see you again."

"Hello, Sister." Amazing how the title flowed from his lips so easily now. He felt a prick of conscience only if he mulled it over.

"Have you brought more distraught parents seeking their children?"

"Not this time." Ned held out the bundle of clothing. "My partner at the station, Patrillo Garza, asked me to bring you this. It's a dress and a few other things that belonged to his wife. For the girl."

"How kind of him. Thank you." Sister Natalie took the bundle.

"How is she doing?"

Sister Natalie looked past him toward the stagecoach. "I don't suppose you can come in for a moment."

"I'm not supposed to even stop. I'm sorry. Wish I could."

"She's making progress. She's still weak, and she had a fever for a few days, but that seems to be waning. She leaves her room for meals with us at least once a day now."

"That's good. Does she understand anything you say?"

"Not much." Sister Natalie frowned. "We've tried English and French. I told the other sisters not to speak French to her anymore. We don't want to confuse her. Learning—or relearning—one language will be difficult enough. But she is beginning to speak a few words."

"She's cooperative, then?"

"Oh, yes. She seems eager to be able to communicate. Yesterday the captain rode out from the fort. I think she was frightened of him at first, but I had Sister Adele bring a slate and help them converse with drawings as well as hand signs."

"That gives me hope. Did you learn anything?"

"The captain brought a list of names that he read to her slowly—children who'd been captured over the last few years. But she didn't show any signs of recognition. He says he's written to the Indian agent at Fort Smith about her and asked for any clues about blue-eyed girls who've been taken."

"Good. I'll speak to the captain myself this evening if I'm able. And if there's time I'll stop again Sunday. I'd best get going now."

"Hey!" One of the passengers was leaning out the door of

the stage. "Are we going to Fort Chadbourne, or what?"

Ned touched his hat brim. "Good-bye, Sister." He sprinted for the stagecoach.

"We brought you another parent who's lost a child." Ned nodded toward the man climbing out of the stagecoach on Sunday. "If he's satisfied that Taabe Waipu is not his daughter, he'll go with us to the home station and then on to Fort Belknap."

"So you'll wait for him," Sister Natalie said.

"Yes. If she's his daughter, he'll stay."

The man wore a dark suit and had the look of a townsman—a shopkeeper, perhaps. A presentable man who should not offer any trouble to the mission enclave.

"Would you mind coming in with him, Mr. Bright?"

"Not at all."

Ned entered the mission with the passenger—Joseph Henderson—and waited with him in the sitting room. Henderson paced, fidgeting with his hat. Ned hoped the sisters wouldn't keep them long. He'd told Brownie ten minutes at most. He had no faith that he'd found Taabe's father. For one thing, Henderson had brown eyes. Ned hadn't bothered to ask what his daughter, Miriam, looked like or how old she was. Everyone with a missing daughter wanted to see the girl, even if she didn't meet their child's description. No words could convince them until they had seen her.

To Ned's surprise, instead of returning to escort them to Taabe's room, Sister Natalie and one of the other nuns—Sister Marie, he believed—came back with Taabe limping between them and leaning on their arms.

She didn't look up as she entered the room. The nuns led her to a stool, and she sat down.

Ned caught his breath. What a difference the nuns had made!

Taabe's hair glinted in the shaft of sunlight from the window. In Elena Garza's long lavender dress with black trim, she looked serene and elegant, though the dress hung loosely on her thin frame. Instead of shoes, her feet were encased in the tall, beaded moccasins he'd found her in. Her blue eyes appraised Henderson then focused on Ned, sending a wave of kinship through him. It was almost like meeting an old friend after a lengthy absence. He hoped she was glad to see him too.

Ned smiled, and Taabe's lips twitched, as though she wanted to respond. His heart surged.

Henderson stepped toward her. "Good morning, young lady. May I ask your name?"

Taabe swung her gaze back to him, but said nothing.

"Shall we all sit down?" Sister Natalie said.

Henderson frowned but took a seat. Sister Natalie sat near Taabe, and Sister Marie stood back, near the door. Ned watched Taabe, who sat quietly, her hands clasped on her lap, her back straight. A ray of sunshine still reached her, perhaps by Sister Natalie's design, to illuminate her face for the visitor's benefit. Her hair gleamed a lighter brown than he'd expected, no doubt thanks to the nuns' patient care. The right side of her tanned face still bore some discoloration, but the swelling had abated, and he judged that she would be deemed pretty in any culture. She did not appear frightened this time, and barely curious. He wondered how many of these sessions she had undergone in five days.

"First of all, Mr. Henderson," Sister Natalie said, "our guest understands only a handful of English words. She calls herself Taabe Waipu, and she appears not to remember her original name."

Ned recalled what Reece Jones had told him. Sun Woman. Now it seemed appropriate. Had her hair been even lighter when she was a child? Perhaps it had floated about her in a golden cloud when the Comanche took her.

"I'm just not sure," Henderson said. "It's been so long, and this young lady looks a bit older than our Miriam. But I realize I'm thinking of her as she was four years ago."

"What about her eyes?" Ned asked.

Henderson hesitated and squinted at Taabe. "They were blue. My wife was German. She's passed on now. This broke her heart—the raid. Losing the children. They took our son, Paul, as well."

"If this is your daughter, she might remember being taken with her brother," Sister Natalie said gently.

Henderson nodded and leaned forward. "Paul," he said. "Do you remember Paul, your brother?"

Taabe gave no response.

"Miriam." Henderson said the name distinctly. They all watched Taabe. She sat motionless, with no change in her expression. Henderson sighed. "What *can* she understand?"

"A few words pertaining to food, clothing, the body . . . not much else yet, I fear," the nun said.

"Does Miriam have other siblings?" Ned asked.

"Yes." Henderson returned his attention to Taabe. "Do you remember John? John. Little brother." He held his hand about two feet above the floor. "And baby Sarah?" He folded his arms and rocked them.

Taabe shook her head.

"Mama?" Henderson asked.

Taabe frowned.

"Mama? Baby Sarah?"

Taabe looked at Sister Natalie, her face filled with bafflement.

"She's not sure what you want," Sister Natalie said. "I'm sorry."

"How old would your Miriam be?" Ned asked.

"Fourteen."

Taabe seemed considerably older, but Ned didn't feel it was his place to say so.

"Did your daughter have any distinguishing marks?" Sister Natalie asked.

Henderson shook his head and blinked. His eyes glistened. "I can't recall any." He rose and walked to the narrow window.

"Anything at all," the nun said gently.

Henderson peered out through the opening. Taabe looked to Sister Natalie, who reached over and patted her arm.

Henderson swung around. "She had stubby little fingers." He held up his hand. "My middle finger isn't longer than the rest, like most people's. Hers were that way too."

Sister Natalie spoke softly to Taabe and held out her hands, with the fingers together. Taabe hesitated and copied her. Sister Natalie looked at Taabe's hands and compared them to her own.

Henderson strode over and stared at Taabe's hands. Ned rose, fighting the impulse to rush over and look.

Taabe's haunted look returned as Henderson towered over her. She drew back her hands and looked up at him, her lips parted and her forehead wrinkled.

"I don't see how she can be Miriam," Sister Natalie said. "Her middle fingers are obviously the longest on both hands."

Henderson's shoulders sagged as he stepped back. "Thank you. I don't suppose I'll ever find our girl. It sickens me, when I think of Miriam living with those natives and being taught their heathen ways." He swiped at a tear and cleared his throat. "Thank you." He turned and stalked past Sister Marie. The door closed with a thud.

Ned drew in a deep breath and stepped toward the women.

"I'm sorry for all the intrusions you're getting."

"It's necessary, I suppose," Sister Natalie said. "The captain questions them and makes sure they are sincere in their search, not just people who want to look at her out of curiosity. I wish we could just let her rest and recover for a few weeks, but people keep coming."

Ned nodded. "She looks fine."

"She's thin yet, but we're working on that," Sister Natalie said.

Ned realized Taabe was watching him, and he smiled at her. "You look very nice." He gestured toward her dress.

Taabe frowned a moment then looked down. Her hands brushed the lavender fabric, and a smile touched her lips. She gazed into his eyes and touched her chest.

"Taabe Waipu." She pointed at Ned and arched her eyebrows. "You?"

He laughed and shot Sister Natalie a glance. "Ned. Ned Bright." He held out his hand.

Hesitantly, Taabe touched it with her long, slender fingers. Ned grasped her hand for a moment then released it.

"Pleased to make your acquaintance, Taabe Waipu." To Sister Natalie he said, "The captain asked me to tell you the fort's surgeon will ride out tomorrow to examine her, and he'll bring crutches."

"Praise God," said Sister Natalie. "She's still weak, but I think she's ready to use them. And it will be good to have the doctor's opinion, though it would have been more useful if he could have come sooner."

"Is it true you are going to open a school here?"

"Eventually. It's taken us a while to get settled, and our garden won't produce until next summer. But we might take in a few girls over the winter, if the parents are willing to donate supplies or money for their board. But we can't handle more than half a dozen at this point."

"And now you have a patient who can't understand you." Ned smiled. "I asked because Señor Garza has mentioned possibly bringing his daughter to you. Since his wife died . . . well, he has four sons and only the one girl, and—"

"How old is she?"

"I believe she's nine."

Sister Natalie nodded. "A good age. We would consider her."

"I'll tell Patrillo."

Taabe stood in the dooryard with Sister Marie until the big wagon left. Ned Bright had climbed on top and sat with another man, behind a team of four mules. Long leather reins ran from his hands to the mules' mouths. The other man who had come and tried to talk to her was now inside the wagon.

Sister Marie pointed to the departing vehicle. "Stagecoach."

Taabe tried to say the word, but the sounds were hard to get her tongue around. Sister Marie repeated it several times. Finally she was happy with Taabe's pronunciation.

"Come." She turned toward the house.

Taabe shook her head. She pointed to the low stone wall that separated the dooryard from a spot where the earth had been worked up. The neat rows in the dirt fascinated Taabe, and she wanted to see them up close.

Sister Marie shook her head and tugged Taabe's arm.

"No, we must go in. Sister Natalie . . ."

Taabe couldn't decipher the rest, but she gathered that Sister Natalie had forbidden the others to take her outside for long. Perhaps it was best. She was very tired. She let Sister Marie help her back to her room, where she lay down.

Within a few days, she was able to hobble about the yard with one of the sisters, using crutches the bluecoat medicine man brought. She didn't like him. He probed her ankle and peered into her mouth and ears and spoke for a long time with Sister Natalie. Taabe could tell he was talking about her. He left the crutches and some white pills that Sister Natalie wanted her to swallow with every meal. They tasted vile, and after the first, Taabe refused.

Sister Riva, who seemed the quietest, took her outside one warm morning and led her through a gate to the place of turned earth. She got across to Taabe that this was to be her garden, and she planned to grow food in it. Taabe knew about growing corn, though the Numinu did not live in one place long enough to cultivate the earth. She had an idea that her old family—her white mother and father—had tilled the soil.

The Numinu didn't grow vegetables. They hunted and raided and occasionally gathered fruit. But in Taabe's heart something stirred as she watched the sister, in her flowing habit, stoop to run a handful of earth through her fingers. This was the way white people got their food, through much labor, rather than stealing it from others.

The people she'd lived with disdained the whites for working so hard. And yet when winter came, they would have food to eat. The sisters would have no starving months, the way the Numinu had almost every year. If you lived with the whites, they would make you work all day, Pia's mother had told her many times. They forced children to work for them and to grow food for them.

Taabe wasn't sure about that. She didn't remember being made to work the earth. Compulsory labor had no place in her memory. Were the whites really so cruel to their children?

Sister Riva insisted that Taabe wear a wide-brimmed straw hat outside, like the one she wore over her head cloth. Sister

Riva never tried to get Taabe to talk, which was restful. She showed her a small wooden bench on the outside of the low wall. Taabe sat there in the sun while Sister Riva worked. She used a spade to dig in the dirt and turn over clumps of sod. She shook the soil off the roots and threw the tops aside.

At the end of an hour, Sister Adele came out of the mission house, smiling and calling to her. Taabe rose, using the crutches to help her balance. Adele beckoned and pointed to the house. Time to go in. Taabe waved to Sister Riva and followed.

The next morning, her fever was back. Taabe wanted to fight the sickness, but every time she tried to rise, her head swam and she fell back on the pillow.

For several days she had risen and dressed herself, then gone to the eating room for breakfast. Now she heard the bell, one Sister Marie rang when a meal was ready, but she couldn't answer the summons. Sister Adele came in search of her.

"Taabe! Are you ill?" She came to the bedside and laid a cool hand on Taabe's brow. "You poor thing. You're hot again. Let me bathe your forehead." She brought one of the pills the uniformed man had left and a cup of water. "Take this, my dear. You must."

Though her words were gentle, Taabe understood her urgency and forced herself to swallow the bitter medicine.

Sister Adele smiled and crooned over her. She poured water from the pitcher into the big bowl and wrung out a white cloth in the water. She pulled the stool beside the bed and sat down.

Taabe closed her eyes and let Sister Adele dab at her forehead with the wet cloth. The nun began to hum. Taabe let her mind drift. She missed the open skies, the camp of many Numinu beside a stream, the laughter and camaraderie with the others. She missed the babies and the horses. She missed her sister, Pia, and Pia's husband. She missed their little girl, her smiles and cooing. Her memory stretched further back to another child—a little boy. Tears burned in her eyes and she made herself stop thinking of the Numinu. She listened to Sister Adele's quiet melody.

How long would she stay here with the sisters? They treated her kindly, but at times she felt imprisoned. They would not let her stay outside long. Taabe understood they feared she would weaken if she tried to do too much. Perhaps they were also concerned that prying eyes might see her. Sister Riva had let her sit in the shadow of the garden wall, but not in the open.

Perhaps Peca and the other men had given up looking for her. But she had known them to chase an escaped slave for weeks. They always brought back the runaway. Or his scalp. She shivered.

Sister Adele began a new tune. After a moment, Taabe caught her breath and listened closely. The words meant nothing, but the tune seemed familiar. She lay perfectly still, anticipating the rise and fall of Sister Adele's voice. She had heard this song before. Not here, and not in the land of the Numinu. Her heart ached as she listened.

The nun stopped singing and spoke quietly, under her breath, on and on. The sisters did that often. Taabe had decided they were speaking to spirits. Sometimes they looked at the little figure on the wall and touched themselves on their foreheads and chests. They all did it the same way, and Taabe felt it was a ritual of some kind. She couldn't fathom its purpose. Someday maybe she would speak their language well enough to ask. If she stayed that long.

When she was well and her ankle would support her again, perhaps she could go on to another place. She must have a family out there. Certainly she didn't belong here with the sisters, though she was beginning to know and even appreciate them. She could be friends with Sister Adele, she was sure.

Sister Marie glided into the room. Taabe heard the rustle of her black dress and opened her eyes.

"She is ill again?"

"Yes," said Sister Adele. "Some tea perhaps, and a little gruel."

"I will bring it."

Taabe was surprised that she understood the brief conversation. In time, maybe she would feel she belonged here.

CHAPTER SEVEN

Ned followed Sister Riva around the back of the mission house. The sister pointed to a low adobe wall with a gate. "That is our garden. Taabe likes to sit there. We don't leave her outside alone very long, but she cannot be seen from the road when she sits inside the garden wall."

"Thank you. How is she?" Ned asked.

"She is getting stronger." Sister Riva smiled. "She tries to help us. Though she is still too weak to do heavy work, she washes dishes and helps with the laundry. She seems amazed at the quantity of hot water we use."

"Is she picking up English?"

"Oh, yes. Sister Adele has begun daily sessions with her, and we all converse with her. It's a bit odd, since we normally don't speak much. But having Taabe here is like having a child about the place."

Ned smiled. "It will be quite a change when you begin to take pupils."

"Oh, yes." Sister Riva frowned. "The Lord will give us grace."

"I'm sure He will." Ned looked toward the garden wall. "Taabe is no longer frightened?"

"Only when strangers come."

"Does that happen often?"

"Almost daily now. The captain sent two men from the fort yesterday with some supplies. He said it was because we've used our resources to care for her. We can always use a bit extra." She smiled. "We don't see much meat, and they brought a quarter of beef. Imagine, for the five of us. Sister Marie is drying some of it. And another man came hoping to find out where his son is."

"His son?"

"Yes. These poor parents, Mr. Bright. They are distraught and would do anything to find their children. This gentleman had lost a boy, but like the rest, he hoped Taabe could tell him she'd seen him."

"Did Taabe speak to him?"

"She looked at the photograph the man brought and said no." Sister Riva sighed. "These visits wear on her, but I think she hopes the right family will come one day."

"You believe she really wants to find her own people?"

"I think that is why she came."

Ned nodded, thinking about that. Had Taabe risked her life to escape the Comanche and find her birth family? It was unheard of—at least for a captive who had been with the Comanche for any length of time. Six months to a year, it was said, and the children would not go back voluntarily. "God works in ways we don't understand."

"Oh, yes." Sister Riva smiled at him. Ned wondered what had brought this woman—all of them—into her role as a nun. Had she fled some dire situation, or run toward what she believed was God's best for her?

"You haven't seen any sign of Indians hereabouts?"

"No, nothing. Of course we don't stand about looking for them, but we have no reason to think they are aware of her presence."

"Thank you, Sister." He ambled to the gate.

Inside the garden, he could hear a lilting voice. Sister Adele, no doubt. She and Sister Marie kept a strong French accent. Would Taabe end up speaking English like a Frenchwoman?

Ned entered the garden, and Sister Adele jumped up from a small wooden bench against the inside of the wall. Taabe scrambled to her feet, using crutches for leverage.

"Oh, Mr. Bright. You startled us." Sister Adele smiled at him and glanced at Taabe. "It's all right. You remember Mr. Bright and the stagecoach."

"Ned Bright." Taabe pointed to him, and he laughed.

Taabe's smile was warmer than the sun on his shoulders. Maybe that was why they called her Sun Woman, though he could now see that golden highlights rippled through her luxuriant hair. Most women wore their hair up, or at least tied back, but Taabe's flowed in generous waves over the shoulders of her lavender dress. The sight of her set his heart pounding, and Ned had to look away.

"It's wonderful to see her looking so well," he told Sister Adele.

"Tell her yourself."

Ned stepped closer and looked into Taabe's blue eyes. He spoke the Comanche greeting he'd badgered Reece into teaching him.

Her eyes widened, and she answered him, smiling.

"You look well, Taabe."

"Thank you," she said carefully.

Ned grinned wide enough to swallow an ox. He glanced at

the items Sister Adele held—a small slate and chalk. "English lessons?"

"Yes. Isn't she progressing marvelously?"

"Yes, and your English is very good too."

"Thank you." Sister Adele's cheeks pinked. "Sister Natalie insists we speak English only with our guest."

"Is that difficult for you?"

She shrugged. "I grew up in New Orleans, speaking French at home, but I learned English in school and from some friends. When I entered the convent, I continued to study English. My superiors felt it was important for our missions."

"Will you be teaching in the school here?"

"I hope so. Teaching Taabe is a fulfillment of my dreams. I never thought I'd have a pupil with a background like hers—or one so apt." She held out the slate, which held several small drawings. "We are using this to learn new vocabulary."

"Horse," Ned said.

"Horse," Taabe repeated.

He chuckled. "Very good." He pointed to a small drawing of a bird and looked at her.

"Bird."

"Yes." He pointed to her. "Waipu. Woman."

Taabe eyed him with raised eyebrows. "Yes. Woman."

Ned pointed to himself and offered one of the last Comanche words he'd learned. "Tenahpu. Man."

Taabe reached out and touched the front of his leather vest. "Yes. Ned Bright. Man."

Sister Adele laughed. "In no time she'll be communicating fluently."

"I think you're right," Ned said. "Taabe, soon I hope to bring another man here. A man who speaks your language."

Taabe frowned, watching his lips.

Ned puzzled over how to get his meaning across. He

pointed at her and then at Sister Adele. "Woman. Woman." He touched his chest. "Man."

Taabe nodded.

Ned gestured as though someone else stood near him. "Man. Another man."

Slowly she nodded.

Ned touched his mouth. "Talk. Man talk . . . to you." He pointed to her.

Taabe turned an uncomprehending frown on Sister Adele.

Sister Adele touched her arm. "Ned Bright will go." She made walking motions with her fingers. "He will come back." She demonstrated, and Taabe nodded. "Another man will come with him." She handed Ned the slate and made two sets of walking legs from her fingers. "He will talk." She moved her lips and at the same time moved her hand, close to her mouth, opening and closing the fingers to signify talking. "To you." She pointed to Taabe.

Taabe nodded, but she still seemed unsure.

"When will you do this?" Sister Adele asked Ned.

"I'm not sure. The next time I take the stagecoach to the fort—which will be Friday—I hope to find someone who can translate for us."

"You're not with the stagecoach today?"

"No. I came with my partner, Patrillo Garza. He brought his daughter to meet Sister Natalie. He hopes she can come here as a pupil."

Sister Adele's eyes lit. "I would like to meet her."

"I'm sure she'd like to meet you," Ned said. "Especially if you are to be one of her teachers. Of course . . ." He glanced at Taabe. "She's especially eager to meet Taabe. Do you think that's possible?"

"I think it's a wonderful idea." She turned to Taabe and made a fluttering motion near her cheeks, like flowing hair. "Woman."

Taabe nodded.

Sister Adele held her hand palm down, about waist level. "Girl."

"Girr."

"Girl."

Sister Adele seized the slate and drew a hasty portrayal of a stick woman wearing a long, triangular skirt. "Woman." Taabe nodded. Beside the woman, Sister Adele drew a smaller figure like it. "Girl."

"Girl."

"Yes. Come, let's go and meet a girl." Sister Adele took Taabe's arm and led her out through the gate.

Ned followed at a leisurely pace and closed the gate. When he reached the front of the house, the door was open, so he went into the cool hallway. In the sitting room to the side, Quinta was chattering eagerly. He stepped into the room and saw that Taabe was the object of the girl's excitement. Patrillo, Sister Adele, and Sister Natalie stood by watching with amusement. Taabe's bright eyes were riveted to Quinta's face.

"Did you have your own horse?" Quinta asked. "Did they let you ride?"

"Horse," Taabe said.

"I knew it! What did it look like?"

Taabe frowned and shook her head.

"Your horse. What color was it?"

"I'm afraid her English isn't that good yet, my dear," Sister Natalie said.

Taabe turned to Sister Adele and took the slate and chalk. She wiped out the simple figures with her palm and sketched the outline of a horse, then added splotches on the animal's side and face.

"You had a spotted horse!" Quinta grabbed Taabe's hand

and bounced up and down. "You must have had a grand time with the Comanche."

"Quinta," Patrillo said sharply. "Her time with the Comanche was not for fun."

"But she got to have her own horse, Papa."

Patrillo sighed and shook his head. "I'm sorry, Sisters. My daughter has much to learn."

"She is charming," Sister Natalie said. "As you know, we expect to take other students. We're preparing rooms for them now. So far we have two interested families. If you think you would like to place Quinta here, just let us know. She is welcome any time."

Patrillo hesitated. "Sister, do you think you will be safe, you and the girls? You have no one here to protect you."

"Yes, we do." Sister Natalie's serene smile seemed to calm him. "We've come here in answer to God's calling. We believe He wants a school here—one where girls can receive a spiritual education as well as an academic one. He will watch over us, Señor Garza."

"But the Indian trouble . . ."

"We have heard of none since we moved here," Sister Natalie said. "Of course, it has only been about two months. I'm sure there will be incidents, but we trust the Lord to protect us."

"Papa," Quinta said.

"What is it?"

She looked down at the floor. "Nothing."

"We can talk later." He smiled at Sister Natalie. "Thank you for showing us the mission. If I decide to send Quinta, I will bring her and her things when the stagecoach comes."

"Very good, Señor Garza." Sister Natalie bowed her head.

"All right, Quinta. Say good-bye." Patrillo nodded at his daughter.

Quinta glanced up at Sister Natalie and Sister Adele. "*Adios*. I mean good-bye." She turned to Taabe, and her face brightened. "Good-bye. I hope to see you again, and you can tell me more about your horse."

Taabe chuckled. "Good-bye."

Patrillo led Quinta out, and Ned nodded to the sisters and Taabe.

"Ladies. I hope to see you again soon." His gaze lingered on Taabe.

She was watching him, and his pulse galloped.

Carefully and distinctly, she said, "Good-bye, Ned Bright."

He nodded and clapped his hat on as he hurried out the door to where Patrillo and Quinta waited.

As soon as she was strong enough to walk about the mission, Taabe began to work. Women always did the work of the family, and in a family of only women, they all had their chores. Sister Marie did most of the cooking. Sister Riva prepared the garden for planting in the spring. She also kept their water buckets and the box beside Sister Marie's stove full. Sister Adele did the laundry and much of the cleaning. Sister Natalie helped with all these things and many others, but she also spent many hours in the dim room the sisters called "chapel."

Taabe saw her coming and going from the room. Once Taabe had drawn back the curtain over the doorway and peered in. Several candles flickered within. Unlike the other rooms, this one had a floor of flat stones. Sister Natalie was kneeling at a low bench, facing the wall farthest from the one slit of a window. On the wall was a figure like the one in Taabe's room, only larger. The dying man on the torture rack. Taabe shivered and dropped the edge of the curtain. Someday, when she knew enough words, she would ask Sister Adele about that man.

Since Sister Adele spent more time with her than the others, and since she seemed so eager to teach Taabe new words, she was the one Taabe most wanted to help. Taabe couldn't carry heavy loads yet, but she could help Sister Adele when she wiped dust from tables and shelves, scrubbed floors, or washed clothing. When Adele went to Sister Marie's kitchen to wash dishes, Taabe followed her. She made her intentions clear by taking the scrub cloth from Sister Adele's hand and saying, "Me." The sisters understood and allowed her to do light work.

After each session, they insisted Taabe rest for a while. She did not like to admit weakness, even to herself, but leaning on her crutches for a short time while she cleaned the dishes did drain her strength.

The day after Quinta's visit, Sister Adele accompanied Taabe to her room to help her remove her outer skirt and settle on her bed. The sister leaned Taabe's crutches against the adobe wall, where she could reach them easily.

Taabe reached out and patted the stool beside the bed.

Sister Adele looked at her in surprise. "You want me to stay?"

"Song." It was one of the new words the nun had taught her. Taabe felt shy, not certain she should ask, but she wanted to hear Sister Adele sing again. Specifically, she hoped to hear the song that had sounded familiar.

Sister Adele sat and began softly to sing one of the songs the sisters sang in the chapel room. Taabe closed her eyes. It was not the one she had hoped to hear, but she would wait.

Every day the sisters went into the chapel at certain times. All of them went early in the morning, and again after breakfast. Late in the afternoon they gathered again, before supper, and once more after the sun had set. Taabe heard their songs, and sometimes quiet chanting.

Sister Adele finished her song and started to rise.

In Comanche, Taabe said, "Wait."

Sister Adele peered at her.

"Song," Taabe said.

Sister Adele smiled and resumed her seat. She began singing—the same song she had just sung.

Taabe's frustration grew. How could she explain? She sat up and felt along the edge of the bed for her parfleche. She took out her small flute and began to play.

Sister Adele's jaw dropped. After a moment she sat back, smiling.

Taabe finished the simple melody and lowered the flute. "Song?"

"That's 'Frère Jacques,'" Sister Adele said. "How clever of you!"

Taabe raised the flute and played the tune again. Sister Adele sang with her, softly.

"Frère," Taabe said, eyeing the nun.

"It means Brother Jacques—or James, I guess." Sister Adele went to a shelf near the door and took down the slate and chalk. She sat and quickly sketched four stick figures. "Family. Father, mother, brother, sister." She pointed in turn to each figure.

Taabe frowned and took the slate. She pointed to the figures and said slowly, "Man, woman, boy, girl."

Sister Adele nodded, smiling. "Yes, but this is a family." She drew a small bundle in the woman's arms. "Baby."

"Baby," Taabe said.

"Yes. Papa, Mama."

"Mama."

"That's right. Baby."

"Baby."

Sister Adele pointed to the boy. "Brother." She drew a line between the boy and the girl and pointed to each. "Sister. Brother."

Taabe was familiar with the word *sister*. She placed her hand on Adele's wrist.

"Sister. You."

Sister Adele laughed. "Yes, I am Sister Adele. We are all called 'sister,' but that's different. In a family—" She tapped the slate with the chalk. "—the sister is the girl." Again she touched the boy and girl figures. "Brother. Sister."

Taabe frowned. It was too confusing.

Sister Adele went through the entire family again. "Father. Mother. Baby. Brother. Sister."

Suddenly it all fit together, and Taabe caught her breath. "Mama." She pointed to the woman.

"Yes."

"Sister." She touched the girl.

"Yes." Adele's face glowed.

Taabe put her hand to her chest. "I. Sister."

"You are a sister?" Adele frowned. "You *have* a sister?"

Taabe thought of Pia, the girl she had grown up with, whose lodge she had lived in after their mother died. She whispered the Comanche word for sister. Her eyes burned with tears. She did miss Pia and her family. The life among the Numinu was a hard one. They had no beds, no stoves, no store-rooms full of food. But she did love Pia and her baby girl. The others of the people she cared about as well. Perhaps she was making a terrible mistake to leave them behind. What lay beyond this temporary life with the sisters?

She touched the nun's sleeve, still confused over the words. "Sister?"

"Oh, I don't have any sisters," Adele said. "Well, not out-side of the church. We're all sisters here because we're sisters in Christ." She pointed to the carved figure on the wall.

Taabe looked up at the man hanging there, more baffled than ever.

CHAPTER EIGHT

The westbound stage arrived a few minutes early, and Ned was still in the ranch house. He grabbed his hat and whip.

"Papa, I don't want to live at the mission." Quinta set the pitcher of milk on the table with a thump.

Patrillo frowned at her. "We will talk about it later. Right now you get the table set. We have three passengers to feed today. Quick!"

Ned followed Patrillo outside, where the passengers—three men who had come from Fort Smith—were taking turns at the water basin.

Patrillo carried the sack of mail straight to the stagecoach. Ned paused under the eaves and called to the passengers, "Dinner is ready, gents. We leave in ten minutes."

The men rushed inside. Ned ambled to the stage and took the pot of grease from Benito. He worked his way around the coach, applying grease as needed to the wheel fittings. By the time he'd finished, the boys had the teams switched, Tree had settled the mail sacks inside, and Brownie had stowed his small bundle of belongings in the driver's boot.

"One of the passengers asked me to put a packet in the treasure box," Tree told him softly.

Ned nodded. So far they hadn't carried much for valuables, other than the mail. It wasn't as if they were in the middle of a mining district. But the desolate miles they traveled made them vulnerable to holdups. Reports had come from other areas of road agents robbing the passengers and stealing the mail sacks. The fact that the stagecoaches came to them after traveling through Indian Territory seemed to lend a little insurance. The tribes between Fort Smith and Texas knew that if they attacked the mail coaches, they would be severely punished and their agents along the route would lose their commissions. Still, a lot of people were leery of riding the stage through Indian lands.

"Are you going to put Quinta at the mission?" he asked.

Tree gritted his teeth. "I don't know. She gets wilder and wilder. Yesterday she rode clear out to the cliffs by herself. I wanted to tan her hide."

"Think the sisters can tame her?"

"I don't know." Tree shook his head. "Sister Natalie thinks so, but I'm not so sure. I'm thinking on it. She'd have to speak English all the time."

"Is that bad?"

"Maybe. Maybe not. I want her to be able to speak good English. People think better of you then, and treat you better."

"Really?" Ned grinned. "Maybe I'll treat you better if you start talking better."

Tree laughed. "Maybe so. Are you stopping by the mission?"

"If I can find a translator."

"I thought maybe I'd send something else for that girl,

Taabe. They're doing a good job with her."

Ned looked up at the sun. "Save it for next time. We need to get rolling."

"Right. I'll go tell the passengers you're ready."

Ned climbed to the driver's box.

The door of the house flew open and Quinta ran out and streaked toward the corral. In her overalls and plaid shirt, she looked like a little boy, except for the long, dark braids that flew out behind her.

Tree looked up at him. "If you see the sisters, tell them I'll bring her to them for a week. They can see what they think."

"Will do." Ned looked at Brownie. This gave him an excuse to stop by the mission, regardless of whether he found someone who could speak Comanche.

Brownie shook his head. "Can't say I envy the sisters."

Taabe sat on the floor in her room, playing her flute softly. She ran through the melody of "Frère Jacques," then mimicked one of the songs she'd heard the nuns singing in their chapel room. Dissatisfied with that—she wasn't quite getting it right, and this displeased her—she went back to the melodies she had learned in the camps of the Numinu.

As she played, images of the people she'd known danced across her mind. Pia, the baby, and Pia's husband, Chano—a stern warrior, but gentle with his family. The older woman who had been her mother for so long, until she died two winters ago in a time of sickness and near starvation. Others who had died—some that she loved dearly. Then there were the Numinu children she had played with as a child, men returning from raiding with painted faces that frightened her, and captives that drew her pity.

Peca. She shuddered at the thought of the man who had

pursued her. She had been here with the sisters many days, but Peca had not come to take her back. Her flight must have angered and shamed him. She couldn't imagine the proud warrior ignoring the slight. No, Peca had followed her. He may have lost her trail, but he had surely found her horse. And so many white people had come to stare at her. If they all knew she was here, Peca would find her eventually.

She continued to play songs of the Numinu, but she stared up at the figure on the wall. "Cross," Adele had said. The man hung on a cross. And he was God's Son. That much Taabe had grasped. The sisters believed their God was bigger than any other spirits. Taabe wasn't sure why His Son was being tortured on the cross, but she knew now that when the sisters spoke with their eyes shut, they were talking to Him. Praying, they called it.

Somehow that seemed normal to Taabe. White people prayed. How did she know this? The soldiers, the farmers, people like Ned Bright the stagecoach driver—did they all pray? In the shadows of her memory she could see white people with their eyes closed, their lips moving, speaking to their spirit God.

She had left her door open a crack, and now it creaked open. Sister Adele came in.

"That is lovely, Taabe. May I sit and listen?"

Taabe understood her name and "sit." She nodded. Adele seated herself on the stool.

"You heard Mr. Bright say that Quinta Garza will come to us soon?"

Taabe hesitated then nodded. Ned Bright's brief visit that morning had left her longing for the chance to spend more time with him—so different from the feelings Peca inspired in her. Ned had greeted them all cheerfully and told Sister Natalie something concerning Quinta. Sister Natalie had smiled and nodded, so Taabe guessed it was good news. And that must mean the girl would visit again.

Adele lifted Taabe's slate from the bedside table. "I will teach Quinta." She pointed to the slate and said again, "Quinta."

Taabe's heart lifted. The girl was coming to learn—perhaps to learn English, as she was. It might be like having a sister again. *Sister*. The word brought such longings. Did she yearn for Pia, her Comanche sister?

A girl with pale hair . . . was that a memory or did she imagine it?

She turned and looked at Sister Adele. "Family." She touched her chest and repeated, "Family." She wished she could speak what was on her heart, but she hadn't the words yet.

Sister Adele looked into her eyes. "Yes. You have a family. Somewhere."

Taabe laid aside her flute and reached for the slate.

She sketched two woman figures, one slightly larger than the other. "Taabe." She pointed to the small one, then the large. "Sister."

Adele smiled. "So. You *do* have a sister."

Taabe nodded, troubled by her thoughts. She certainly had a sister among the Numinu. But maybe she also had a white sister. Other white people hovered at the edge of memory. Who were they? Slowly she drew another woman, larger than the others. "Mama."

Adele caught her breath. "You remember your mother?"

Taabe's heart pounded. What was real, what was wishful thinking, and what was a remnant of the fears her Numinu mother had pounded into her? A beautiful white woman with a book in her hands . . . did that thought come to her because of the numerous times she had seen the nuns holding books? But the woman in her mind wore no head covering. Her pale hair made a soft cloud about her face. And she held a book and read from it aloud to Taabe and the other girl.

She lifted the flute and blew into it. Slowly she played several notes to a song she did not learn in the Numinu village. One that should be sung, but she couldn't remember the words.

The bell rang, clanging softly through the house. Sister Adele stood. "I have to go now. It's time for prayers. Thank you for playing for me."

Taabe nodded and watched her go out and shut the door soundlessly. She scrambled to her bed on her knees and grabbed her parfleche, opened it, and felt inside. Her hand trembled as she took out the folded and tattered piece of paper. Should she show it to the sisters? They might be able to tell her what it meant. Why had she kept it all this time?

"Couldn't get anyone?" Brownie spat over the side of the stagecoach.

Ned gathered the reins and released the brake. "Nope. Nobody seems to know anyone who speaks the language well."

"You'd think there'd be some buffalo hunters who would."

Ned shook his head. "The captain says one of their scouts is good, but he's off with a detachment. And somebody thought there was a boy who'd spent six months or so with the Comanche, but I couldn't find out where he lives. Might be just a rumor. Have you heard of any captured kids being recovered?"

"Not for a while, and then it was south of here."

Ned chirruped to the team and they broke into their road trot, smooth and easy. He settled back and enjoyed the drive. The cool breeze of early November was amplified by their speed, and he was glad he'd worn his leather jacket over a wool shirt.

"You stopping at the mission today?" Brownie asked.

"Just for a minute. Got a man on his way to Fort Smith who heard about the school. He wants to talk to the nuns."

Brownie nodded.

It was almost a scheduled stop now. If Ned had an excuse, such as people who hoped to identify Taabe or Catholic parents considering sending their daughters for schooling, he felt less guilty about delaying the mail.

When he halted the stage outside the large adobe, he wasn't surprised to see Tree's wagon in the dooryard. Inside he found his friend in the small parlor with Sister Natalie.

"Hello, Mr. Bright." The sister smiled. "Mr. Garza has brought us our first pupil."

"Glad to hear it," Ned said, though he still felt uneasy about a defenseless house full of women and girls. He nodded at Tree and introduced the man he'd brought.

"Sister Riva is with Quinta," Tree said, "helping her settle into her room."

Ned held out a bundle he'd brought from the fort. "I reckon you'll want to leave this with her."

"Oh, yeah, thank you." Tree took the parcel wrapped in brown paper and handed it to Sister Natalie. "Like I told you, Sister, Quinta's grown so much this year that her dress is very short. I asked Ned to pick up some material for a new one. I don't know if you will be teaching her any sewing . . ." His dark eyes gleamed with hope.

"Of course." Sister Natalie laid the bundle on a bench. She glanced at the man Ned had brought, then back to Tree. "Domestic skills are a big part of any girl's education. We'll train her in sewing, cooking, and housework, as well as spiritual studies, reading, history, English, music, mathematics, and, if you wish it, French."

Tree swallowed hard. "My Quinta can learn all of that?"

"I'm sure she can. She seems to be a very intelligent child."

"Well, she is that." Tree glanced at Ned. "But you might have some trouble keeping her in a chair long enough to pass all of that on to her."

Sister Natalie's smile was so faint, Ned felt a stab of pity for Quinta. "She's already pretty good in the kitchen," Ned said. "She and her brothers take turns cooking and cleaning up."

"That's right." Tree threw him a relieved smile. "We have quite a crew of men at the ranch—me and my four boys, Ned, Brownie, and a couple of men who help with the freighting business. That's a lot of frijoles and tortillas."

"I'm sure your daughter will benefit from learning some additional skills in the kitchen," Sister Natalie said. "Sister Maria will take charge of that portion of her instruction."

"Uh . . . well, good." Tree nodded. "I'd best be going, then."

Ned pointed toward the bundle. "I got a double dress length like you asked me to. It's a dark blue . . ." He gazed meaningfully at Tree.

"That's right." Tree nodded in Sister Natalie's direction. "I asked him to bring some for the captive girl, so she could have a new dress too."

"Mrs. Stein suggested I get some plain white muslin, too," Ned said. "For . . . well, whatever ladies need it for."

"Use it as you see best, Sister," Tree said.

Her smile was warmer this time. "Thank you, gentlemen. That is most gracious of you. Perhaps Quinta and Taabe can have sewing lessons together. Mr. Bright, may I take a few minutes to introduce this gentleman to our school?"

"Yes, ma'am. Would five minutes be enough?"

"Barely, but I understand you must keep your schedule."

"Thanks," Ned said. "I'll be by again on Tuesday." He walked outside with Tree, disappointed that he hadn't seen Taabe or Quinta.

They walked to Tree's wagon and paused beside it.

"It's going to be quiet at the ranch without Quinta," Tree said.

The ranch was never quiet, but Ned knew what he meant. "You can come see her any time."

Tree grimaced. "Sister Natalie asked me to leave her alone for the full week. She's taught at other schools, and she said some girls are homesick the first few days. If they see their parents, they'll cry and want to go home. But after a week, they're usually settled in and want to stay."

Ned pressed his lips together and nodded. He could imagine Quinta's misery when she began missing her brothers and her favorite mustang, not to mention her father. Tree doted on her. Who would cajole and spoil her at the mission?

"By the way," Tree said, "you need to change teams at the ranch and keep going."

"Keep going?" Ned stared at him. Doing so was part of the mail contract, but so far he hadn't needed to make extra runs.

"Charlie Peckham's too sick to drive. And you might have to go all the way to Fort Phantom Hill. A rider came in just before I left home—the driver on that stretch up and quit."

"How come?"

Tree shrugged. "There's talk of Indian trouble up there. You'll have to see what they know at the swing station when you get there."

Ned blew out a breath. "All right. Can you pack up a clean shirt and socks for me and have supper ready when I get there?"

"I sure can." Tree climbed onto the seat of his wagon and touched his hat brim.

Ned looked toward the mission door. His passenger had better hurry up. He had a long day ahead of him.

CHAPTER NINE

Taabe helped Sister Marie in the kitchen the next morning after breakfast, while Quinta had lessons in the parlor with Sister Adele and Sister Natalie. Quinta disliked being kept indoors all morning to work on her slate and read, but the nuns had promised she would be allowed to go out each day after the noon meal.

Taabe found she could sit on a high stool and wash dishes for Sister Marie without hurting her ankle, and she'd begun doing this each day. Sister Marie seemed happy for her help. She chattered away or hummed lilting melodies while she cooked. Sometimes Taabe understood what she said. Sometimes Sister Marie seemed to launch into another language. She would say something, shake her head, then repeat the words slowly in English.

Sometimes she would give Taabe a knife and a pile of vegetables to peel or chop. Within a few days, Taabe understood how she wanted most of them prepared, and Sister Marie would smile at her and say, *"Bon."* Then came the head shaking, and "Good. It is good."

Late in the morning, Sister Adele came to the kitchen. Taabe climbed down from her stool and took off her apron. It was one of the sisters' prayer times. She was accustomed now to being summoned each morning and evening to join them in the chapel. For a few minutes the sisters all knelt and prayed. Taabe usually sat quietly until they finished. If they sang one of their songs, she hummed along.

Since Quinta had come yesterday, the girl joined them as well, and Taabe watched her.

Today they entered the chapel and sat down, with Sister Adele between Quinta and Taabe. Quinta smiled faintly at Taabe, as though she wasn't sure she wanted to be here. Taabe understood. At first she'd felt bewildered. Now she found this time peaceful.

The other sisters knelt between the benches. Quietly, they all began to pray.

Sister Adele said something to Quinta. The girl clasped her hands, closed her eyes, and rattled off a long string of words.

Sister Adele said nothing until she had finished, but when Quinta had uttered her "amen" and opened her eyes, the nun touched her arm.

"English," Sister Adele said softly.

Quinta scowled at her.

"You and Taabe must both learn your prayers in English."

So Quinta also spoke another tongue. But it was not the language of the Numinu.

Sister Adele looked at Taabe and held up her clasped hands. Taabe folded her hands in her lap and closed her eyes.

"Our Father," Sister Adele said.

Taabe repeated the words. After a moment, Quinta also said, "Our Father."

They continued through the prayer, which was not long. At the "amen," Taabe opened her eyes and looked to Sister Adele.

The sister nodded and smiled at her, then at Quinta. Taabe sat quietly for the next few minutes, eyes on her hands, while the nuns continued to pray, each in her own place. Taabe knew that if she looked past Sister Adele's kneeling form to Quinta, the girl would smile at her and make humorous faces, which would cause her to laugh. It was dangerous to look at Quinta during the morning and evening prayer times.

A few minutes later, Sister Natalie rose, and the other sisters rose too. They all made the odd motions, touching their foreheads and chests. Taabe now realized, thanks to Sister Adele's tutelage, that they were pretending to draw a cross—the torture rack. It seemed to be a symbol of their faith and commitment to their God. This was something Taabe could not remember ever seeing. But then, she was sure she'd never known anyone quite like the sisters in her old life.

Her people—her white family—prayed. She felt certain of that. But the rest of it? She wasn't sure.

After Sister Natalie and the other two nuns walked silently out of the chapel, Sister Adele led her and Quinta into the hall. She turned to them with a smile.

"Now we will sew."

Quinta scowled.

Taabe looked to Sister Adele for an explanation. "What is . . . ?"

"Sewing." Sister Adele made a stabbing motion with her fingers then a pulling motion. Taabe didn't understand. The nun lifted a fold of Taabe's skirt and made the gestures again, as though poking something into the fabric, then pulling it out.

"Ah!" Taabe smiled. This she knew. They would stitch.

Would they be mending the sisters' clothing? Or making something new?

Sister Adele took them to the parlor, where they entertained guests. On a table, she spread out a long piece of dark blue cloth.

"Dresses." She pointed at each of them in turn. "For Quinta. For Taabe. Dresses. New dresses."

Taabe grasped her meaning with joy. She and Quinta would make new dresses for themselves. She looked at Quinta, smiling. "Dress."

Quinta hung her head, still frowning. "I don't want a new dress. I hate dresses."

Taabe blinked and looked at Sister Adele. She wasn't sure what "hate" meant—it was not a word the nuns had tried to teach her. But Quinta's feelings about the new dress were clear.

"And I hate to sew," she said.

Sister Adele patted Quinta's shoulder and spoke rapidly and softly. She pointed to the hem of the dress Quinta wore, which fell halfway between her ankles and her knees.

Quinta sighed, folded her arms, and scowled. Taabe stared at her. Quinta was far too big to pout. The Numinu would send her outside the camp for that.

She reached out to touch the blue fabric. It felt soft. She could hardly wait to wear it. Sister Adele had been teaching her color words, and she said softly, "Blue."

"Yes," the sister said with delight. "Blue cloth."

Taabe looked at Quinta. Slowly, she said, "Quinta, dress. Taabe, dress. Blue."

Quinta looked at her, emotions warring in her expression. "Yes. We'll have dresses alike. I'd rather have my overalls."

An idea came to Taabe. She grabbed Sister Adele's hand and said, "Wait," in Comanche, because she couldn't remember the English word. She turned and hobbled as quickly as she could to her room, swinging along on her crutches.

Her parfleche lay as always on her bed, against the adobe wall. Taabe opened it and took out the little deerskin pouch. She carried it back to the parlor and laid it on the fabric.

"What's this?" Sister Adele asked.

Taabe opened the pouch and spilled a few of the colored glass beads on the cloth. Against the deep blue material, the red, yellow, white, and black beads glistened. She spoke the Comanche word for them.

"Ah," Sister Adele said. "Beads."

"Beads," Taabe said. She looked at Quinta.

The girl showed some interest. "Beads for our dresses?"

"Yes," Taabe said and grinned at Quinta. "Dresses. Beads. Pretty."

All of them laughed.

Sister Adele said, "I don't see why you shouldn't add a few beads to your dresses, though I'll have to make sure Sister Natalie doesn't mind. I hope she won't think they're heathenish. Taabe, perhaps you can teach us how to do the beadwork."

Taabe frowned, trying to follow the rapid words.

Quinta touched her sleeve, and Taabe turned to her.

"You," Quinta said, pointing to Taabe. "You. Teach. Sewing. Beads."

Taabe smiled. She could do that. She could show Quinta and Sister Adele how to stitch the little rounds of color into a pattern at the cuffs and collars, just the way Pia's mother had taught her. Remembering those long afternoons spent at beadwork when she was a girl brought tears to her eyes. Those quiet times had calmed her, soothed her. The Indian woman's patient instruction had helped her not to fret about her real mother and the rest of the family she had lost.

"Yes," she said. "I teach. Beads."

⟵ ★ ⟶

The stagecoach rolled past the ruins of Fort Phantom Hill to the house that served as a temporary way station for the Overland line. They arrived well after dark, and Ned had been driving a good fourteen hours. He didn't like driving at night, but at least he was familiar with the road from freighting days. He'd dropped Brownie at an earlier stop where he'd changed teams. Brownie got to hitch a ride home while he went on.

Beside Ned rode Henry Loudon, half Kiowa and known as a sharpshooter. Henry lived west of Phantom Hill and made no secret that he felt lucky to have secured a paying job as a shotgun rider for the mail stage.

"Too bad they put all that effort into building this place," Ned said as they rattled past the old powder magazine and commissary. Along with a stone guardhouse and several stark chimneys pointing skyward, they were all that remained of the fort.

"Yeah, and too bad it burned," Henry said. The fort had been used for only four or five years, and was abandoned in 1854. "Butterfield's going to have some repairs done, so we can have a comfortable home station here. At least that's what the division agent said when he came through."

"That right?" It would be an improvement and a boon to passengers, though the shortage of good water that had forced the army to abandon the post would likely be a problem for the stage line as well. A handful of houses stood near the old fort. Ned couldn't call it a town, though it did have a trading post and a saloon.

The station agent met them and assured Ned that his run was over. "You can get some sleep and head back in the morning."

"Great," Ned said. He and Henry went into the house and

ate supper, after which Henry prepared to leave for the night.

"Watch yourself on your way home," the agent said as Henry reached the door. "We heard there was some Indian trouble up the line."

Henry grunted and left.

"Would they bother him?" Ned asked.

"Comanche would. They don't care who they raid."

"Say, do you know anyone who speaks the Comanche lingo? I asked Henry, but he said he doesn't speak it well, and he wouldn't want to go all the way to Fort Chadbourne. Too far from his ranch."

The station agent scratched his head. "You might try over to the saloon. There's a buffalo hunter hangs around there when he's in these parts. Isaac Trainer. He claims he spent a winter with them."

Ned pulled on his leather gloves and turned up his coat collar against the chilly November night.

His mother back in Alabama would weep if she knew he was headed for the sordid little shanty of a saloon. But she need never know. Even so, Ned silently renewed the promise he'd made her five years ago, when he left the family farm, that he wouldn't do anything that would shame her and his pa.

He missed the family, but with seven siblings, he'd felt the cramped walls of the farmhouse and longed to get out on his own, to try his hand at something other than dirt farming. In Texas he'd found opportunity. Patrillo Garza had taken him on to help with his new freighting business, and the growing family had made Ned feel at home—though he had his own room at the ranch house. He'd worked hard. Patrillo liked him and his penchant for figures, which had helped them save a lot of money. By the time the mail contract came along, they were full partners in the business.

He wondered how Quinta was doing at the mission. Was

she homesick and bawling her eyes out? More likely she was up to mischief. She'd be good for Taabe—a distraction from the uncertainties that must plague her.

Thoughts of the beautiful young woman hastened his steps. More than anything, he longed to know her full story—how long she had been with the Indians, if she had escaped on her own, and how she had survived.

And was she safe now? The scattered rumors of Indian unrest bothered Ned, but there was nothing he could do to ensure that the nuns and their guests wouldn't be harmed. He paused outside the saloon and looked up at the star-filled sky.

"Lord, You know my intentions of going in here, so I figure You'll overlook it." He shoved aside the twinges of conscience and pushed the saloon door open.

Inside, the air was hazy with smoke. He succeeded in holding back a cough as he searched the small room. A black-haired woman of indeterminate age tended the bar, and three men stood before it. Two more sat at a rickety table with glasses at hand, playing cards. Ned looked the five men over and decided one of the card players was the most likely candidate for a buffalo hunter.

He sauntered toward the table, staying aware of the other people around him. The woman at the bar watched him from beneath lowered lashes.

"You Trainer?" he asked the older of the two card players.

The graying man looked up at him. "Nope."

"I'm looking for Isaac Trainer. Do you know him?"

"Yup."

Ned tried not to let his frustration show.

"Whatcha want him for?" asked the man's companion, who looked a bit younger but also had a tanned, creased face. His dark beard blended in with his shaggy hair near his ears, and he kept his dark brown eyes riveted on his cards.

"I need someone who can translate for me," Ned said. "I heard he speaks Comanche."

"He does. Whatcha payin'?"

Ned eyed him cautiously. "Are you Trainer?"

"Maybe."

Ned pulled out a chair and sat down. "Listen, mister, I don't want to broadcast this, but the army's got a returned captive. They want someone who can speak the lingo to question this person and see what they can find out."

For the first time, the man looked directly at him. "Where's this captive at?"

Ned hesitated. "Not here. It would involve a few days' travel, but I can get you a pass on the Overland stage if that would help. If you're Trainer, that is."

The man's eyes narrowed. "What else?"

"We'd pay your expenses and send you back here after."

"And?"

Ned swallowed hard. "Ten dollars."

"Hard money?"

"Dollars."

"American or Mexican?"

Ned's patience had reached its limit. "American paper money. Take it or leave it."

The man folded his hand of playing cards and laid them on the table. "I'm out, Reg. You take it."

The older man scooped up the few coins of the table.

"I'm Trainer," said the younger man. "When we leaving?"

Though Quinta apparently disdained sewing, she accepted the challenge of laying out the patterns on the blue fabric to the best advantage. Sister Adele and Sister Riva used Taabe's and Quinta's dresses as patterns and cut pieces of brown wrapping paper the same shape as each portion of the dresses. They showed Taabe and Quinta how to arrange those patterns on the fabric close together, so little cloth was wasted, and Quinta eagerly moved them around until all agreed she'd found the best arrangement.

Throughout the next step—cutting out the pieces of the new garments—Quinta muttered and complained. Taabe couldn't understand most of what she said, but Sister Adele chided her gently, both to speak English and to think on beautiful things.

The sentiment came from the Holy Book—the Bible. Sister Adele had read from it many times to Taabe while she worked at her language lessons. Taabe loved the black book. She had seen such a book before, she was certain. That must have been part of her distant childhood. That verse particularly spoke to her heart. Sister Adele read the portion aloud to her first while she still lay feverish in bed, and it flowed like a poem.

"Whatsoever things are true, whatsoever things are honest, whatsoever things are just, whatsoever things are pure, whatsoever things are lovely . . . think on these things." Once she grasped the meaning, Taabe found the verse comforting and often repeated it to herself. She wanted to think about things that were lovely and pure and honest.

Quinta, however, had other things on her mind. She scowled and thumped the cutting tool down on the table, muttering to herself.

"Think on things that are lovely, Quinta," Sister Adele said. "Your new dress will be lovely. Think on that and our Lord's sacrifice for you. And speak English, please."

A few minutes later Quinta came out with a word that caused both nuns to stare at her in horror. After a moment, Sister Adele cleared her throat.

"My dear, when I asked you to speak English, I did not mean for you to use such language. It is better if such words are not spoken aloud in any tongue."

Quinta folded her arms and lowered her chin. "The shears are dull."

Taabe reached for the tool. "I cut," she said. "For you."

Quinta blinked at her but said nothing. The sturdy fabric did resist the blades, but Taabe persevered, holding the shears the way Sister Adele had showed her, with the bottom blade touching the table.

When she had cut free the large piece that would be the front of Quinta's skirt, Sister Adele patted her shoulder. "Nicely done, Taabe. Those shears *are* dull. Perhaps Mr. Bright can take them to Fort Chadbourne for us the next time he comes through, and someone could sharpen them for us. I believe the blacksmith at the fort might have a grindstone."

They labored on, and Quinta meekly took another turn at cutting. By the time Sister Marie rang the bell for the midday meal, the pieces for both dresses lay neatly folded on the table.

"Excellent," Sister Adele said. "After lunch, the two of you should go outside for a while."

Taabe strung together the words in her mind. A walk in the open air with Quinta appealed to her, but she had made it a habit to wash dishes every afternoon.

"I help Sister Marie," she said, then corrected herself. "I *will* help."

Sister Adele smiled. "That's good, Taabe. Perhaps you could both help in the kitchen, and then you would finish faster and get to walk about outdoors sooner."

Taabe thought she grasped the meaning and glanced at Quinta.

"Sure," Quinta said with only a small scowl. "I do know how to do dishes—it's one thing I've done a lot of."

Sister Adele took that comment with grace. "I'm sure Sister Marie would be most appreciative if you offered. And since you and Taabe are both used to spending a great deal of time outdoors, we would like to allow you some freedom for exercise."

Quinta opened her mouth but said nothing. She looked at Taabe.

Taabe shook her head, not sure she understood Sister Adele's point, other than that she would get to go outside with Quinta after the two of them helped clean the dishes.

Over the two weeks she had spent with the sisters, Taabe gathered that they had lived in the adobe house only a few months. Every day if there was no rain, Sister Riva toiled in her garden, preparing the soil for the next crop. She took the two girls out with her that afternoon and walked with them around the perimeter of the plot she'd been spading up. Next to it was a fenced corral, but no animals grazed there. Taabe supposed the people who had lived here before the sisters had kept horses and maybe some cattle. Perhaps the sisters would add livestock later on. The only domestic animals about the place were a small flock of chickens. Sister Riva locked them up every night in a small house at the edge of the garden and let them out every morning to forage. They produced a few eggs and an occasional dinner of roasted chicken, followed by chicken stew the next night. Taabe eyed them with a greedy desire for another chicken day.

One of the hens followed them as they strolled about the garden, and Sister Riva crooned to it occasionally.

"I shall plant carrots and potatoes here." Sister Riva waved her arm in a sweeping movement that encompassed the far end of the garden. She'd spaded long rows to within a few yards of the edge of a pine woods beyond.

Taabe had seen her pull a small cart with sticks on it, and she supposed this was where the sisters gathered firewood for cooking, though she'd seen quite large, split sticks in Sister Marie's wood box. Perhaps a man from outside the mission provided firewood for them.

As she gazed toward the trees, she caught a flicker of movement. She stood absolutely still and waited, peering toward where she had seen it. Was it only the branches swaying in the breeze? The air was calm today, and the trees did not move as she watched. Something darker among the pine trunks moved—a shape that didn't belong drew back and lost itself among the boughs.

CHAPTER TEN

Taabe's throat dried and she stopped breathing.

Sister Riva touched her sleeve. "Come."

Taabe didn't move, still staring toward the pines.

"What is it?" Sister Riva stood close to her and followed her line of sight. "You wish to walk in the forest?"

Taabe shook her head. She pointed to her eye and then toward the trees.

"You saw something?" Sister Riva's whisper held a note of alarm.

Quinta moved to Taabe's other side. "What's the matter?"

Taabe hesitated. Perhaps it was nothing. A squirrel scampering among the trees. But she'd heard no chirring since they'd come out here today, and she saw no further movement now. She forced her gaze upward, to the treetops. Shouldn't there be squirrels and birds flitting about? She'd seen them on other days she'd come out here with Sister Riva.

"Don't know," she said. Her stomach felt odd, the way it had one summer day when Pia's mother ran into the tepee and grabbed her wrist. "Bluecoats," she'd said. "You hide."

Taabe and Pia had run to the edge of the creek and hidden in tall reeds for two hours before their mother came and told them the soldiers had gone. Apparently a small detachment had stopped by the camp, spoken to the leaders, and left again without any discord. But Taabe learned from that and other incidents that when a stranger came around the camp, it was best for women and children to hide.

"We go in."

"Yes." Sister Riva took their arms and turned them back toward the house, casting an anxious glance over her shoulder.

They walked as quickly as Taabe's ankle allowed, back across the field, through the gate in the garden wall, and around to the door of the mission.

Sister Riva left her and Quinta in the small parlor and hurried off, returning a moment later with Sister Natalie and Sister Adele.

"What has happened?" Sister Natalie asked, drawing Taabe to one of the chairs they kept for visitors. "My dear, tell me as best you can."

"I . . ." Taabe looked around at the three nuns and Quinta. If only she had the words to tell them.

"She saw something in the pine woods," Quinta said.

Taabe nodded.

"An animal?" Sister Natalie asked.

Taabe shrugged.

Sister Natalie sat and peered into her eyes. "Do you think it was a man? Men?"

Again Taabe raised her shoulders helplessly.

"Sister Riva, bar the door and check the kitchen door as well."

"Yes, Sister." The younger nun hurried out, and Taabe heard the heavy wooden bar thud into its brackets inside the front entrance.

Sister Adele stepped forward and held out Taabe's slate and chalk. "Perhaps this would help."

Taabe seized it and sketched a small animal with a sweep of bushy tail.

"Squirrel," Quinta said at once.

Taabe nodded but then shrugged. On the slate, she drew another animal, a little bigger and with perked ears.

"Dog?" Quinta asked.

"Coyote," Sister Adele said.

Taabe nodded and spread her hands to indicate their guesses about the picture were correct, but she wasn't sure what she'd seen. Finally she drew a human stick figure.

"Man?" she said, her voice raising in question. She drew several trees over and around the figures, pointed to her eyes, then to the slate. "What?"

Sister Adele placed her hand on Taabe's sleeve. "My dear, do you think men would come to find you? To harm you?"

Taabe's heart raced. She looked around for a rag, saw none, and wiped the slate with her sleeve. Sister Natalie opened her mouth to protest, but sank back with a shake of her head.

On one edge of the slate, Taabe drew a crude horse, with a stick figure on its back.

"Horse and rider," Sister Adele said. They all watched for what she would draw next.

Behind that drawing, Taabe left a space then added three more horse figures with men on their backs. In the leader's upraised hand, she drew a line with an arrow tip. A spear.

"They are chasing the other man," Quinta cried. Her face sobered. "Or were they . . . chasing you?"

Taabe pointed to the fleeing figure. "Taabe." She pointed to the leader of the pursuer. "Peca. Man."

"Peca?" Sister Adele frowned. "Is Peca a man's name?" She touched the figure on the slate. "Peca."

"Yes," Taabe said. "Peca . . ." She hesitated. How could she communicate anger? She made a wrathful face and shook her fist.

"He's mad," Quinta said. "This Peca is mad at you and he chased you."

"Yes." Taabe smiled with relief.

"You ran away," Sister Adele said.

Taabe nodded, drained of the strength she'd felt when they walked out into the sunshine.

"Can't we do something?" Quinta asked. "Taabe is scared."

"Indeed we can. We shall pray, of course, but there are other precautions we can take." Sister Natalie rose, her face somber. "Come with me, ladies."

She led the way to the kitchen, which jutted off the back of the house. Sister Marie looked up in surprise from her bread kneading.

"I beg your pardon," Sister Natalie said. "We must disturb you for a moment." She looked around at the others. "It's good that we are all here. As nearly as I can tell, Taabe saw something outside and is frightened that perhaps she has been followed here by an angry Comanche warrior. I think it best that we let her in on our crisis plan and show her the hiding place."

Taabe watched her as she spoke, but much of the meaning escaped her. But Sister Adele strode forward, moved aside a small work table, stooped to lay back a woven floor mat, and lifted a section of three short floorboards of uneven lengths.

Sister Natalie pointed to the hole. "This is our root cellar. We keep it covered so it is not obvious. Anyone in the cellar can fasten two hooks that will keep the boards in place unless someone above rips up the boards with tools. There is space for two or perhaps three people to hide for some time. Do you understand?"

Taabe nodded slowly, and Quinta, her eyes gleaming, also nodded.

This was a secret refuge where they could go if anyone attacked them, or where the nuns could hide Taabe if someone she feared came searching for her.

"We will place a jar of fresh water in the cellar now," Sister Natalie said. "Sister Adele, please take care of that."

"Yes, Sister."

"And some parched corn as well, and a blanket. A person in hiding could survive down there for some time if necessary."

"And now, I shall take a short stroll in our yard—not far. Just to see if there is any obvious activity about the mission." Sister Natalie looked around the circle, her gaze resting briefly on each of the nuns, Taabe, and Quinta. "Sister Riva, you will accompany me. We will take walking sticks. Our guests shall remain in the house until further notice."

The nuns murmured their assent, and Sister Riva tucked her hands into the openings of her wide sleeves and quickly left the kitchen.

"Come, Taabe, Quinta." Sister Adele smiled at them. "You may help me place the provisions in the cellar, and then we'll do some reading in the sitting room."

"Prayers will be on time unless something unexpected occurs," Sister Natalie said. She left the room.

Sister Marie hurried to a shelf and took down a large water jug with a cork stopper. "Use this, Sister. And there is plenty of parched corn in that keg."

Taabe helped Sister Adele fill containers and carry them to the hole while Quinta ran to get an extra blanket from the alcove where the nuns kept linens.

Sister Adele climbed down the short ladder into the hole and lit a candle. She held it up so Taabe, peering from above, could see into every corner of the refuge. The hiding place was square, only about as wide as Taabe was tall. An open barrel of potatoes and one of carrots took up much of the space. Several candles and a tinderbox lay in one corner, and in another was an empty wooden bucket. A prison—or a haven. Taabe nodded at Adele, who gazed up at her. Quinta returned with one of the pieced blankets and handed it to Sister Adele.

Taabe stood back from the hole and watched as Sister Adele climbed out and replaced the cover, the mat, and the table.

The hole was not big enough for all of the sisters. What would the others do if the mission were besieged?

Ned watched the tenders hitch the fresh team to the stagecoach. The Phantom Hill station agent held the door for the passengers. Isaac Trainer climbed inside with five other men, and the agent closed the door.

Henry Loudon ambled toward Ned, his shotgun resting on his shoulder. "Where's Trainer going?"

"I'm taking him to Fort Chadbourne to see if he can talk to that Comanche captive I was telling you about."

Henry shook his head. "I wouldn't trust that one."

"Oh?"

"He's thick with the Injuns."

"I figured he'd be useful."

"Mebbe so." Henry headed for the stage, and Ned followed. Once on the driver's box, he gathered the reins and released the brake. He clicked to the mules and steered them onto the road westward.

He glanced at Henry. "You think I'm making a mistake?"

Henry shrugged and pulled a plug of chewing tobacco from his pocket. "Hard to say. He might be just the man you need. On the other hand, I wouldn't turn my back on him."

Taabe sat with Quinta in the small parlor after morning prayers, sewing the bodice of her new dress. Stitching the factory-made cloth was different from sewing leather. In some ways, it was easier—certainly she needed less effort to run the needle through the material. But Sister Adele scrutinized her work frequently, and she was very particular. She demanded tiny, even stitches on every seam.

Quinta muttered darkly as she worked on one of her sleeves. Taabe could sympathize, but she would rather use her energy to master the craft. She had learned the painstaking art of beadwork from her mother among the Numinu. That had taken many sessions and hours of exacting labor. Her Indian mother, if anything, was more strict than Sister Adele when it came to stitching.

But the Garza household had been without a woman's influence for some time. When Quinta visited the mission, and again when she arrived to stay, no mother came with her. Over the last few days Taabe had engaged in several conversations with the high-spirited girl and learned much through simple words and drawings on their slates.

Quinta had four brothers, and her mother now rested somewhere in a grave marked by a cross. The girl had sketched a graveyard with several such markers. For the first time, Taabe connected the crucifixes hanging on the walls throughout the mission with the crosses white people put over their loved ones' graves. Somehow the cross was a symbol of their belief in the tortured man. Scraps of knowledge teased at the fringes of her mind, and Taabe often lay awake at night pondering what it was she didn't know—but once knew—about the cross.

"The stagecoach is coming." Sister Marie popped her head into the parlor and was gone again before Taabe could look up.

"It's Ned!" Quinta threw down her blue fabric and ran for the entrance.

Taabe realized she'd heard the hoofbeats, but had been so lost in her thoughts and her stitching, the significance hadn't penetrated the fog. She tucked her needle into the cloth and laid her project aside.

She heard the nun lifting the bar on the front door, and Quinta's chatter. She stepped to the doorway behind them as the coach rolled into the yard. Ned halted the horses and lifted his hat.

Taabe couldn't help smiling. When Ned and his friend, Brownie—who never came inside unless there were supplies to unload—arrived at the mission, everyone smiled. Ned was the sisters' link to the outside world. For Taabe, he was more than that. She looked forward to his visits with an eager optimism. Ned brought treats and special supplies for her and the sisters. He brought people who were eager to help her find her family. He brought her hope, and his arrival always made her feel more alive in this new life she had chosen.

"Ladies! I have a visitor for you." Ned hopped down and opened the door of the stagecoach.

Sister Natalie and Sister Adele came into the hallway.

"Is it Mr. Bright?" Sister Natalie asked.

"Yes." Taabe stepped aside and let them pass her, following Sister Riva and Quinta outside.

Quinta ran straight for Ned. The sisters waited near the door. Taabe was about to step out with them to greet Ned when she caught sight of his passenger. She caught her breath and scanned the bearded man alighting from the coach. She had seen that man before.

Taabe backed away from the doorway, then turned and ran to the kitchen.

Sister Marie was peeling potatoes at her work table. She looked up with startled eyes as Taabe dashed across the room and shoved the small table aside.

"What are you doing?"

Taabe flipped the mat away and clawed at the boards.

CHAPTER ELEVEN

Sister Marie gasped and ran to her side, still holding her paring knife. She stooped and put a finger into a small crevice at one edge of the trapdoor and raised the section of connected boards.

"Quickly, friend, quickly!" Sister Marie held the cover while Taabe scrambled down the short ladder.

The hole was deep enough for her to stand upright. She beckoned to the sister to replace the boards. An instant later, darkness engulfed her. Taabe stretched out her arms. Her right hand touched a cold wall of earth. She sucked in a breath. Her heart raced, and she pressed her hands over it, willing herself to calm.

The cellar smelled of dirt, with a faint trace of Sister Marie's baking. Taabe bent over and felt about. She found the barrels and tried to orient herself. Over her head came a dull thumping, then a scrape as Sister Marie moved the mat and table back in place.

Taabe's cold fingers touched the woolen blanket. She

opened it one fold and sat down on it. Looking up, she couldn't see even a crack of light. She inhaled deeply and let the breath out slowly, through pursed lips.

She imagined the bearded man going from room to room of the mission, searching for her. He had been to the Numinu camps many times. He had brought the chiefs gifts. Peca had sat down with him and smoked and told stories. Was he here to find her for Peca? Would he tell the Numinu where she was?

She wished she had brought her parfleche and all of her Comanche things down here so the buffalo hunter would have no chance of seeing them. If things turned out all right today, she would ask Sister Natalie if she could put all her things in a bag down here.

Over her head, Sister Marie's comforting footsteps moved about the kitchen. Taabe's heart pounded, and she made herself breathe slowly and deeply. In her mind, words formed. *Help. Do not let him find me.*

But to whom were those words aimed? Was this prayer? Did the Father God hear such desperate thoughts? She couldn't remember the English prayer Adele had begun teaching her and Quinta. The nuns knelt when they prayed, but Sister Adele said you didn't have to do that. You could just talk to God and He would listen.

Taabe clasped her hands so tightly, her fingers hurt. "Please hear me," she whispered.

Ned walked to the cluster of nuns with Quinta hanging on his arm. She lifted her feet, putting her whole weight on him while she peppered him with questions about home.

"Is my mustang all right? Has Diego ridden him? Does Papa miss me?"

"Here, *chica*, you've got legs of your own. Use them." Ned

laughed and plopped her on the ground. "Your papa's fine, and we all miss you."

"Tell him I'm learning to sew. He'll like that."

"I will." Ned grinned and addressed Sister Natalie. "Ma'am, the man I brought today speaks Comanche. I thought maybe we could speak to Taabe Waipu and learn a little more about her background."

"Yes, I'm sure that would be helpful." Sister Natalie turned and looked to the doorway, then frowned. "Sister Adele, please find Taabe and ask her to come to the parlor."

Sister Adele hurried off, and Sister Natalie smiled at Ned. "Our guest is making great progress in her language lessons, but there is still much to be learned. Won't you bring the . . . gentleman into the parlor?" She eyed Trainer, taking in his worn buckskins, tangled hair, and scruffy beard. "Sister Riva, some coffee for our guests, please."

They had been seated with Sister Natalie only a moment when Sister Adele appeared in the doorway. She glanced at Ned and Trainer, then approached her superior and spoke in hushed tones.

Sister Natalie rose. "Excuse me a moment, won't you, gentlemen?" She glided out the doorway with Sister Adele in her wake.

Ned heard quiet murmuring in the hallway, but he couldn't make out a word. Perhaps they were speaking their native French. He hadn't liked the way Sister Natalie's eyebrows had quirked when Sister Adele came in and whispered to her. Not one bit.

"What's going on, do you s'pose?" Trainer asked.

"I'm not sure. I expect we'll find out soon." Ned rose and paced the room. Maybe Taabe was ill again.

Sister Natalie returned, and Ned stepped toward her before Trainer could get up.

"I'm so sorry, Mr. Bright, but the young woman you're seeking is no longer in the house."

Ned blinked at her. "Excuse me?"

Sister Natalie smiled apologetically. "It seems I was mistaken when I said she would be able to meet with you. She's not in the mission just now."

"Not . . ." Ned eyed her. He was sure he'd seen Taabe in the shadows of the doorway when he first drove up. She was standing back, behind the nuns, and his pulse had quickened with anticipation. Then Quinta had distracted him, and he'd had to introduce Trainer. Something had happened in those moments.

"Here, now!" Trainer's loud voice seemed out of place in the quiet, dim adobe. "What is going on here? I rode a good many miles to see this young woman. Why can't you produce her?"

Sister Natalie's brown eyes hardened. "As I said, Mr. Trainer, I was mistaken. Our acquaintance is not in the house just now." She spread her hands in supplication.

"Well, where is she?" Trainer glared at her.

"Not here."

"Is she out back, or in that barn yonder?"

"I assure you she's not," Sister Natalie said calmly. "I am sorry to disappoint you."

Ned shot a glance at Sister Adele. She stood near the door with her hands folded, but she kept her eyes on the floor. Something was up. The nuns had closed ranks, and he could think of only one reason—to protect Taabe. Sister Natalie had met him at the door and invited them in to see the young woman. Now she claimed Taabe had left—of all the insane notions. He knew she was here. They wouldn't hide her away and refuse to let him see her, would they? The girl had seemed happy here. She'd always come out to talk to people who wanted to see her and ask about captives. She'd given no impression she wanted to leave until her birth family came and claimed her. Only one thing was different this time.

Trainer.

Ned looked at the buffalo hunter. Trainer's breath was too shortened, his face too red. He was angry, but why? He'd be paid for his time, whether he saw the girl or not.

The hair stood up on the back of Ned's neck.

"Sister Natalie, I'm sorry we've disturbed your day," he said.

"What?" Trainer reared back and eyed him. "You're going to just leave it at that? These women are up to no good."

"I'm not sure what you are suggesting, Mr. Trainer," Sister Natalie said, "but I think it's time for you to leave."

"Yes," Ned said. "We need to keep our schedule." He clapped Trainer on the shoulder. "Come on, we'll be at the fort soon, and I'll get you some dinner."

"Hold on," Trainer said. "I want to know what happened to that girl. Did she run away, or what?"

"Sorry. We aren't supposed to stop here—it's not a regular stop on the line—and if we're late with the mail, we'll get in all kinds of trouble." Ned steered the shaggy man toward the door. "If the girl's not here, we'll just have to forget it."

"I could stay here and look for her. I'll bet I could track her. Yeah, that's what I'll do. I'll walk to the fort when I've finished."

"No, Mr. Trainer, you will not." Sister Natalie's voice had gone cold. "When I tell you the person in question is not here, you can rest assured that it is true. I cannot tell you where she has gone, but I tell you one last time, she is not in this house. Please do not come back. Good day."

Ned propelled him outside and toward the stagecoach. He glanced back at the three nuns standing like blackened statues under the eaves of the adobe. He longed to know what had happened, but a stronger instinct told him to get Trainer away from the mission. Brownie, who had joined him at the Bright-Garza station, replacing Henry Loudon, had climbed down and stood near the mules' heads. He eyed Ned curiously as they approached. Ned yanked open the door of the coach.

"Get in, Trainer."

"Leave me here. I could—"

"No. You heard the sister. They don't want you here, and this is private property."

"But she thought the girl was here when we came. Either that nun is lying—which I wouldn't be surprised to hear—or something's happened to the girl. She's run away or something worse."

"Like what?"

"I don't know. Been snatched, maybe, or hung herself in the barn."

Nat stared at him, shocked by his bluntness. "How could you think that?"

"Easy. Those captives can't adjust when they come back. If she did herself in, she wouldn't be the first. And if they're trying to hide something like that—"

"They wouldn't," Ned said. "They'd be deeply grieved. But I've met this girl several times. She isn't like that. She wouldn't hurt herself."

"You don't know that."

"I do. It's more likely she got back enough strength to travel and decided to go back to her people." As Ned almost shoved him into the coach, he met Brownie's quizzical gaze. "Let's go," he said, and climbed quickly to the driver's box. He shook out the reins and set the mules into a quick trot. "Make sure he doesn't jump out."

Brownie's eyebrows shot up, but he immediately looked back. "Trouble, Ned?"

"Maybe." Ned gritted his teeth and reached for the whip. He wouldn't make it easy for Trainer to jump out. And his first act at Fort Chadbourne, once the mail was taken care of, would be to consult Captain Tapley about Isaac Trainer and the incident at the mission.

Dear Lord, what have I done to that poor girl?

CHAPTER TWELVE

"We'll take you back to our home station tomorrow," Ned told Trainer when they'd bar-reled in to Fort Chadbourne a half hour early. He'd punished the mule team, but he'd make Mr. Stein, the station agent, understand why. "And I'll make sure you've got your through ticket back to Fort Phantom Hill."

Trainer looked toward the fort's parade ground, his eyes narrow slits. "I might just decide to stay here a while. Where's the best place to get a drink?"

"Probably yonder." Ned pointed toward the town that had grown up around the fort. He knew at least three saloons had opened, along with the trading post, a blacksmith shop, and a laundry. Probably more businesses had popped up since the last time he'd paid attention.

"Your outfit is paying my expenses, you said." Trainer waited, not smiling.

"Yeah." Ned reached in his pocket and took out two dol-lars. "This should get you a meal and bed. And breakfast." With the ten he'd promised Trainer for coming and the price of his ticket back to Phantom Hill, Ned would be strapped for cash until he got paid again. And for nothing. Less than nothing—for endangering Taabe Waipu, unless he was mistaken.

Trainer took the money and walked toward the saloons, staggering a bit as he got his land legs under him.

Brownie came around the back of the stage. "We taking him back tomorrow?"

"Yes. And we're not stopping at the mission."

"What happened there?"

Ned sighed. "I'll tell you when we eat. Right now I need to go see the captain."

Stein was already unloading the mail sacks, so Ned walked over to the fort. His discussion with Captain Tapley didn't satisfy him.

"I'll have Trainer brought in later and talk to him, if he's sober," the captain said. "I'll see if I can get anything pertinent out of him. He may have seen captives in some of the Comanche bands when he was out hunting. He might even give us an idea of where this young woman came from."

"That's what I'm afraid of." Ned's chest felt as though a stack of rocks sat on it. "She saw him, and she hid. She's afraid of him. That means she knows who he is—she's seen him before. So if he saw her, he'd recognize her too. And that might be bad."

The captain leaned back in his chair with a sigh. "It may just be that she's afraid he'll give away her whereabouts. Or it could be something more sinister. Perhaps there's bad blood between Trainer and some of the Comanche."

"I wish we had a good translator." Ned shook his head. "That's all I was trying to do."

"I know." The captain sat forward. "We'll keep an eye on Trainer and make sure he doesn't leave the fort tonight."

"Maybe my shotgun messenger can help," Ned said. "Brownie Fale—he's a good man. He's over with the Steins now. Maybe I'll ride out to the mission this evening and talk to Sister Natalie. I think without an audience, she'd tell me what's up. I can borrow a mule from the stagecoach's string."

"I'll lend you one of my horses," Tapley said. "I've got a good gelding that will get you there quickly."

An hour after sunset, Ned rode into the mission's dooryard. He knocked at the door and called softly, "It's me, Ned Bright."

A moment later, the door opened a crack. One of the nuns stood within; he couldn't tell which in the darkness.

"I'm alone, Sister. I came to see if everything is all right."

Sister Adele let out a breath. "Mr. Bright, come in. You are always welcome, of course. We hoped you'd understand our rudeness this afternoon."

"I think I might, but I'd like to talk things over with Sister Natalie, if she doesn't mind. But first, is Taabe all right?"

"Yes, but she has chosen to remain in hiding until the stagecoach has passed tomorrow, in case your passenger comes by again. At least, I think that's what she meant. She was quite frightened."

Ned nodded. "She knew Trainer's face."

"That is what we think. She can't express to us why she fears him, but she obviously thinks that showing herself to him will put her in jeopardy. We respect her judgment."

"Of course." He held out a stoppered jug. "Frau Stein sent you some milk. She said that if you want to keep a cow, she'll start looking for a likely heifer for you."

"How kind of her." Sister Adele smiled. "If we're going to have children living here, it's almost a necessity. Please thank her and tell her we accept." She led him farther into the house. "You are a friend, Mr. Bright. If you'd like to wait in the sitting room, I'll inform Sister Natalie that you are here."

Ned had paced the small room only half a dozen times when the older nun joined him. Close behind her came Sister Marie with a tray.

"Would you care for some coffee, Mr. Bright?" Sister Natalie asked.

"That'd be nice. And thank you for seeing me. I'm sorry for disturbing you this afternoon."

"I'm sure it wasn't your intention to upset anyone." Sister Natalie sat down. Ned took a chair close to her, and Sister Marie poured coffee for them both. "Thanks to you and Frau Stein, I can offer you milk to go in it."

Ned usually drank his coffee black, but he poured a few drops from the small pitcher into his cup.

"I met Trainer up at Fort Phantom Hill, and I thought he'd be a good translator. Guess I was wrong."

"Taabe recognized him. She ran to the hiding place we'd prepared. None of us realized she'd gone until I sent Sister Adele to get her. Sister Marie told us she'd helped her hide and that Taabe was greatly agitated. That was enough for me. I did my best to get you to take the man away without alarming him."

"He was suspicious," Ned said, "but under the circumstances, you did well. I took your statements to mean that Taabe was not within the building, though she was close by."

"That is correct." Sister Natalie raised her cup to her lips. She seemed perfectly calm now.

"I also inferred that she hadn't run away."

"No. She is safe. I wish I could say she was in her own bed now, but she won't come out of the refuge. I believe she's afraid that man will come back in the night, looking for her."

Ned took a sip of his coffee and set his cup down. "I spoke to Captain Tapley at the fort. He and his men will try to make sure Trainer stays put tonight. I think the captain understands how important it is to keep her whereabouts quiet—though that's difficult with so many people wanting to try to identify her. So many already know where she is that it's probably no longer a secret."

"Yes." Sister Natalie sighed. "The poor child. And Quinta!"

"Was she frightened?"

"Not really. But she is very tenderhearted. She insisted on staying hidden with Taabe, to keep her company."

"Will that endanger Taabe?"

"I don't think so. Quinta takes the matter seriously. She's an unusual child, Mr. Bright."

Ned smiled. "Isn't she? She's had it a little rough since her mother died, but she hasn't lost her spirit. And she is much loved."

"That is good. I sensed that her father brought her to me, not to be rid of her, but because he truly felt she needed a feminine influence. That and religious instruction."

"I'd say that's a fair assessment. Patrillo cares deeply what happens to his children. But he's so busy, he's afraid Quinta isn't getting all she needs from him and the boys."

Sister Natalie placed her cup and saucer on the tray. "Would you like to see her and Taabe?"

The final weight lifted from Ned's chest. "I would like that very much."

The sister rose. "I think it's safe to bring her out while you are here."

"If it's not too much trouble." Ned stood.

"It's not. She is only steps away. Let me refresh your coffee, and I'll bring her." She refilled his cup and left the room.

Ned couldn't hear her footsteps, but a few muffled sounds came from another room. He forced himself to sit and sip the coffee.

Sister Natalie returned, entering the room first, with Taabe behind her.

"Quinta fell asleep, so we didn't disturb her." Sister Natalie stood aside and let Taabe pass.

She bounded toward him, her face glowing.

"Ned Bright!"

She held out her hands, and he clasped them, smiling down at her. Her hair shimmered over her shoulders in the lamplight. Her upturned face held a sweet eagerness.

"Hello, Taabe. You have a new dress."

She glanced at the navy blue fabric. "Yes. I sew."

"You made it yourself?"

She nodded, smiling. "And Quinta and Sister Adele."

"That's wonderful. The beadwork is very pretty."

"Beads." Taabe put a hand to her collar, where the colored beads caught the lamp's glimmer.

"If you will excuse me for a moment," Sister Natalie said.

"Of course." Ned tried not to let his surprise show. The nuns usually hovered like hens over their one chick. Perhaps she thought Taabe might say something to him that she hadn't expressed to them, or wouldn't in her presence.

Sister Natalie picked up the coffee tray and left the room.

"Come sit down." Ned drew Taabe to the two chairs drawn close together, where he and the sister had talked. They both sat, and he gazed into Taabe's eyes. They seemed a darker blue tonight, perhaps because of the dim lighting and the dark cloth of her dress. Within their depths, he found the same delight he experienced. He would do anything to keep her safe and to help her find her family. If that family couldn't accept her as she was—though he couldn't imagine that—he would undertake to help her find her new place in life. More than anything, he would strive to see her happy.

"Man," Taabe said. "Stagecoach."

"Yes. I'm sorry I brought him. I thought he could help us talk. He speaks Comanche."

She frowned and nodded.

"Numinu." Ned had learned the Comanches' word for themselves. "Talk. Man, you, me."

She said something in the tribe's language.

"I'm sorry, I don't know those words."

Taabe looked about in frustration. She rose, pressing down on his hands, indicating he should stay where he was, and hurried out of the room. A minute later, she returned carrying her slate and chalk, with Sister Natalie following.

"Taabe asked me to return," the sister said. "Perhaps she feels that among the three of us, we can communicate better."

"I'm sure you understand her better than I do," Ned said. "I believe she's trying to tell me something about Trainer."

Taabe drew a four-legged beast Ned eventually realized was a buffalo, and a man. A line extended from the man to the buffalo.

"Yes," Ned said. "Trainer hunts the buffalo."

Taabe nodded and sketched several triangles in the distance.

"Tepees?" Ned asked.

She drew an arc from the man to the triangles.

"Perhaps she's signifying that Mr. Trainer visited the Comanche village," Sister Natalie said.

"Yes." Ned touched Taabe's wrist. "Man came to your people? The Numinu?"

"Yes." Taabe held her hand up and tilted it, as if she were drinking. She did it several times and tapped the sketched village with the chalk.

"He . . . ate with your people?" Ned asked.

She shook her head and made the motions again.

"He *drank* with your people."

Taabe rose and staggered about the room.

Sister Natalie cleared her throat. "It seems to me that Mr.

Trainer gave the Comanche some alcohol."

"That makes sense." Ned stood and took Taabe gently by the arms. "When Trainer went to your camp, what happened?"

She frowned and shook her head.

Frustration overwhelmed Ned. "We need a translator."

"Yes," said Sister Natalie. "But her language skills are improving rapidly. I shall ask Sister Adele to concentrate on vocabulary that will help her explain to us her life among the Comanche. I fear that until this point, we've been more concerned with helping her learn to cope in this world. But if she can tell us her story, that may help us find where she truly belongs."

Ned rubbed the back of his neck. "Maybe it would help if she visited the fort."

"The fort?" Sister Natalie's eyes widened.

"It's possible she might recognize the place. Or if it set off some other memory for her, that might be a big step forward in finding her family."

"But everyone would see her."

"I doubt anyone would know who she is, except the few military men who know she's staying with you, and possibly the Steins. But dressed the way she is now, she bears little resemblance to a Comanche woman."

Sister Natalie rose and surveyed Taabe from head to foot. "What if she were dressed as we are?"

"You mean . . . in a habit?"

"Yes. Then she would be almost invisible."

Ned realized that when he'd first encountered the nuns, he'd done everything he could to not look directly at them or attract their attention. Anyone at the fort who wasn't Catholic would probably feel the same unease and avoid speaking to the sisters.

"That's a good idea," he said. "She'll need shoes, though, not those moccasins. I could ask Mrs. Stein . . ."

"I think we can take care of that," Sister Natalie said.

"Good. When I come next Tuesday, if I don't have any passengers along, I'll take you and Taabe and maybe another of the sisters. Whatever you think."

"And Quinta?"

Ned grinned. "Even better."

Taabe stepped forward and spoke a few words in Comanche, looking from him to Sister Natalie with a puzzled frown.

Ned pointed to her and smiled. "You. Stagecoach."

Her eyes flared, and she turned to Sister Natalie. "Stagecoach? Taabe?"

The nun smiled and patted her shoulder. "Yes, dear. We'll talk about it. I'll see if Sister Adele can get it across to you. But there's nothing to worry about. Mr. Bright will make sure of that. Won't you?" She turned a stern look on Ned.

He felt suddenly like a guilty schoolboy. "Yes, ma'am. I surely will. It's getting late. I should get back to the station."

"Thank you so much, Mr. Bright."

He clapped his hat on and looked at Taabe. She still seemed mystified.

"See if you can explain why I won't be here tomorrow," he told Sister Natalie. "And Tuesday I'll be back."

Taabe went back to the cellar. Her anxiety was eased, but she did not want to be caught in a vulnerable position if the buffalo hunter returned. Besides, Quinta lay sleeping on her blankets in the hole. Taabe didn't want her to awaken and find herself alone.

Sister Adele helped her climb into the hiding place and put the trapdoor partially into place. "We'll leave a space, so more air can get in." She replaced the mat almost in its usual position and pulled the table closer, so that if the alarm were given, one of the sisters could quickly close and cover the trapdoor.

Taabe curled up next to Quinta. The girl stirred.

"Is it morning?"

"No." Taabe patted her head and lay down on her pallet. In a few days, she would ride in the stagecoach Ned Bright drove. He would take her and one of the sisters to another place. She thought she was too excited to sleep, but the next thing she knew, the trapdoor was moved aside and light poured into the cellar.

Sister Marie smiled down at her. "Good morning."

Taabe nodded and rose, careful not to jostle Quinta, but her eyes were already open. She jumped to her feet.

"I'm starving, Sister Marie."

The nun chuckled. "Then climb up here and go get washed, Miss Quinta. Put on your school dress, and you can help me fix breakfast."

That day all of the sisters moved extra quietly. They went to the yard often and looked about. When Quinta asked to go outside, Sister Natalie refused her.

"I want to see Ned when the stagecoach goes by."

"Not today," Sister Natalie said. "Next time."

Quinta's face drooped. "Is it because of that man he had with him yesterday?"

Sister Natalie glanced at Taabe. "Yes, Quinta. We're not sure he is a friend, and we'd rather you and Taabe stay inside until we know he's no longer in this area."

That seemed to satisfy Quinta, and she went about her lessons with more enthusiasm than usual. When her schooltime was over, she coaxed Taabe to play her flute. They sat on Taabe's bed, and Quinta hummed along as she played the Numinu songs softly.

After she'd finished one melody, Taabe held the flute out to Quinta.

"You."

"Really?" Quinta's eyes glittered as she gingerly took the thin wooden instrument. "What do I do?"

Quinta was able to blow a few different notes on the flute and tried to make a melody of them. Taabe showed her again how the Indians produced the simple, flowing music, and the girl tried to imitate her.

They spent an hour together, laughing and singing in different languages. Some of the songs Quinta knew didn't even sound like English to Taabe's ear, but they were happy songs. She was glad the girl had come to the mission. The nuns were kind to Taabe, but Quinta seemed more normal, more like the people she thought she had known long ago. The sisters were from another place, another culture.

Of the black-robed women, Sister Adele seemed to understand Taabe's longings and fears the best, but even her friendship did not take away Taabe's loneliness. Adele was one of the sisters, and every few hours when the bell rang, she hurried to the chapel. She spoke little except during their lessons. Every time she allowed Quinta and Taabe to laugh or speak loudly, Sister Natalie seemed to appear, frowning.

But Taabe's times with Quinta took her back to a place of warmth and happiness. Quinta sometimes fell into a bad temper, and often she reacted childishly, but she was always interesting. At the end of their beading and music hours, Taabe realized she was not lonely when Quinta was near.

Quinta lowered the flute and rested her small hand on Taabe's arm. Taabe looked at her and smiled.

"Are you sad?" Quinta asked.

Taabe wasn't sure what she meant. It wasn't a word the sisters had taught her. She raised her eyebrows in question.

"Sad. You know." Quinta made fists and scrubbed at her eyes.

Taabe smiled. She streaked her fingers down her cheeks like tears.

"Yeah, that's what I mean." Quinta gazed at her soberly. "Are you sad, Taabe? Do you miss your family?"

Taabe knew the word "family," but not which family Quinta meant—the Numinu family she had abandoned, or the white family she barely knew existed.

CHAPTER THIRTEEN

Ned was glad to be home. The sixty-mile run to Fort Chadbourne seemed to get longer every time—especially those times he didn't stop to see Taabe.

They rolled into the ranch's barnyard after dark. The new driver and shotgun rider were waiting to take over for the run to Fort Phantom Hill, and Tree's sons changed the teams out quickly. Trainer lurched inside the house with the other three passengers and ate a hasty supper. The stage would take them as fast as possible to their destinations, but they would have to sleep in the mail coach.

Ned waited until they were ready to board again. He stopped Trainer as he left the house.

"Here's your ten dollars."

The buffalo hunter took the money and crammed it in his pocket. "Too bad it didn't work out."

"Yeah." Ned hesitated. "I guess she went back to the Comanche."

"You couldn't have stopped this morning and asked if they'd found her?"

"Could have, but I'm not supposed to. The captain will let us know. Look, don't broadcast it about the girl, will you?"

"What, that she ran away?"

"Anything."

"I thought you wanted to find out who she is. The only way to do that is to let people know."

Ned scowled. "Folks would be awfully disappointed if they went to see her and she wasn't there, wouldn't they? And we wouldn't want anyone bothering the nuns. We've been telling folks to see Captain Tapley if they're looking for a missing girl."

"Time to board," Tree called from beside the stagecoach.

Trainer nodded at Ned and strode to the coach.

Ned let out a sigh and leaned against the wall of the ranch house. The stagecoach pulled out, and Tree walked over.

"Everything all right?"

"Not exactly."

"Come on. Marcos made plenty of tortillas, and I think there's some gingerbread left, though we weren't expecting so many passengers to feed. How's my *chica* doing?"

"Quinta's fine. Full of chili peppers." Ned chuckled. "I'm supposed to tell you she sewed a new dress. And she's picking up a few words of Comanche."

"Well, there," Tree said. "Pretty soon she'll be able to translate for you. That girl chatters all day long."

"You may be right. I hope she has Taabe chattering back pretty soon—in English. Quinta misses her horse, and I expect she misses her brothers too, though she didn't say as much."

"She is missed here," Tree said. "I will go and see her soon. It's too quiet, you know?"

"Yeah, I know." Ned hung up his hat and sat down at the long table.

Diego brought him a heaped plate of tortillas, beans, beef, and applesauce.

"That looks good. *Gracias*." Ned bowed his head for a moment and silently thanked God as well.

"There's been some Indian trouble farther up the line," Tree said.

"Bad?"

"They raided a couple of ranches. Stole some horses and wounded a man." Tree poured himself a cup of coffee and brought it to the table. "Ned, do you think Quinta's really safe at the mission?"

Ned swallowed a bite. His throat suddenly seemed tighter. This was his question all along—and now Patrillo was having second thoughts.

"They have a hiding place," he said. "Don't mention it to anyone. But yeah, I think she'll be safe. I hope."

"You don't sound sure. Maybe I should bring her home until things quiet down again."

Ned grimaced. "Let me tell you what happened with Trainer, and you see what you think."

Quinta always made Taabe laugh. No one could drive away her anxiety the way the dark-eyed girl could. She talked constantly unless the nuns chided her to keep still. Taabe soon realized she was fluent in both English and her native language—Spanish—and was rapidly learning Comanche. The morning Quinta attempted to make a joke in Comanche, Taabe not only laughed until her sides ached, she also realized Quinta could be her link to the outside world—and to the past.

Sister Natalie announced at the noon meal that another girl—perhaps two—would arrive in two weeks to attend school. This news brought a stare of dismay from Quinta.

Taabe patted her shoulder. "Is good. You have new friend."

"*You're* my new friend," Quinta said.

"Now, Quinta, finish your luncheon," Sister Natalie said. "You've got arithmetic and sewing yet to do this afternoon."

"I've been thinking about the man who chased Taabe," Quinta said.

The dining table fell silent. Taabe and the four nuns waited for her to continue.

"We should have a plan, in case he hears where she is and comes looking for her."

Sister Natalie caught her breath. Sister Adele looked anxiously at Taabe. None of them had spoken directly of this fear since the day they'd shown Taabe the hiding place. While the nuns calmly accepted the situation and went about their daily routines, the nine-year-old girl had obviously been considering what should be done about it.

"Has Taabe spoken to you about this man?" Sister Adele asked, with a glance at Sister Natalie.

"A bit. His name is Peca, and he left six horses outside Taabe's house. Well, not house, but the tepee or whatever—where she lived."

"Six horses?" Sister Adele's eyebrows shot up, and the nuns gazed at one another.

"Why did he do that?"

Quinta frowned. "I think he was hoping she'd take care of them for him."

Taabe puzzled out what she meant and shook her head. "For family."

"Oh," said Sister Marie. "He gave your family six horses?"

Taabe nodded slowly.

"That was kind of him," said Sister Marie.

"No. Not good."

"Not?" Sister Marie was clearly baffled.

"He must be a bad man," Quinta said. "Was he the one that stole you?"

Taabe frowned. "Stole Taabe?"

"You know. When the Indians raided your parents' ranch and snatched you."

Taabe looked helplessly to Sister Adele. "When . . . ?"

Sister Adele cleared her throat and glanced at Sister Natalie before speaking. Her superior made no protest and Adele said, "I believe Quinta is referring to the time when you were a child. When the Comanche took you. You were young, like Quinta. You remember when they took you from your home?"

Slowly Taabe nodded. She did remember her terror those first few weeks. Riding, riding, day and night, with only a mouthful of food now and then—food that seemed foul at the time. She thought she would starve. When she fell asleep on the horse and tumbled to the ground, they had tied her on. She'd wept and wept until she felt as dry as an old corn husk. And at last they'd come into a deep canyon with houses built along the cliff wall—fantastical palaces, she'd thought. A wrinkled Comanche woman had taken her and fed her and laid her on a pallet of buffalo robes and let her sleep.

Quinta tugged at her sleeve. "Was Peca the one who kidnapped you?"

Taabe stared at her, troubled at the memories flooding her and the fact she didn't know the words Quinta used.

She turned to Sister Adele, lifting her hands.

"It means stole," Sister Adele said. "We call it kidnapping—stealing a person."

Taabe gazed toward the wall where the crucifix hung. After a long moment, she said, "Peca did not steal me."

"But he wants to steal you now," Quinta said.

Taabe's throat tightened. She looked into Quinta's open face. So innocent and blunt, this girl was.

"Yes. Peca kidnapping now."

"We've seen no sign of the Comanche," Sister Natalie said. "Unless . . ."

No one spoke of the shadow in the woods.

"It's what I said." Quinta looked at the sisters. "We need a plan."

"We have the hiding place," Sister Marie said.

"Yes, but we need a warning system. So that if one of us sees Peca—or any suspicious men—skulking about, we can warn each other at once."

Taabe was confused by Quinta's words, but she waited to see what the sisters said.

"That's an interesting idea, and it's not far off from thoughts I've been having," Sister Natalie said. "Tell us what you have in mind, Quinta."

"Whistles are good." She turned to Taabe. "Don't the Comanche use whistles to signal each other?"

Taabe frowned, studying Quinta's face and trying to force a meaning on the words that tumbled from her mouth.

Quinta pursed her lips and gave a sharp whistle. Taabe flinched.

"Like that. Or how about an owl?" The girl gave the eerie call they had heard outside the mission walls in the evening.

Taabe smiled. "Good. Man come—" She repeated Quinta's owl call. "Bad man." She hooted again.

Quinta's grin revealed her white teeth. "That's it! We can all tell each other without having to run inside."

"You had *better* run inside if you see a bad man," Sister Riva muttered.

"And won't the Comanche know the owl's call is out of place?" Sister Marie said. "They don't usually come out in the daytime."

"We can use different birds." Quinta's brow furrowed. "We

could invent a whole language of signals."

"I think it would be best to keep it simple," Sister Natalie said. "That way we're not apt to become confused."

Quinta pressed her lips together, and Taabe almost laughed. The girl must feel sorry that all these older women feared they couldn't remember a dozen or so different whistles and keep them straight.

She placed her hand on Quinta's wrist. "Good. You tell us. Good man. Bad man. Run." She shrugged.

"Yes," said Sister Adele. "Two or three distinct whistles. We shall all have to practice them, and Quinta, you will be the teacher for this lesson. You must make sure we all make the signals correctly."

Sister Natalie cleared her throat. "Shall we have our whistling lesson right after arithmetic class?"

"Why not before?" Quinta asked.

"Oh, I think not," Sister Natalie said. "Arithmetic is very important, and there are not likely to be any kidnappers about before sunset, do you think?"

Taabe couldn't wait to suggest the signal she'd thought of. She touched Quinta, and when the girl turned to her, she said, "Stagecoach."

"Stagecoach?" Quinta's eyebrows shot up.

Taabe made a mournful call of several notes, dropping low at the end.

Quinta laughed. "Yes! Perfect." She turned to the nuns. "That will mean the stagecoach is coming—it's a roadrunner."

On Tuesday morning, Quinta gave her roadrunner call. Taabe lifted the hem of the long, black robe she wore and ran out to the entrance. Sister Natalie had refused to let her go to the fort in her regular dress, but had conceded that she would probably not be recognized if she wore one of the Ursuline habits.

All the nuns gathered in the yard to watch the coach roll in. Ned blew a blast on a gleaming brass horn, and Quinta clapped her hands, bouncing with glee.

Brownie jumped down and held the lead mules' heads while Ned strode toward them, grinning.

"Good morning, ladies! We've no other passengers today. How many of you are going?"

"Just Sister Adele, with Taabe and Quinta, if you think it's safe." Sister Natalie nodded toward Taabe.

Ned's eyes widened. "You have a new nun." He stared at the fifth "sister."

Taabe wondered what he was thinking. He almost looked disapproving. He liked the sisters and treated them with respect and kindness, but he didn't seem to like her wearing their dress.

"A postulant, we would call her," Sister Natalie said, "and she wouldn't wear this habit if she truly were here for that purpose, but . . . well, you and I agreed that this is probably best."

Ned nodded slowly. "Yes. I just didn't . . ." He cleared his throat. "It makes sense. No one will look closely at her in that getup. Not at all what they'd expect of a returned captive."

"That was my conclusion as well," Sister Natalie said.

Both of them looked anxious as they surveyed her. Was she doing something wrong by wearing the black dress?

Ned knelt and held out his arms to Quinta, who had waited impatiently, dancing about on one foot. "Come here, *chica*!" She catapulted into his arms, and Ned placed a hearty kiss on her cheek. "That's from your papa. He asked me to tell you that he'll try to come and see you Thursday, when I'm at home to tend to business for him. And he sent you this."

Ned held out a silver chain with a diamond-shaped pendant.

The necklace held a blue stone, and Quinta sucked in her breath and grabbed it.

"Oh! Where did he get it?"

"From one of the Mexican traders."

Quinta examined it briefly, then flung her arms around his neck, spewing Spanish.

Sister Adele laughed. "What did she say?"

"That he's the dearest papa in the world." Ned smiled. "I'm not sure how you say 'spoiled' in Spanish . . ."

Quinta slugged his shoulder.

"Hey! First hugs, then hitting?"

"Quinta," Sister Natalie said. "That is not how ladies behave."

"Gentlemen don't go about insulting ladies." Quinta drew back, her lips in a pout, and carefully pulled the chain over her head.

"That looks lovely on you. I'll tell your papa." Ned ruffled her hair. "Shall we go? We haven't much time to spare today." He turned his smile on Taabe.

Her heart lurched. So he wasn't angry with her for wearing the black robe. Was that gleam in his eyes all for Quinta, or was a little of it for her? She hoped he was happy that she was going with him. She would ride in the tall stagecoach for the first time. No, that wasn't right. Sister Adele had told her that Ned had brought her here in the coach when they'd first found her, lying in the road injured.

She barely remembered when she'd opened her eyes and stared into a horrible white face. She'd feared for her life. Now she knew that face well—it was Sister Natalie, who was kind if somewhat severe. In her haze of pain and confusion, she'd wondered if a skeleton had come to steal her spirit. Sometimes the Numinu spoke of such things. And there had been a man. Ned. He'd lifted her and carried her. She didn't remember riding in the coach. But she would never forget that she'd felt safe for the first time she could remember when he lifted her. She had relaxed and stopped trying to fight the pain and fear.

They all walked out to the stagecoach. Brownie nodded and called, "Good morning."

The three sisters who weren't going along watched as Ned gave each passenger his hand and helped them into the coach. Quinta slid across the middle seat and stuck her head out the window on the other side. Sister Adele climbed in carefully and smoothed the skirt of her habit as she settled on the back seat, facing Quinta.

Ned held out his hand to Taabe. She reached for it, as she'd seen the others do. When he clasped hers in his big, warm hand, she caught her breath. Why did this man have such an effect on her? She lifted her skirt enough to allow her to put her foot on the metal step. Sister Natalie had insisted she wear a pair of black shoes belonging to Sister Marie, and they felt heavy and awkward. But no one would believe she was a sister if she wore her Comanche moccasins.

As she pushed against his firm hand and rose, Ned placed his other hand gently on her shoulder. She wanted to linger there in midair, but that was impossible. She leaned forward and brought her other foot up, into the stagecoach. Several bulging sacks sat on the floor between the front and middle seats. She settled beside Sister Adele, so she'd have the cushioned back to lean against. Quinta's seat was covered in leather, but had no back, so the passengers using it could face either way. The inside of the coach smelled like leather and wood.

Ned closed the door firmly. Sister Adele leaned forward and looked past her, waving at the three somber figures standing outside.

"Good-bye!"

Kneeling on the seat, Quinta leaned out the other window and yelled, "Blow your horn, Ned!"

A moment later, a clear, loud blast sounded, making Taabe's spine shiver. Quinta pulled back inside, laughing and clapping.

"Ned's a very good driver. I'll bet he's the best driver on the whole Overland Mail route."

Sister Adele smiled faintly. "Don't say 'I'll bet,' Quinta."

The stagecoach started forward with a slight jerk, and Quinta's knee slipped off the edge of the seat. Sister Adele caught her arm and slowed her tumble to the floor.

"There now, sit down as you should."

Quinta frowned but took her seat, bracing herself with her feet and holding on to a leather strap that hung from the ceiling.

Taabe gazed out the near window as they bowled along the dirt road. She didn't recognize anything. The hills and fields wore drab shades of brown. The few scrubby pines they passed didn't impress her. Nothing about this land drew her.

They passed a small adobe house that had a barn four times its size and several holding pens.

"Do you think you've been here before?" Sister Adele asked.

Taabe shook her head.

In less than an hour, Ned guided the team into the barnyard at another house, but this one lay close to a town. Taabe had seen several large buildings, and many people walking about, riding horses, and driving wagons. She couldn't remember ever seeing so many people, except at a winter camp of the Numinu, when several bands settled close together along a river for a few months, and never so many whites.

Another blast of the horn sounded, and Taabe jumped. Quinta shrieked with delight.

"Settle down, Quinta," Sister Adele said. She seemed to

have taken on Sister Natalie's role.

The coach came to a stop, and Ned appeared at the door. He opened it and swept off his hat. "Welcome to Fort Chadbourne, ladies. If you wish, you can eat dinner with Mrs. Stein, in that house, for twenty-five cents each. If not, I'd be happy to escort you to the trader's after the mail is seen to."

Taabe looked to Sister Adele.

"We brought our luncheon, to eat on the way home." Sister Adele patted the bag that hung from a strap across her habit.

"I want to pat the horses." Quinta dashed toward the nearest corral.

Sister Adele opened her mouth, but closed it again. She watched Quinta with anxious eyes. "I suppose it's all right, so long as we can see her."

"Her father knows the people here very well," Ned said. "I don't think you need to worry." He reached into the coach and hauled out one of the gray sacks. "I'll take this inside and be right back."

A few minutes later as they walked toward the trading post, Taabe was surprised to see several groups of Indians mingling with the whites and Mexicans about the fort.

"Are those Numinu?" Quinta asked, tugging Taabe's hand.

Taabe swallowed hard.

"Quinta, please keep your voice down," Sister Adele said.

Taabe stooped and said softly to Quinta, "Kiowa." She avoided looking toward the Indians as they continued their walk.

Just outside the door of the trader's establishment, Sister Adele touched Quinta's shoulder. "My dear, please remember that we do not wish to call attention to our friend. You must call her 'sister' if you speak to her, and please avoid speaking about anything related to the Comanche while we are inside. Can you do that?"

Quinta's stricken face showed she realized her mistake.

She nodded and looked up at Taabe with tears in her dark eyes. "I'm sorry, Ta—Sister."

Taabe smiled and took her hand. "Come. You show me trader."

They went inside, with Ned right behind them. Several women were among the shoppers. Taabe eyed their costumes, gratified that all of them wore dresses of calico or plain materials that hung in the same general shape as the dresses she and Quinta wore at the mission. Most wore their hair pulled up on their heads, though none wore the constrictive head coverings the sisters chose. Instead they wore cotton bonnets or hats of woven straw. One woman's hat had a wide brim and a band of green ribbon around the crown. A bird perched on one side. Taabe stared at the bird, waiting for it to move, until Sister Adele lightly pushed her further down the store.

"My dear, it's impolite to stare."

Taabe blinked at her. "Bird." She looked over her shoulder.

"It's stuffed," Sister Adele hissed.

Taabe's jaw dropped.

"I think it's awful to put a dead bird on your hat." Quinta placed her hands on her thin hips and glared back toward the offending woman.

"Please, dear," Sister Adele said, "we'll discuss it later. Let's not be rude. Sister Marie asked me to get some cloves and sugar for her, as well as a supply of dry beans. We must ask the trader to get those for us."

While the trader filled the order, they walked slowly about the store, past shelves, barrels, and bins of merchandise. Taabe stared, unable to take in the abundant array of goods. Enough food lay in this one room to feed her band for a year.

A tiny sound startled her, and she whipped around.

Quinta said, "Ohh!" and stooped, extending her hand before her.

Taabe looked beyond Quinta to a shadowy crevice between

a barrel and a stack of crates. A small, furry animal peered out at them. It rubbed against the bottom crate, watching Quinta's approach, and made its noise again—*meow!*

Taabe's heart leaped. This wasn't a wild creature. She knew this orange animal, and the knowing sent a warm, happy feeling surging through her. This animal belonged to her past, before the Numinu.

She whirled and grabbed Sister Adele's sleeve.

"Fluffy!"

CHAPTER FOURTEEN

Ned stared at Taabe. "Fluffy?"

She nodded, laughing, with tears spilling down her cheeks. "Fluffy. Kitty."

Ned looked to Sister Adele, who seemed as astounded as he. "Have you talked about cats?"

"No, I don't think so. It hasn't come up."

Quinta reached for the cat, and it flitted between the crates and a rack of shoes. A muffled mewing came from within.

"She's got kittens in there," Quinta cried. A moment later, she stood with a small ball of orange fur in one hand and a calico kitten in the other. "Look, Ned! Aren't they *precioso*?"

Ned laughed. *"Si!"* He reached for the orange kitten and held it in his palm. The little creature wriggled, and he patted it gently. He smiled at Taabe. "Would you like to hold it?"

"Me?" Taabe wiped away a tear.

He nodded. "Hold out your hands."

Taabe cupped her trembling hands, and he deposited the

kitten in them. A look of wonder came over her face. Slowly she raised the kitten and touched her nose to its furry back. The kitten reached up a paw and swiped at her cheek. Taabe laughed and lowered her hands slightly. She adjusted her hold and patted it. The kitten purred and licked her finger. Taabe laughed again and looked up at him with such joy, Ned's heart tumbled.

"You like cats?" he asked.

She nodded, her eyes glowing.

"Did you have a cat when you were young? Fluffy?"

She caught her breath. For a moment, her blue eyes darkened. "Fluffy." She nodded, then smiled. "I . . . my . . . kitty."

Ned looked over at Sister Adele, who was also teary-eyed. "Those kittens look as though they might be big enough to leave the mother."

Sister Adele nodded. "I agree. And I'm sure Sister Natalie would not object. Sister Marie has found mice in her pantry of late. Oh, Mr. Bright, this is the first thing she's remembered, or at least that she's told us she remembered. Except one song—I thought she was trying to tell me once that she knew a song I sang to her, back when she was ill."

Ned bent down and peered at Taabe until he caught her gaze. "Would you like to have a kitty? At the mission? I can ask the trader."

Taabe's mouth opened in incredulous delight.

Ned chuckled. "I'll take that as a yes."

"Are we really getting a kitten?" Quinta bounced. "Can I have one too?"

Sister Adele held out her hands. "Let me hold that one."

The mother cat meowed plaintively.

"She's got two more." Quinta passed the calico kitten to Sister Adele and dove for the dark recess. A moment later, she stood up holding another orange fluff ball.

Ned shook his head at the sight of the three cooing over the kittens. He'd have to tell Patrillo's sons he'd discovered the way to a woman's heart.

"Excuse me, ladies. I'll go have a chat with Mr. Lassen." He walked to the counter and waited while the trader finished a transaction with a trooper from the fort.

"Help you, Bright?"

"You selling those kittens?" He nodded toward the back of the store.

Lassen smiled. "A lot of people want 'em."

"I'll give you a dollar for one."

"You'll have to pay more than that."

Ned leaned on the counter. "How much? It's for the nuns at the mission."

"Oh, well, for the sisters . . ." Lassen scratched his chin. "Of course, I'll lose a good sale if I let them have one cheap. Five dollars?"

Ned straightened, eyeing him critically. "Are you serious?"

"I am. I've only got four, and I could sell every one of them five or six times."

Ned reached in his pocket and pulled out all the cash he had on him. He didn't have much to spend money on—if you didn't count things like hiring Isaac Trainer. Tree paid Ned whenever they got money from a freight contract or from the federal government for the mail contract, but his living costs were part of the business expenses and came out of the ranch funds.

He counted out ten dollars. "I want two."

"Two? Aw, come on."

"Yup. The orange one with a white chin and the calico."

Lassen sighed and picked up the money. "They ought to stay with their mother another week."

"You know those nuns will hand feed them if they have to. They couldn't ask for better care."

"All right, all right. But have they got a cow?"

"No. Guess we'd better have a jug of milk too."

They rode back to the mission in the Steins' wagon, with the two kittens in a sack, but they hadn't gone a mile before Quinta and Taabe, sitting in the wagon bed, had them out to play with.

Sister Adele had cheerfully paid for a large can of milk, along with some other supplies for the mission. She'd also picked up the sisters' mail, which included several letters addressed to "the School at the Ursuline Mission" or "Headmistress, Ursuline School."

"I'm sure we'll have a full complement of students soon," she told Ned. "We have room for eight, and their fees would make us self-sufficient."

"It will be good for Quinta to be with other girls her age," Ned said.

"Yes, though she's doing very well. It's taken her some adjustment to living in a houseful of women, instead of having nothing but men around her." Sister Adele glanced at the two in the back and smiled. "She's grown very close to Taabe, and I believe it's doing them both a world of good."

When they arrived at the mission, Sister Marie and Sister Riva fawned over the kittens. Sister Natalie smiled and murmured something about the rodent problem. She invited Ned to stay and eat supper with them. He accepted and got only a nod in return. More and more, the sober nun reminded him of his dour aunt Alla.

Sister Adele handed her the mail, and Sister Natalie retired with it while the others carried in the supplies. Taabe disappeared for a few minutes and returned wearing her lavender dress instead of the habit. Ned spent a half hour watching her and Quinta introduce the kittens to their new home. He couldn't remember laughing so hard.

"We need to take them out to the garden, where the ground is soft, so they can do their business," Quinta said after a while.

Taabe looked puzzled, and Ned hid his laughter. Quinta picked up her kitten and gestured for Taabe to do the same. Ned followed them outside and around to the garden gate. Dusk was falling, and Taabe looked around carefully before going outside the wall by the house.

Quinta turned to Ned, still holding her kitten close to her chest. "You keep watch." She pointed toward the pine woods at end of the field. "There, especially. We don't want anyone sneaking up on us."

"Do you think that's likely?" Ned asked.

"Taabe saw something once. We want to be ready."

"Whoa! Taabe saw someone out here?"

Quinta nodded soberly. "She wasn't sure it was a person. It could have been an animal." She crouched and set her kitten on the ground, her hands poised to seize it if it tried to bound away.

Ned looked at Taabe. "You think you saw someone lurking around near the mission?"

Taabe nodded slowly. "I think . . . man. Maybe man."

"When?"

She shook her head and looked up at the sky. "Maybe ten suns. Days."

"Before I brought the buffalo hunter."

She nodded.

"That's why you had the hiding place ready. I should have realized."

She seemed to have lost the meaning of his words.

"I'm sorry," Ned said. "We shouldn't stay out here. Maybe I could fill a box with dirt for the kittens and they could use it inside."

"Sister Natalie wouldn't like that," Quinta said. "But Sister Marie would probably let us. We could put it in the kitchen."

"Yes. Let's go in and ask her," Ned said. "If she thinks it's all right, I'll fix the box for you."

"Do we have to tell Sister Natalie?" Quinta asked.

Ned considered that question. He wanted to say no, but he didn't want to weaken his alliance with Sister Natalie by doing anything concerning her household without her approval.

"I'd better speak to her."

"She'll say no." Quinta screwed up her face, and Ned feared tears were imminent.

"Don't worry. She's not going to send the kittens back, and she wants you to be safe."

Deep creases formed at the corners of Sister Natalie's mouth and eyes when Ned explained the need.

"I know it's inconvenient," he said, "but the girls mustn't be going outside all the time to meet the kittens' needs—especially after dark."

Sister Natalie sighed. "I suppose you're right. And we do need to do something about the mouse situation."

Ned considered the victory complete when they were going in to supper and he saw Sister Natalie pause and bend to stroke the calico kitten surreptitiously as the others left the room. He didn't let on that he'd seen her.

After they'd eaten Sister Marie's roasted chicken, potatoes, squash, and rye bread—a meal that rivaled Mrs. Stein's but without the gravy and dessert the German lady would have added—Ned prepared the "necessary" for the kittens. Quinta took it upon herself to make sure the two little creatures understood its purpose. Ned left her with a quick hug and a promise to see her again soon.

Taabe walked with him to the door. Ned was surprised none of the sisters followed. He took the bar down and turned to say good-bye. Taabe gazed up at him. What was going on behind those blue eyes? Ned didn't want to leave, but staying was out of the question. He put his hand to her cheek and held it there for a moment.

"Taabe, I will do everything I can to find your family. Do you understand?"

She nodded and lowered her eyelashes. She reached up and touched his face, letting her warm fingers graze his cheek, then more confidently rest against it.

"Thank you, Ned Bright."

The overwhelming longing to protect her rolled over him. He stood looking down at her for several seconds. At last he touched her hair lightly. Its softness rivaled the kittens' fur.

"I'll see you soon."

"Yes."

He went out to the wagon and drove to the fort, seeing her sweet face in his mind and holding her touch in his heart. She had to be safe at the mission compound. He'd seen nothing to alarm him, yet their defenses were so flimsy. Was Sister Natalie right, that God would protect them? He hoped so, but it wouldn't hurt to add his prayers to the sisters'.

After two days of rain, Taabe chafed to get outside. Quinta and the kittens, as well as an unexpected visit from Señor Garza, provided welcome distractions, and she plunged into the work of preparing the mission for additional pupils. Her ankle had healed to the point where she felt only an occasional twinge of pain. She insisted on helping with the heaviest work—laundry, mopping floors, and moving furniture into place for the students the sisters expected.

At times of prayer, Taabe went to the chapel and sat behind the nuns. She thought much about God and His Son, Jesus. The idea of the cross no longer seemed strange, and she wondered if facts and impressions she'd long forgotten were gradually making their way back, sifting into her heart. At the same time, painful memories of hurts and sorrows during her time as a Comanche began to heal. She would not forget, but she would move beyond that life.

Of one thing she was certain—she'd made the right decision when she left the Numinu. The longing in her heart would never have let her be content with them. She might not belong here at the mission, but somewhere in this world she would find her place.

The weather broke on Friday, and Sister Natalie consented to let her walk outside—if she would wear the black habit.

"My dear, I hope it is not distasteful to you, but I fear for your safety. If you wear these garments and have another sister with you, and perhaps if we put Quinta on watch to warn us if anyone comes, then perhaps you could walk about the yard for a few minutes in safety."

The compromise did not take away Taabe's restlessness. She ambled about in front of the mission house with Sister Riva, longing to be free of her new constraints. In this she felt a kinship with Quinta, who bemoaned the loss of her mustang. Give them a pair of spirited horses, and the two of them could have a good gallop across the plains. Both would probably be more content afterward with the quiet life of the mission.

Instead they had to content themselves with exploring the barn and chasing Sister Riva's chickens back into their pen.

"One of the hens is missing," Sister Riva said.

Taabe counted and looked carefully at each one. The sister was right—the chicken that often followed her about the garden was nowhere to be found.

"I suppose a coyote got it," Sister Riva said.

"Or an Indian." Quinta's dark eyes gazed at them, defying them to say that was nonsense.

They searched for the hen halfheartedly and even walked out to the road, but never toward the woods, and never out of the sister's sight.

That evening Sister Natalie came to her room and sat down on the stool. Taabe sat on the edge of her bed, waiting for her to speak.

"Taabe, are you frightened? We could take you to Fort Chadbourne, and you might be safer there."

"I stay here." Unless . . . she searched Sister Natalie's face. Did the nuns want her to go? Her presence could bring trouble on them. Perhaps they felt it was time for her to take responsibility for her safety. "I go if . . ."

"If?" Sister Natalie asked.

"You want Taabe to go?"

The nun shook her head. "No, dear. We have come to love you. All of us are trusting God to keep us safe and to help us keep you safe. But if you are afraid that isn't enough, we will see that you get to the fort, at least for a while."

The lines around her eyes seemed deeper, and her face a little grayer than when they first met. Taabe reached out and touched Sister Natalie's bony hand.

"I stay. We pray."

Sister Natalie smiled. "We all pray every day that the Lord will watch over us, and that He will send your family here to find you."

Taabe nodded. "I pray too."

"That brings me great joy, child. I am sure God brought you here, and you've been a great blessing to us." Sister Natalie's rare smile melted Taabe's heart.

"Thank you," she whispered. She wasn't sure yet what she believed about the Numinu's spirits or the white man's God, but she was here, and she was still safe. Did the sisters' constant prayers really protect them? They believed Peca and other men could harm them, or they wouldn't take precautions against it.

"What if they come?" she asked.

Sister Natalie frowned. "Do you mean the Comanche?"

Taabe nodded. "Peca mad."

"He is angry. When Quinta says he is 'mad,' she means he is angry."

Taabe wasn't sure about the distinction between those words.

Sister Natalie patted her hand. "If they do come, we will not give you up to them."

"Men hurt . . . hurt sisters. Hurt Quinta and Taabe."

The nun sighed heavily. "That could happen. I don't think God will allow it, but you're right, it's possible. But even in such a terrible time, God would be here with us. He would watch over us. And if the worst should happen and any of us were killed, He would take us up to Himself, in heaven."

Taabe puzzled over that. Sometimes when Sister Adele read from the Bible, they talked about weighty matters such as this. Heaven was the place the Bible said God's people went when they died. That much she understood.

"I fear we've been slow in your religious instruction," Sister Natalie said. "We wanted to be sure you healed well and that you understood enough English to benefit from it. Sister Adele tells me you have questions when she reads to you."

"Yes. She is very kind."

Sister Natalie smiled again. "I'm glad. And you may come to any of us with your questions. Perhaps it is time for more formal training. You may sit in Quinta's classes if you wish. We'll not force you to, but . . ."

"I learn," Taabe said. She thought much about the older

nun's words, and she began sitting in the room during Quinta's lessons—especially her Bible lessons—whenever she wasn't helping in the kitchen.

The week after their trip to Fort Chadbourne, all the residents of the mission anticipated the stagecoach's arrival. Taabe sat in the parlor sewing while Quinta had her arithmetic lessons. The girl could not concentrate on her studies, and she fidgeted continually.

"Sit still," Sister Adele said for the third time.

"It's almost time for Ned and Brownie," Quinta protested.

Sister Adele sighed. "All right, we will go outside for a short while. Will you join us, Taabe?"

They went for their wraps. A few minutes later, all three stepped out into the blustery front yard.

"May I go to the road?" Quinta asked.

"Yes, but stay where I can see you," Sister Adele said.

Quinta ran up the short lane and stopped where it met the road and stood staring eastward, watching for the stagecoach. A few minutes later, she let out the roadrunner's call. Taabe ran inside to inform the others, and the nuns quickly filed out into the damp dooryard to meet their friends. Taabe lingered inside and watched from the parlor's narrow window. Since the buffalo hunter came, she always waited to be sure no unwanted visitors got off the stagecoach. She was eager to see the new pupils, but more anxious for a glimpse of Ned. Would she get to talk to him today?

A man and a woman emerged from the stagecoach, followed by two girls perhaps a couple of years older than Quinta. She could hear Ned's introductions to Sister Natalie and the other nuns. They would come in soon, and Sister Natalie would bring the parents into this room.

Taabe scurried out to the kitchen. Sister Marie had a kettle of water steaming on the stove and a tray laid out with cups, saucers, and spoons. Taabe filled the small pitcher they used for milk when guests came and put it on the tray.

Sister Marie hurried in. "Thank you, dear. I'll fix the tea, and we'll be ready. Did you see the new girls?"

Taabe nodded.

"The one girl's parents brought her and her friend. The two new girls are already acquainted. I hope they won't shut out our Quinta and only want each other for friends."

Taabe frowned, working out the gist of that. "Quinta is . . . young."

"Yes, you're right. She's younger than either of them." Sister Marie shook her head. "If all goes well, we will soon have a girl the same age as Quinta. And how I'll keep up with the cooking, I don't know."

"Girls help?"

"Some, but not too much or they'll complain to their parents. But Sister Natalie is telling the parents each pupil will have daily chores, to help teach them diligence and discipline."

Taabe shook her head. To her, most of this was incomprehensible chatter.

Sister Marie smiled at her. "I'll take the tray in. I don't think Sister Natalie is ready to let the visitors see you. Of course, you'll meet the new girls later."

Taabe stayed in the kitchen feeling a bit forsaken. She understood why she was excluded from the gathering. She wished to meet as few people as possible. But she would also enjoy being included.

Footsteps drew her attention to the kitchen door. It swung open, and Ned stood in the doorway, smiling. Her loneliness vanished. This was what she'd really wished for—contact with the handsome stagecoach driver.

"Taabe!"

He reached out to her, and she placed her hands in his. Her

friendship with Ned was different from that with Sister Adele and the others.

"Ned."

"It's so good to see you."

She gazed up at him, her heart full. This man had become the focus of her new life. What did it mean that she lived from one stagecoach day to the next, thinking of Ned? And what would happen when they found her family and she had to leave the mission?

For Ned, the five miles from the mission to Fort Chadbourne flew by. Brownie stayed quiet, chewing tobacco and thinking his own thoughts. Ned's heart was full of thoughts of Taabe. He'd followed Sister Adele's whispered directions and found her in the kitchen. Her bright eyes and unrestrained smile when he took her hands would stay with him among his memory treasures.

Delivering the new pupils from Fort Belknap to the mission seemed a fitting event. Now the nuns' school would grow and progress rapidly. Sister Natalie said three more girls would join them within a month, and she had several additional inquiries from parents across Texas. They might even have to hire men to add on to the mission house. Ned hoped they did—it would allow them to extend the garden wall around the compound. If they built new rooms around a courtyard in the Spanish pattern, they would gain a layer of security. Sister Natalie had said she hoped they could also have larger windows facing the courtyard, lightening the interiors of the new schoolrooms she was planning.

"We picking those folks up on our way back tomorrow?" Brownie asked.

"Yup. Sister Natalie asked them to stay overnight at the mission."

The couple accompanying the new students had accepted the invitation, eager to see more of the girls' new environment rather than journey on to rough-and-tumble Fort Chadbourne.

When Ned and Brownie pulled in to the home station beside the fort, the tenders were waiting with the fresh team harnessed. Herr Stein hurried to the stagecoach before Ned could gather his things from the driver's boot.

"The captain wants to see you."

"All right." Ned jumped down and took the mail sacks out of the stagecoach. Captain Tapley's summons must pertain to Taabe. He and Herr Stein carried the mail inside, and Ned left his personal gear in the drivers' room. He scrubbed the dust off his face and hands, whacked his hat against his thigh a couple of times, and brushed off his clothes. Then he walked over to the fort.

"Bright, come right in." Tapley didn't wait for the sergeant to greet him, but stood as Ned came through the door. "There's a fellow here who may be able to help you. Cat Thompson. Ever hear of him?"

"Don't think so."

"He's half Apache, does some scouting for the army. I've worked with him before, and we use him quite a bit. He's considered trustworthy, and he's no friend of the Comanche, though he speaks their lingo pretty well."

"Sounds worth looking into. Think he'd go to the mission with me?"

"Yes. I mentioned I might have a small job for him to do today and sent him over to the mess hall to get some dinner. I'll stand for his day's wages if you want to take him out there. He has a horse. You can take one from our remuda. I'll give the order, if you want to do it."

"Thank you. I'd appreciate it."

"There's one other thing," Tapley said. "I've received a letter from the Indian agent at Fort Smith. He's sent the names of several children who were captured in Texas. Of course, it's possible the young woman at the mission was seized someplace else, but this is a start." He picked up a closely written sheet of paper. "In addition to the ones we already knew about, he mentions two boys—brothers—taken about three years ago, and another who disappeared last year and is assumed captured."

"No girls?"

"There was one down Victoria way, but that's a long ways from here, and it was twelve years ago."

Ned whistled softly. "That's a long time."

"Yes. I hardly think . . . but you never know."

"How do we contact them?"

"The agent sent along her older brother's name and address. Seems the father's deceased and the brother has handled the correspondence regarding the girl. He's written to the governor and the Bureau of Indian Affairs in Washington, and anyone else he hoped could help. I thought I'd write him and ask for a description and tell him about the young woman you found. It would be nice, though, if we had more information from her."

"Maybe we'll learn something today."

"I hope so. I've written out the names of the known captives for you, and those about whom we've received inquiries from the families. Ten in all so far. I'm sure there are more. You can ask her if she recognizes any of the names. Cat can ask her, that is."

"You're sure he's safe?" Ned asked.

The captain grimaced. "As sure as I can be of anyone out here."

"All right, I'll go find him."

Thompson wasn't hard to locate in the troopers' mess hall.

He was the only man not in uniform, but his complexion and long, black hair would have given him away anyway. Ned got a cup of coffee and ambled over to the table where the scout was eating.

"Cat Thompson?" Ned sat down opposite him.

Thompson eyed him as he chewed and swallowed. "You the stage driver?"

"Yes."

Thompson nodded. "The cap'n told me you might have business with me." The man looked to be about Ned's age. He studied Ned in return, his dark eyes guarded. "What's it about?"

"Can you translate for a former captive?"

"Maybe. Probably, if he was with the Comanch or the Apache."

Ned glanced around, but none of the other men were close enough to hear over the chatter of conversation around them. "It's a she. You'll have to keep quiet about it. Where she is, where she's been, all of that."

"I can keep my mouth shut."

Ned nodded.

"She might not want to talk to me," Thompson said. "Depends on how her people feel about the Apache right now and how they treated her. Depends on a lot of things."

Ned started to reassure him but held back, remembering Taabe's reaction when she saw Trainer. "You're right. But if she's convinced you won't send her back to the tribe, I think she'll cooperate. She wants to find her real family."

"I'm willing to try."

"Good. I'll get something to eat over at Steins' and get me a saddle horse. Say half an hour?"

"I'll come over to the stage stop after a bit."

"Thanks." Ned stood and left, nodding to a couple of the soldiers he recognized.

Thompson kept his word and showed up at Steins' a short while later riding a broomtail dun mustang. The horse looked as wiry and trail savvy as his rider.

They rode swiftly to the mission with barely a word spoken. When they loped into the yard, Ned heard the incongruous call of an owl and saw the front door close on a diminutive figure in swirling green skirts. What was Quinta up to?

They dismounted, and Thompson reached for Ned's reins. "Maybe you go in first?"

"Good idea. They're a little gun-shy."

CHAPTER FIFTEEN

Taabe scrubbed the potatoes for Sister Marie, removing every bit of dirt and cutting out bad spots. Fluffy, the orange kitten, tumbled about the floor with her sister, batting at the hem of her skirt and each other. Tonight's dinner was very important. If the new pupil's parents didn't like the meal, they might think their daughter would not be fed well and take her away—or so Sister Marie said.

The sister was hard at work nearby, cutting up the chickens she would fry, when Quinta galloped in, pigtails flying.

"Taabe! Ned Bright is here again, but nobody heard my bird call."

"Ned?" Taabe stared at her. Why would Ned return after only a few hours?

"He has another man with him," Quinta said.

Taabe looked at Sister Marie.

"Quickly!" Sister Marie ran to the hiding place and yanked the table aside.

Taabe threw back the mat.

"Take Sister Riva out to speak to him," Sister Marie told Quinta. "Go!"

Taabe scrambled down the ladder and reached up to help fit the trapdoor in place. Her heart pounded.

"Wait!" Sister Marie snatched up the orange kitten and all but flung Fluffy into Taabe's hands.

"You will be safe," Sister Marie promised.

The sister's anxious face was the last thing Taabe saw as the trapdoor settled in place.

She groped around the wall to where the blankets were neatly folded and sat down. She clutched the kitten to her chest, inhaled deeply, and held her breath, listening. She could hear nothing but the kitten's tiny mew.

"You must be quiet." She stroked Fluffy and made herself relax. Gradually, the kitten settled on her lap and began to purr.

Now would be a time to pray. Taabe took several deep breaths before she formed the words. "Father God, let me be safe. Let man be good." She stopped, frustrated that she didn't have the words to speak to the Creator in English. Sister Adele said sometimes she spoke to God in French. Would He hear her if she spoke to Him in the Numinu language?

That didn't seem right. The God of the sisters didn't seem to belong in the Numinu world. But she was certain she'd known about Him before she was captured. Her family had prayed. She knew that now. They had read from God's book. When had she stopped knowing that—and when had she stopped talking to God the Father? Perhaps it was when she'd started to forget English.

Her Comanche mother had forbidden her to speak English. She had soon learned that the rule came with consequences. On several occasions, Taabe had gone without food for an entire day because she'd uttered a few words in the banned language.

With the perspective of years and distance, had she really been well treated? She hadn't been beaten much after the first few weeks, but deprivation and frequent humiliations had forced her to conform. She remembered many times she'd cowered in the shadows, whispering English words to herself—poems? verses of Scripture?—and hoping none of the Numinu would notice her and call for her to do more work for them.

Tears ran down her cheeks. She wiped them away with her sleeve and cuddled Fluffy close. The kitten meowed and licked her hand. She hoped the calico kitten wasn't sniffing about the trapdoor, trying to find her sister.

Light footsteps moved across the kitchen overhead. Sister Marie. All was well.

Taabe sat back feeling calmer. Sometime she would have to ask Sister Adele if God would listen to anyone, in any language.

Before Ned could reach the front step, the door flew open. Quinta charged out to embrace him.

"Ned! What are you doing here? Did you forget something?"

Sister Riva was only a step behind her.

"Good afternoon, Mr. Bright," the sister said as Ned disentangled himself from Quinta's hug. "We didn't expect you again so soon." She looked past him to where Cat held the horses.

"I've brought another translator. Captain Tapley vouches for him. He scouts for the army, and they've found him reliable. Could you please ask Taabe if she's willing to see him?"

"Of course. And I will fetch Sister Natalie."

"Thank you," Ned said.

Sister Riva turned and went inside.

"Can I ride your horse?" Quinta asked.

"He's not mine, *chica*. I borrowed him, so I think not."

"Aw, just around the dooryard?"

Ned laughed. "All right, but you have to give your word not to go farther."

They walked out to where Cat waited. Ned picked Quinta up, tossed her on the bay gelding's back, and smoothed her skirt down to cover her black stockings.

"Now, this is a cavalry horse, so don't go blowing any charges, will you?"

She gave him a tolerant smile and accepted the reins from Cat, eyeing him curiously.

"This is Mr. Thompson," Ned said. To the scout he added, "She's Patrillo Garza's daughter."

"The freighter?"

"Yes. She's a student here."

Cat nodded and smiled up at Quinta. "Call me Cat."

"I'd be delighted to."

Both men laughed as she turned the gelding and urged him into a smart trot around the yard.

"No doubt she's happy to have permission to call a grown-up by his first name," Ned said. "On the other hand, she likes cats."

Cat smiled. "She seems like a firecracker, that one."

"Oh, yeah. Just wait a few years." So far, Ned liked Cat. He hoped his trust and the captain's were not misplaced.

The door to the mission house opened, and Sister Natalie came out. Her lips smiled, but her eyes raked over Cat. She seemed satisfied by the time she reached them. "Mr. Bright, won't you come in and bring your guest?"

"Thank you, Sister. This is Cat Thompson."

Sister Natalie bowed her head slightly. "You are welcome here." She looked at Quinta as the girl brought Ned's horse around to where they stood. She frowned. "Quinta, perhaps you could take both the gentlemen's horses into the barn."

Ned raised his eyebrows. She'd never made this offer before.

"As a precaution," Sister Natalie said. "We have no livestock of our own, but Sister Riva and Quinta have been working to make it habitable for the cow Mrs. Stein is procuring for us. I think your horses will find it acceptable for a short time."

As Quinta slid to the ground, her skirt caught on the stirrup, exposing a quantity of petticoat and pantalets. Sister Natalie reached over to swat the skirt down. "Modesty, Quinta. Always remember modesty is the best cloak for young ladies."

"Yes, Sister."

Ned was impressed by the girl's meekness. Quinta did not seem cowed by the severe nun, but obeyed instantly. She always rambled on happily whenever he talked to her. It seemed she had made a successful adjustment to life at the mission school.

Quinta took Cat Thompson's reins and turned to walk both horses to the barn.

"Can you handle them both, señorita?" Cat asked.

"Easy as pie."

Cat grinned at Ned. "You're right. Her father's going to have his hands full."

"Our new pupils, Laura and Kate, and Laura's parents are in the parlor with the girls and Sister Adele, discussing the curriculum," Sister Natalie said. "I've asked Taabe to meet us in the dining room. Right this way, gentlemen."

The door to the sitting room was closed, and Ned heard the soft murmur of voices as they passed. He wondered if the out-of-towners had met Taabe yet. Would they object to leaving their daughters in a household that contained a young woman who'd lived with the hated Comanche?

The dining room was empty when they entered. Sister Natalie said, "Mr. Thompson, won't you take a seat, please? And Mr. Bright, if you could join me in the kitchen for just a moment."

Mystified, Ned followed her into the adjoining room. Sister Marie looked up from her work table, where she was preparing food, and nodded.

Sister Natalie closed the door. "Taabe is in hiding again. She refuses to come out until you tell her it is safe."

"I trust this man," Ned said.

"But you don't know him."

"No, but in the short time I've spent with him, I don't see any deceit or slyness about him. The captain said he's served the army well, and he's promised to keep this visit quiet."

Sister Natalie nodded. "You trusted Mr. Trainer as well, I believe."

Ned huffed out a breath. "No. I didn't really, but I was desperate. I shouldn't have brought him here. But it's different now. Even if we didn't have a translator, in time I'm sure Taabe would learn enough to tell us the details we need. But time is important too. The captain has inquiries from several families of lost children and new information from the Indian agent. The sooner we find her family, the better."

"I agree," Sister Natalie said. "You may rejoin Mr. Thompson. I will ask Taabe to come."

Ned heard a small creaking. He whipped toward it, searching for the source. The small rag rug under a table moved, pushing upward. The floorboard beneath it rose until a crack a couple of inches wide showed.

"I will come now," said Taabe's voice.

Sister Natalie touched his sleeve. "Help me move the table, Mr. Bright."

A moment later, Taabe stood next to him, holding her orange kitten. "Man good," she said.

"Yes," Ned replied. "I believe he is."

Taabe nodded. "We talk."

She set Fluffy down on the floor with the calico kitten and looked at Ned expectantly.

"Come then," Sister Natalie said. "In the dining room."

Ned sent up a swift prayer as they walked the few steps. If Cat betrayed Taabe's whereabouts to the Comanche, things could get ugly.

The scout was peering out the narrow window in the dining room when they entered. It faced the back of the house, toward the garden. Was he looking at anything in particular? Ned shook away the doubts.

Cat turned. His gaze homed in on Taabe. He gave a slight smile and a nod.

Taabe looked at Ned, then back at the stranger. The change in her expression was subtle, but Ned could detect some hesitation as she and Cat looked each other over. Taabe wore the lavender dress again—the one that had belonged to Elana Garza. The soft hue gave her an air of gentle femininity.

Cat looked impressed. What had he expected—a filthy, half-wild creature?

"Taabe Waipu, may I present Mr. Cat Thompson?" Sister Natalie said. "He is here to translate for you and Mr. Bright."

Taabe made a shallow curtsey, no doubt one of the graces the sisters had taught her.

Sister Natalie pulled out a chair, and Ned hastened to hold it for her. Cat watched then went around the table uncertainly and held a chair for Taabe. She looked at him with astonishment in her eyes.

"It's all right, Taabe," Sister Natalie said. "It is one of the courtesy gestures we've been speaking about in Quinta's deportment class. Gentlemen in our culture hold a lady's chair for her."

Taabe sat down cautiously, eyeing Cat sidelong as she positioned herself in the chair. Cat went to the end of the table and sat down. Ned was glad Cat had distanced himself enough that Taabe shouldn't feel too intimidated by his presence. Sister Natalie was their chaperon and would not budge during the interview. In Ned's opinion, this spoke more about her willingness to leave Taabe in his care for short periods than about her lack of trust in Thompson. Sister Natalie would never imagine leaving a young lady alone with two men, one of whom was an unknown quantity.

"Taabe, thank you for letting me bring Cat Thompson," Ned said.

She nodded and darted a glance at Cat.

Cat spoke to her in Comanche, what seemed a rambling greeting.

Taabe listened, her eyes downcast, then nodded. In a whisper, she spoke the simpler words of greeting Ned had learned.

Cat looked to Ned. "What do you want me to ask her? I believe we'll have no trouble communicating."

"Please ask her to tell us what she remembers about her capture."

Cat spoke to Taabe. She replied, hesitantly at first, but then her words poured out. She began by looking at Cat, but after a moment shifted her gaze to Ned. He felt that she was speaking to him from her heart, as she had longed to do at other times.

After several sentences, she paused and looked at Cat.

He cleared his throat. "She says it was many years ago. She was small, scarcely tall enough to reach your belt when you are standing."

Ned nodded with a smile.

"She does not remember her white name or where she lived, but she recalls a few things about that day. She was riding a horse. A dark horse, and very beautiful. It was her own mount, though she was young. She stresses that."

Ned watched Taabe's face while Cat talked. A girl scarcely eight or ten years old had her own horse. He shouldn't be too surprised—Quinta had a mustang she claimed as her own at the ranch.

"Go on," he said.

Cat nodded. "She was riding out across a field to see someone. To meet someone. She doesn't remember who. She crossed a stream, and the Numinu rose up out of the grass beyond. Three of them. They caught her bridle and pulled her off the horse."

Ned sat still for a moment. His heart was racing as he imagined the little girl's terror. He wasn't sure he wanted to hear what happened next.

His voice cracked. "And then?"

"One of the Numinu took her horse. It had a saddle on it. He got on, but the saddle was too small. He cut the girth and dropped it."

Ned nodded, watching Taabe. Tears stood in her eyes.

Cat spoke to her for a moment. Taabe flicked him a glance, then returned her gaze to Ned and began to speak again.

Ned listened to the cadence of her voice. He couldn't guess what she was saying. She showed no grief, except for the unshed tears. Finally she paused and Cat began translating.

"The warrior rode her horse. Another took her on his mount—a sorry, brown-and-white spotted one. She remembers thinking how thin all their horses were, compared to hers. They met up with more Comanche men, and they rode for many days and nights. They gave her only a little food and a mouthful of water when they ate."

"Ask her how many there were, and what direction they went. And if there were other captives."

Cat relayed the questions, and Taabe answered.

"She says there were at least six, maybe eight. She's not sure now. The others had a boy with them. She tried to speak to the boy once, and the warrior she rode with slapped her. Later she heard the boy speak, but she didn't understand him. She thinks now he was Spanish."

"Or German," Ned said, thinking of the names on his list. "Ask her what became of the boy."

When Cat spoke to her, Taabe shrugged and gave a brief reply.

"She doesn't know. They separated after a while, and she never saw the boy again that she remembers."

"All right, we can see if any boys were taken about the same time as a girl. That may help us identify her. What about direction and distance?"

"She said the sun was in her eyes in the afternoon. She was relieved when it went down and didn't hurt her eyes. Sometimes it was behind them, though. They rode for many days, hardly stopping. Then they began to stop at night. They traveled more than a week, she thinks. Perhaps two."

"They were heading west." Ned frowned. "North and west? Heading for the Llano Estacado?"

"They may have started far south of here, or east of here, nearer the coast," Cat said.

"True."

Ned turned to Sister Natalie. "I should have thought of it—would you have something I can write on? I want to be able to tell the captain and the Indian agent these details, and I don't want to forget anything important."

Sister Natalie rose and left them for a few minutes and returned with paper and a pencil.

Cat continued to prompt Taabe, and Ned jotted notes.

"She had a family. She believes she had a sister. She remembers a girl with golden hair, older than she was."

"That's progress." Ned wrote it down. "What else?"

"She remembers men—tall, like you. One she thinks was her father. And a mother who made sweet cakes. She missed her mother's cooking for a long time, until she got used to the Comanche ways."

"I can understand that," Ned said. "What about names? Does she recall any of their names?"

Cat spoke to Taabe, but she shook her head.

Ned looked into her eyes across the table. "Taabe, do you know the name 'Morgan'?"

Frown lines appeared on her forehead.

"There was a girl named Billie Morgan," Ned said slowly. "She lived in a place called Victoria, on a ranch. She was about your age, and she had blue eyes and dark blond hair. Billie Morgan."

Taabe's face showed pain or extreme concentration, but she shook her head slightly.

"Billie," she whispered, still frowning.

Ned sighed. "What about the cat? Ask her about Fluffy."

At his mention of the name, Taabe's eyes cleared. "Fluffy."

Cat spoke to her in Comanche. Her face lit up and she spoke with more animation than Ned had seen before.

When Cat turned to him a minute later, he was smiling. "She had a kitten. It was orange. Its name was Fluffy. How did you know?"

"That's what she named her new kitten here."

"I see." Cat spoke to her again and then told Ned, "Her cat was the same color as the one you bought her at the fort. Did I get that part right?"

"Yes, I got it from Lassen."

"She loved it a great deal, it seems. And she remembers horses, lots of horses. All of them were dark brown or black. No pintos or palominos."

"That's odd."

Cat shrugged. "She admits she's confused. The Comanche had lots of horses. But she thinks that where she came from, most of the horses were solid colored. And one thing she held against her captors was that she never got her horse back. Later, when she was allowed to ride, she had to use a poorer mustang. One of the chiefs claimed her original mount as his war horse. The day came when he went out raiding and came back without it, riding a different horse. She never forgave him."

"Wow." Ned sat back and looked at Sister Natalie.

"I don't know about you gentlemen, but I'm exhausted," she said. "Would you like some coffee?"

"That would be nice, ma'am," Cat said.

Ned added his thanks.

"I should check on our guests as well," Sister Natalie said. "As much as I'd like to hear the rest of her story, I'd probably better send in one of the other sisters while I entertain them."

Taabe rose when Sister Natalie did.

"Where are you going, Taabe?" the sister asked.

"I go. I come back."

Sister Natalie nodded and smiled at Ned. "I'm sure she'll return in a moment."

"Yes, ma'am."

The two women left the room.

Ned turned to Cat. "What do you think?"

"I think she's being honest. What else do you want me to ask her?"

"I'd like to know more about her life with the Comanche. Where did they take her? Did they treat her well? That sort of thing. And if she can give you the names of the chiefs she had contact with, it would help the captain pinpoint where she's been."

"All right," Cat said. "I'm not sure what to make of the white people she described. It seems her memory is hazy on that. She may have just fixed her mind on you because you were the first white man she'd seen in years, or at least the first one who was nice to her. That stuff about the tall men with all the horses . . . it could be a mishmash of things that have happened to her."

"All right." Ned found that thought disappointing. "Let's also go over this list of captives with her. If she recognizes any of the names, it will be a breakthrough for Captain Tapley. He'd love to be able to tell the Indian agent where some of these abducted children are."

Taabe appeared in the doorway, and the two men stood. She held something that looked like a thin stick.

Ned peered at it.

"What is that, Taabe?"

"Music." She held up a small, hand-carved flute.

CHAPTER SIXTEEN

Taabe held the flute out so Ned could see it.

"Can you play it?" he asked.

She nodded. The eager light in his brown eyes made her happy. She looked at the army scout called Cat. "Ask him if he wants me to make music," she said in Comanche.

"I'm sure he does," Cat said.

She smiled and walked to the other side of the table. Slowly she turned to face them and held her flute to her mouth. She played an eerie Comanche melody, with notes wandering up and down, reaching for the wind.

When she stopped, Ned clapped his hands together. "That was beautiful! Thank you."

Taabe needed no translation.

"Where did you get the flute?" Cat asked.

"From He Sits by the Fire—an elder." Her throat tightened. "He is gone now. He played one day when I had first come there, and I reached for the flute. He was surprised, but he let me take it. I played on it, and he was surprised even more."

Cat laughed. "I believe that."

"He made me a flute of my own, smaller than his, and I have had it ever since."

Cat turned to Ned and translated what she'd said.

She positioned the flute again and launched into a spirited rendering of "Frère Jacques."

Ned laughed. "I know that song."

"What is it?" Cat asked.

"It's a French song. I think it's called 'Frère Jacques.' About a lazy priest."

Taabe lowered the flute and said, "Sister sing."

"One of the sisters sings that?" Ned asked.

Taabe nodded, but felt she wasn't being clear.

"Which one?" Ned asked. "Sister Adele?"

"Yes, but . . ." She turned to Cat and said swiftly in Comanche, "Tell him my own sister sang it. When I was a child, I heard this song. Then Sister Adele sang it here, and I knew it."

Cat's jaw dropped. He turned to Ned and spoke earnestly. "She knew the song before she came here. She says her sister sang it. Her own sister, she said. I think she means in her real family—her white family."

Ned's face froze. "Is her family French?"

Cat walked closer to Taabe. "Your family—before the Comanche. Were they French, like the nuns here? Did they speak French?"

Taabe shook her head. "English. No French, no Spanish. English."

Cat laughed and translated to Ned.

"They make music," Taabe said in English. "Much music."

"Your family was musical?" Ned asked.

She frowned. "I think yes." She looked at Cat for help and launched into Comanche. "I played another instrument—with my hands." She held her hands out before her and wiggled her fingers.

Ned and Cat stared at each other.

"The piano?" Ned asked. "You don't suppose she played the piano?"

Cat shrugged. "Anything is possible. The nuns don't have one, do they?"

"I'm sure they don't." Ned smiled at Taabe. "Do you remember any other songs your family sang? Anything at all? It may help us find them."

Cat relayed his message to be sure she got the full meaning.

Taabe hesitated. One melody had haunted her, tickling the edges of her memory. She said to Cat, "I tried to play this once for Sister Adele, but she didn't recognize it. And I'm not sure all the notes are right. This flute does not play as well as the old one, and it is long, long since I heard someone sing the song."

After he translated, she put the flute to her lips and began to play softly, reaching for the elusive notes.

Ned walked slowly around the table, wonder on his face. "I know that song. Taabe, I know it."

She lowered the flute.

"It's called 'Amazing Grace.' But—" He glanced at Cat. "The nuns might not know that one, because I think it's a Protestant song. I don't know if Taabe understands about Catholics and Protestants and . . . Oh, just tell her I know the song and it's a good one. We sing it in church. It's about God's love for us and His grace. Do the Comanche have a word for that?"

Cat smiled. "Just stop talking and let me try to explain to her. She may understand more than you think."

Taabe listened carefully to Ned's talk, but many of the

words he used weren't known to her. She waited impatiently for Cat's turn.

"Ned knows this song," he said in Comanche.

She nodded. "I thought so. He likes it."

"Yes. It is one his people sing in church—when they worship God. You know about church?"

"It is . . . like the chapel room the sisters have, only bigger?"

"Well . . . I suppose so. But Ned believes differently than the sisters do."

She frowned. "Not all white people have the same God?"

Cat glanced at Ned and said quickly, "No, not a different God. . . . It's hard to explain, but I think the church the sisters follow have some different teaching from this other church that Ned goes to."

"Like the Numinu and the Kiowa?"

"Uh . . . maybe. Not really." He frowned. "They all worship God and His Son, Jesus."

"Jesus." Taabe nodded. Sister Adele was teaching her more about Jesus, and she'd been sitting in on Quinta's class they called "catechism," where one of the sisters asked questions about God, and Quinta was expected to give the correct answer.

"Well, the two churches have different songs," Cat said.

"I understand."

"Good." He seemed relieved. "The first song you played was not a church song. But the second one was. It is about God and how . . . good He is. How He gives people things they don't deserve."

Taabe cocked her head to one side while she thought about that. "What are the words to sing with it?"

Cat turned to Ned. "Can you sing the song for her?"

"I guess so." Ned cleared his throat, obviously self-conscious, and stepped a little closer. "It goes like this: Amazing grace, how sweet the sound, that saved a wretch like me. I once was lost, but now am found, was blind but now I see."

Taabe was charmed by Ned's true, clear voice, but Cat gritted his teeth. "I'm not sure I can translate that."

Ned looked upset, and Cat said quickly, "But I'll try."

He closed his eyes for a minute then spoke in Comanche. "Ned says it's about God's gifts that he doesn't deserve, and how wonderful they are. How sweet and unexpected." He eyed her doubtfully, but Taabe nodded, so he went on. "Ned says he had lost his way but someone found him—God, I think. And he couldn't see, but now he can." Cat held up both hands. "But that's not real. I mean, he wasn't really blind. I think the song means it like . . . in a story. You say a man is as tall as a mountain, but he's not really. And this song says he was blind, but it means . . . I think it means he was blind to God. He couldn't see the things God wanted him to see, but now he can."

Taabe stood still for a long moment, letting that soak in. She turned and looked at Ned. He might have been holding his breath, he was so still, and his expression was one of dread.

He is afraid I won't understand—but I do!

She smiled at him. "Sing again."

Ned let out a short laugh. "Play again."

She raised the flute and played the notes softly. Ned made the words fit with the music, and she knew they were right. Those were the words she couldn't remember. *I once was lost, but now am found.* God had found her. He'd brought her here—one of His unexpected, wonderful gifts to her.

Ned's heart caught as the last notes died away. Singing to Taabe's music had hit him hard, like catching a rock in the chest. Unless he was mistaken, she had tears in her eyes. Even Cat seemed to be moved by the song.

Taabe spoke quietly to Cat, then jerked her head and her eyebrows toward Ned.

"She wants me to tell you that she used to play an instrument in her old life. It was somewhat like this flute, but it was made of metal. She's had this one that the old man made her for a long time. Her Comanche family liked to hear her play."

"It's amazing." Ned gripped the back of a chair. "Ask if she is ready to listen to the names. I'd like to read her the list now."

Cat spoke to Taabe. She nodded and laid the flute on the table.

They spent another hour going over the list and talking in their awkward way about life in the Comanche village. Ned had never felt so drawn to a woman. Every new detail he learned about Taabe pulled him closer to her, until he wanted desperately to find the shadowy family she remembered—the ones who had given her a horse and a flute and a cat. No doubt they had loved her deeply.

If only they had some proof of her identity.

"Ask if she has any birthmarks or scars that would help her family identify her."

Her answer saddened him.

"She believes any scars she carries were made after her capture."

Ned sighed and gazed across the table at her. What sorrows had she borne? What pain had she endured?

"I wish I knew what questions to ask," he said. "I'm sure there's much more we don't know that could help us."

Cat spoke gently to Taabe, and she answered at length. He turned to Ned. "She says that when she was taken, the Comanche band rode north for many days until they reached a place where white men never go."

"What sort of place?"

"I expect she is talking about the Valle de las Lagrimas."

Ned puzzled that out. "The Valley of Tears?"

"Yes. That is what the Spanish call it. I don't know what the Comanche call it—they never speak of it to outsiders. It's an isolated canyon deep in Comanche country. The Indians take captives there because they know that no one can follow them there."

"How can that be?"

"It is secret, it is very defensible, and the entrance is well guarded. No white man has gone there except as a captive. Ever. It is said that they raid and take captives and then keep them in the valley until they either sell them to the Comancheros or else they are acclimated to the Comanche culture to such an extent, they will not want to leave." He shrugged. "If they know they will keep the captive and adopt her into the tribe, they might not take her there. I can't say that's the place, but it's a guess."

Ned gazed at Taabe. "Obviously they were not successful in assimilating this one."

"You mean?"

"She did not forget everything. She never stopped wanting to return home."

Taabe spoke again, in the Comanche tongue, and Cat listened.

"She says she tried for a long time to keep from forgetting English, but she was with them too long. They forbade her to speak it and punished her if she did. When you brought her here, she couldn't remember any of the language or read the nuns' books." Cat's eyes bored into Ned. "That's important to her. She knows she could read at one time."

Ned looked at Taabe. "You once read books?" He held his hands together like a book.

She nodded with tears in her eyes. "I read. I write too. I

write long . . . long story. Not story, but . . . something." She turned to Cat and spoke in Comanche.

"She says she had lessons, like Quinta is having now. She learned to do a great many things. She wrote long essays—at least that's what I think she means. Many sheets of paper."

Ned nodded.

Taabe held out her hand to him across the table. Ned leaned forward and clasped it.

"I am one of you," Taabe said in a fierce whisper. "I am not one of them."

Ned's heart lurched. Perhaps she was telling him more, beyond the surface of those few words. Did she have feelings for him too?

"I will write letters," he had Cat tell her. "I'll write to anyone who is looking for a girl who might be you. We'll find your family, Taabe. We'll find where you belong."

Her eyes glistened as she squeezed his hand. He wanted to say more, but not through a translator. She released his hand, and he knew it was time to go.

Ned and Cat took their leave of Taabe, saying a brief good-bye to Quinta and the nuns.

Sister Adele accompanied Quinta out to the barn with them. "This visit was helpful?" she asked Ned.

"Very. There is much more I'd like to ask her, but we're all tired. Perhaps another time." He sighed. "I didn't learn much about the time between her capture and her escape. Just generally how she lived and that she wasn't kept as a slave exactly. She had a Comanche family, and she said she was treated as well as anyone else. But I know there's more we never touched on."

"Perhaps Mr. Thompson can come again."

Cat shrugged. "I wouldn't mind. But the captain needs me to go out again with some troopers tomorrow. I'm not sure when I'll be back."

"We can discuss it," Ned said. "Maybe you can let me know."

Sister Adele paused outside the barn. "Quinta wishes to give you messages for her father and brothers. We told her that she might."

"All right." Ned listened to all of Quinta's chatter and her requests for trifles from her father.

"I have something else to tell you," she said, drawing him aside.

"What is it?"

Quinta beckoned him closer. He bent down and turned his head so she could whisper to him.

"Sometimes Taabe cries. She doesn't want the nuns to know, but my room is next to hers, and I hear her at night."

Ned swallowed hard. "Why? Why does she cry?"

Quinta shrugged. "I think she said that she misses her baby. That can't be right, can it? Maybe I should ask her again . . ." She eyed him anxiously.

Ned's heart plummeted. "No, *chica*. If she wants to tell you more, she will."

As he and Cat rode back to the fort, Ned ruminated on what Quinta told him. A baby. What did it mean? All sorts of possibilities presented themselves, but the strangling feeling wouldn't leave. For the past few weeks, Ned's life had centered on Taabe and his visits to the mission. He still knew very little about her, yet he cared for her deeply. What would something like a baby—a half-Comanche baby—do to their friendship?

No, Quinta must be mistaken. Taabe had wept for someone else's baby. Her Comanche sister's, perhaps. He would say nothing of that, to anyone, until he heard from Taabe what it was about.

And the place Cat had spoken of—the Valley of Tears. How close had Taabe come to being sold as a slave to the Comancheros, the Mexican traders who came up to swap goods with the Comanche? He uttered a silent prayer of thanks for her deliverance.

"I can see why you were so determined to help her," Cat said as their horses jogged along the road.

"You'll keep quiet—" Ned stopped and shook his head. "Sorry. I know you will."

Cat nodded. "My word is good. I'll tell no one about her, and if anyone asks me, I will send them to the captain."

Cat left Ned at the parade ground and headed for the troopers' barracks. Ned went to Captain Tapley's office and gave him a quick overview of what he'd learned.

"Would you like to write to this rancher down near Victoria?" the captain asked. "The Morgan girl seems by far the most likely candidate. If you give him some of these details you've learned, he should be able to tell you if this is his sister."

Ned spent an hour wording his letter to Judson Morgan. He described Taabe Waipu, with her light brown hair that might be blond in the summer sun, and her eyes as blue as an August sky. He told of her musical ability and her memories of songs and playing a flute or similar instrument and also a piano, and about the herd of dark horses and the kitten named Fluffy. At last he sat back and reread the letter.

If these people claimed her, what would happen? Taabe would go away, that's what.

He added another paragraph, advising the man not to set out too hastily. Better to correspond until they were certain than to take a journey of three hundred fifty miles and then learn they were wrong. He asked if Billie Morgan had any scars or other unmistakable physical characteristics. He emphasized that Taabe had forgotten English, her family, and even her name.

His steps dragged as he walked to the front of the station to give the letter to Herr Stein. It would go out in the next sack of mail heading south. If this was the Morgan girl, surely the things he had told them would confirm that. If not, they might still hope and insist on seeing her.

Ned stopped at the front door and looked eastward, toward the mission. His jaw tightened and he reminded himself to breathe, but the anxiety didn't lessen. He had to force himself to enter the building with the letter. He handed it to Herr Stein and watched him place it in the sack.

As he trudged back around the house to the room he would share with Brownie that night, the question weighed heavily on him. He wasn't sure he wanted to answer it, but it hounded him.

Did he really want to find Taabe's family?

The changes at the mission confused Taabe and sometimes frightened her. Girls were flitting everywhere. Though the sisters admonished them to be quiet and to move slowly, she could often hear raised voices and running footsteps. Another girl came to stay, and all of the small bedchambers now had occupants. If more students arrived, the girls would have to double up.

As colder winds and rain settled in, Taabe often donned a habit and went outside with the girls and one of the sisters. The students eyed her with curiosity, but seldom tried to draw her into conversation. Taabe assumed that Quinta had given them her own explanation of her presence. She was glad to see Quinta joining in games with the others and leading them in excursions outside the mission house. The energetic youngster performed her chores heartily, setting an example for the older girls, who seemed less eager to carry water, sweep the floors, and wash dishes.

Quinta also led the class in mathematics. Eager to learn

more about numbers, Taabe sat in on this class, which Sister Adele taught all four pupils daily. It was not a discipline the Comanche cared about, beyond the usefulness of being able to describe quantities and keep track of their horses. Taabe found the precision of numbers refreshing. Her fingers flew as she wrote them on her slate and solved the arithmetic problems Sister Adele set her each day. Her only true rival was Quinta.

In all the other classes—literature, history, French, deportment, domestic arts, and catechism—Quinta lagged behind the others. Taabe thought this was because she tended to daydream and much preferred action to studies.

Another mysterious body of knowledge to Taabe was the calendar. Sister Adele and Sister Riva spent many hours teaching her the rudiments of measuring time. At Sister Riva's suggestion, each girl constructed her own calendar. Quinta's featured her drawings of horses around the borders of each page. Next Sister Natalie set the girls and Taabe to stitching calendars for the following year—1858—as samplers. This exacting work frustrated Quinta, but Taabe found it soothing as she placed the tiny stitches and saw the procession of days flow from her needle.

"If I ever finish this, I shall give it to Papa for Christmas," Quinta said as she and Taabe sat in the parlor working on their samplers while the older girls took their grammar lesson with Sister Adele in the dining room.

Taabe planned to hang hers on the wall in her room, to help her track the stagecoach days in the new year. But the idea of giving gifts seized her attention. She had heard people speak of Christmas several times, and Sister Adele had explained that it was a celebration of Jesus's birth.

"Give to Papa?" She raised her eyebrows at Quinta, which usually elicited an outpouring of information from the chatterbox.

"For his Christmas present. You know. Or do you?" Quinta looked stricken. "Have you gone without Christmas for years and years? How tragic!"

"Jesus," Taabe said.

"Yes. And we give gifts to the people we love. I shall make something for each of my brothers, and for Ned. I've asked Papa to send me some oil-tanned leather so I can braid a new set of reins for Marcos and one for Benito. I'm not sure about the others yet. Perhaps I could sew something—although I doubt I'll finish this sampler in time to sew anything else before Christmas." Quinta frowned and jabbed her needle through the linen. "I'm only up to February on my calendar, and that means ten more months to go."

"Sister Adele says be patient," Taabe said.

Quinta grimaced. "My horse calendar only took me two days to make. This will take me two months. And it's all time I could spend doing other things that are so much fun."

The kittens tumbled in from the entry, swatting at each other, and rolled together across the floor. Quinta laughed and jumped up, casting aside her needlework.

Taabe felt she ought to call Quinta back to her task, as any of the nuns would, but she didn't want to. Instead, she laughed as she watched Fluffy and Mimi, the calico, chase the skein of floss Quinta waved before them.

Many times Taabe felt she stood between adulthood and childhood, between responsibility and freedom. Quinta's presence accentuated that. It was another tearing of her character, as was the tugging between the white world and the Indian. Most of the time she wanted to live in the world of the whites. She belonged here. She had the strong conviction that if she persisted in relearning the white culture, she could take her place in it again.

But sometimes she looked back to her life with the

Numinu and sadness caught her. Would she never see her sister, Pia, again? The tiny baby girl Pia had borne last summer had seized her heart, and Taabe loved holding the baby and helping care for it—though it reminded her of her own loss. Sometimes she shed tears when she recalled cradling a warm little body close to her heart. She'd come to love the little scrap of a child she'd had once—and had resolved at that time to be content as a Numinu woman.

But that season had passed, and with it came much sorrow. When Peca began making advances, she had backed away. Pia and Chano saw no reason why she should not marry the warrior, but the idea troubled Taabe. When he staked out the horses before their lodge, Taabe's uncertainties fled, and she had settled her mind and her heart once and for all. She had one last chance to be free, and she would not tie herself forever to the Numinu. She would never become the wife of a man like Peca.

Although she'd accepted much of the Comanche life as normal, she never quite felt it was normal for *her*. Always, even when she could no longer remember the English words to the songs she used to sing, when she no longer knew the name of the little girl she had been, even then she could not bring herself to accept again becoming the wife of a raiding warrior.

Now it seemed she had escaped that life. Ned spoke of a family who had lost a child who sounded like her. Would she soon meet her true family?

The faint call of the horn reached them through the narrow window. Quinta's head jerked around.

"Stagecoach!" She leaped to her feet and ran to the entry to unbar the door.

Taabe rose and put away her embroidery so the kittens wouldn't play with it. She wanted to fly as Quinta had to the front yard. Ned was here—that knowledge always tugged her toward him. But now she always waited to see if he had strangers with him.

Two of the sisters hurried past the doorway. Sister Adele paused and poked her head in. "You are all right, Taabe?"

"I wait here."

Sister Adele nodded. Taabe leaned against the cool wall by the window, trying to see the stagecoach, but all that came within her view at first were the mules pulling it. They stood, stamping and snorting, and then she saw him. Ned strode past the leaders, lifting his hat then settling it onto his head. Taabe put her ear to the opening but couldn't make out his words to the sisters.

A moment later, Sister Adele came to the door. "Taabe, Mr. Bright is here to see you. He's alone."

The nun stepped aside and Ned walked in smiling. His face was smoothly shaven this morning. The trail must not be dusty today, since rain had fallen lightly in the night—his blue flannel shirt looked fresh. He held his hat in one hand and extended the other to her.

Taabe stepped forward and took his hand for a moment.

"I have a message for you," he said. "I hope it makes you happy."

She waited, not wanting to hope too much.

"I wrote to the people near Victoria. The Morgan family."

"Billie Morgan," she said, remembering the name he'd pressed her about two weeks ago. The more she repeated the name to herself, the more it seemed to belong.

Ned's eyes widened. "Yes. That was the name of the child they lost. She was nine years old, as I told you before. And she had a kitten. Taabe, Billie's kitten was named Fluffy."

Tears rushed to her eyes so quickly, Taabe had no time to stop them. They flowed unhindered down her cheeks. She raised her hand to her face, overcome with relief, but not knowing what to do, how to act. She looked to Ned for a hint, and he held out his arms to her.

CHAPTER SEVENTEEN

Ned stood for a minute, holding Taabe close and stroking her back with small, tender pats. She clung to him as Quinta would in a time of stress, and he tried not to read too much into that. Still, he couldn't stifle the rightness of it. This was meant to be. God had placed her in the path of his stagecoach on that first mail run, meaning for him to find and protect her. Yet he was the messenger who brought the news that meant she would leave him.

He rested his cheek against her cool, silky hair. "I believe you are the Morgan girl, Billie," he said slowly, pronouncing each word carefully. "That is your name. Your brother wants to come and get you. If you want me to, I will tell him to come. Sister Natalie and the other nuns can help you prepare."

Her shoulders quaked, and she gave a small sob. Ned reached into his pocket for a handkerchief, and she disentangled herself and stood back. She took his bandanna, mopped her tears, and handed it back to him.

"Write." Taabe made gestures as though writing with a pencil.

"You want to write to Mr. Morgan?"

"Write. Billie Morgan." She made the motions again.

Ned smiled. "You want to write your name."

She nodded. In her eyes, Ned saw a longing and a resolution. This was a definitive action—the moment she would claim her true name. She would leave Taabe behind and become Billie.

For a moment he wanted to discourage her—to tell her she should wait until Mr. Morgan came and they were certain. But that would only prolong her distress. In his heart there was no doubt, and he could not make her wait any longer.

"I'll tell the sisters." He touched her shoulder gently. "I'm sure they will help you learn to do that, and that it won't take you long."

She gave him a watery smile. "You write letter."

"I will. I'll do it tonight."

"How long?"

"How long before he comes here?"

"Yes."

Ned shrugged. "It will take the letter several days to get there—perhaps a week or more. And he'll have to ride . . ." He thought about the way the Comanche rode, day and night, disregarding hunger and fatigue. Would Judson Morgan ride that way, coming to reclaim his sister? Or would he take a stagecoach partway, or perhaps even drive his own wagon to take her home in?

"I don't know. I guess it will be a couple of weeks, maybe longer." A thought struck him, and he smiled. "Not before the next full moon."

She nodded in perfect comprehension, and he hastened to qualify the statement.

"I'm guessing. It may be longer, but not before then."

"I will . . . be ready."

He smiled, a bittersweet smile accompanied by stinging in his eyes. "I'm sure you will. But I'll miss you, Taabe. If you go with the Morgans . . ." He shook his head and looked away.

She laid her hand against the front of his jacket.

"You." She pulled her hand back and touched her heart.

"Aw, Taabe, I don't know what I'll do if you're that far away." He looked at her face, wanting to say all kinds of things. But he couldn't make any sort of declaration now—that might confuse the issue with her family. She had so much to think about, it wouldn't be fair to ask her for promises when she didn't know what her future would be. He managed a smile. "I'd better go now, or I'll be crying next. Quinta wouldn't understand, and Brownie would rag me all the way to the home station."

She pressed her lips together, as though unsure whether to smile. "You come back."

"I will. I'll be here on Friday."

Her lips curved upward. "Stagecoach day."

"Yes. Friday is a stagecoach day. You've got my number, haven't you?" Her blank look made him laugh. He reached for her hand and pressed it firmly. "It means you've got me all figured out. I wish I had *you* figured out. I'll see you soon." He went out, settling his hat as he walked down the steps. Quinta and Sister Adele were talking to Brownie, while Quinta stroked the nose of the near lead mule.

"All set?" Brownie called.

Ned nodded. "Let's move. I'm afraid I took more time than I intended."

"Is Taabe leaving us?" Quinta asked.

"Maybe. Her brother wants—that is, Mr. Morgan wants to come and meet her and probably take her home. If he really is her brother. But . . ." He looked at Sister Adele. "I can't see much room for doubt. He was excited to hear about the music and the horses. It's all true. But the kitten is what clinched it."

Sister Adele smiled. "This is what we've prayed for all these weeks."

"Yes," Ned said with less conviction than he should. He tweaked Quinta's pigtail. "I'll see you Friday, *chica*."

"You'd better."

He grinned as he climbed to the driver's box and gathered the reins. Brownie let go of the leaders' bridles and clambered up on the other side. "Let 'em tear, boss."

Ned slackened the reins and clucked to the mules. "Tear, you fools."

The mules set out in a smart road trot. Ned looked at Brownie and shrugged. "Awful hard to get mules to break any faster than that."

Brownie shook his head mournfully. "You wasn't hardly tryin'."

Billie woke each morning thinking, "Soon I shall leave here."

The sisters seemed more dear, now that she had this understanding, and each of their small kindnesses moved her. Quinta shadowed her whenever the nuns didn't require her presence elsewhere.

"I'll show you your name, Taabe," Quinta said the same day Ned brought the news. She fetched her slate and chalk and sat down beside her.

"I am Billie. I am not Taabe Waipu."

"That's right," Quinta said. "You must call yourself Billie now, and think of yourself that way. I will help you by calling you Billie."

She wrote *B-I-L-L* on the slate and stopped, frowning.

"Hold on." Quinta rose and walked over to Sister Riva who sat nearby mending. "Is it Billy with a *Y* or with an *I-E*? I'd think the *Y* way is for a boy."

Sister Riva smiled. "It is *I-E*. Mr. Bright showed us the letter from Mr. Morgan. She is named for her father, Bill Morgan, who died fighting—" She hesitated and her gaze flickered over Quinta. "I believe he died in battle."

Billie barely had time to realize she had understood not only what Sister Riva said, but also what she'd left unsaid—that her father had died fighting the Mexicans. Riva had swallowed that detail in deference to Quinta's heritage. Billie's love for the quiet nun swelled.

Quinta nodded and returned to Billie's side.

"Did you hear that, Billie? You are named for a hero."

"Yes." She smiled at Quinta and patted the cushion beside her. "You show me."

Billie's English lessons continued with Sister Adele, and Quinta broadened her vocabulary considerably, including a sprinkling of Spanish sayings.

Ned was right about Billie's quickness—she learned to write her new-old name perfectly by the next time he returned. He brought another visitor, a white-haired man looking for his granddaughter. Billie met with him, but the gentleman left disappointed. His lost grandchild would have been only eleven now, and she had green eyes. Billie wondered why people made these arduous journeys when the captain had written to them and told them she was likely not their loved one.

While Brownie helped the tired old gentleman back into the stagecoach, Ned stole a moment with her. He hadn't received any news from the Morgan family yet—not enough time had elapsed—but, to Billie's delight, he still wanted to spend a few minutes with her.

Sister Natalie sat nearby, reviewing the four students' most recent essays, while Ned assured Billie he would bring her any news the moment he received it.

"I practice," she said to him.

"What do you practice?"

"I talk English. I write. I sew. I play the song about God's grace."

Ned smiled and glanced toward Sister Natalie. "It's hard to believe how far she's come since she arrived here."

Sister Natalie looked up and nodded. "We shall miss our Taabe."

"Billie."

They both looked at her, and she repeated her true name. "Billie. Not Taabe."

"Of course, child." Sister Natalie's face held a wistfulness that Billie regretted. She had put that expression there, had caused new worry lines near the dear sister's mouth.

Ned had almost the same set to his face. They were grieving already. Grieving because she would be gone.

But she couldn't ignore the joy that burgeoned inside her when she thought about meeting her brother. Anxiety, however, was that joy's constant companion.

She turned to Ned. "This man—brother . . ."

"Judson Morgan."

"Yes. What happens . . ." She reached for the small word that changed a meaning so drastically. "If . . . what happens if he does not love me?"

Ned inhaled and looked at her for a moment before speaking. "They already love you. They want you at home. They have loved you all this time. If you are Billie Morgan, they have been looking for you and hoping for twelve years."

She nodded slowly. Had it been that long? She supposed

it had. So much had happened to her since she went to live with the Numinu.

"*If* that happened," Ned said, "and they changed their minds—I'm sure it will not, but if it did—you must remember that you have people here who care about you. You will never be without a home again."

Sister Natalie spoke with a tremor in her voice. "That is true, child. You will always be welcome here. No matter how many pupils we gain, you were our first, and we will always love you. If you leave us and you have troubles in the world, you may come back at any time."

Billie knew it was true. Even if the sisters knew every detail of her life in the Comanche camp, they would accept her and treat her with compassion. And now that she had spent time with them, she truly loved each of them, and she felt their love in return. "Thank you," she whispered.

But what about Ned? He sat beside her, so confident, pouring out his friendship. His feelings for her went beyond what a man would normally feel for a neighbor in need—she knew that. But did she dare think he would love her?

Her emotions soared whenever he was near. She must be careful for many reasons. Because Ned did not know everything. When Judson Morgan came, she would tell him—her brother. But she wasn't sure she would tell Ned. Mr. Morgan could decide whether he would claim her for a sister—or not. But what about Ned? She felt the risk was greater with him. Would he feel the same about her if he learned all?

Ned rode with Tree to the mission several days later. Tree had clothing and sweets for Quinta, and gifts of cheese and beef for the sisters. Ned just wanted to see Taabe—Billie—again, when he didn't have to hurry to keep the stagecoach schedule.

She had seemed worried about meeting her family, and he didn't blame her. She had every reason to feel insecure. Everywhere he went he heard stories about captives who couldn't make the adjustment back into normal life, and about the families who tried to rehabilitate them but were afraid of their own children. Some returned captives were shunned. Others were stared at and pestered by the curious. What was Jud Morgan thinking as he made his way north?

Ned tried to look at the situation from Billie's perspective and couldn't imagine her turmoil. Though he'd meant every word he told her—she was loved here—he couldn't speak for the Morgans. They might reject her or treat her badly because of her past. Ned only knew that if he were in her shoes, he'd be petrified.

Quinta dashed out from the dining room, where she'd been having lessons with the other girls, and into her father's arms. Ned smiled as he watched Tree shower her with kisses. He was forgotten when her papa was near, and that was the way it should be.

Sister Natalie brought Billie into the sitting room. She entered with a shy smile for Ned. He stood and held out his hands to her. She wore the dark blue dress with her beadwork at the collar and cuffs. Her hair still floated free about her shoulders, though all the girls wore theirs in plaits. As he took her hands, Billie caught her breath. She cast a quick glance up at him, then lowered her gaze.

"Sit down," he said softly. "Talk to me."

Once they were seated on the sofa, Sister Natalie withdrew. Tree had claimed an armchair—a new acquisition the freighters had brought the previous week—and sat with Quinta on his lap, hearing her excited account of a spelling bee Sister Adele held among the students.

"Billie," Ned said.

She looked up at him, her blue eyes wide, her face calm and expectant.

"I know I've asked you before, but the captain wants me to inquire again, now that your English is better. Billie, when you were with the Numinu, were there other children? Other white children they had taken?"

She nodded slowly.

"Did you meet other children who were captured like you were? We've read names to you and asked you about specific children who were kidnapped, but it seems to me you wouldn't know their English names. But you've seen others among the tribe? Ones they've adopted? White Indians?"

"Yes." She spoke in a small voice, and her eyes took on an anxiety Ned didn't like. "Sometimes. They don't stay where I am. Was. Most of them go with other bands."

"Remember the first man and woman I brought to see you here—the Cunninghams? At the time, I'm sure you didn't understand most of what we said to you. But they had a daughter, Sally. She was also taken, about two years ago, not far from here. She was younger than you. She'd be twelve years old now." He held up all ten fingers, then two. "Twelve. You understand?"

"Yes."

"Have you seen a girl like that in the last two years?"

Billie shook her head. "Not now."

"Not recently?"

She nodded doubtfully, and Ned wasn't sure she caught his meaning.

"Other girls?" he asked. "Boys?"

"Boy." She touched her hair. "White hair."

"A boy with white hair."

She nodded and pointed to Quinta. "Small like her."

"When?" Ned asked.

Billie shrugged. "Hot. Men raid much. Very hot."

"Last summer?"

"Yes, summer. Bring back boys. One is . . . brown face. One is white. Hair very white."

"A Negro boy and a blond white boy?"

"Yes. But . . . they trade them. Peca trade the white hair boy."

"Peca?" Ned caught something in her manner when she said the name. A slight squint of her eyes and a touch of hardness to her voice.

Quinta climbed down from her father's lap and walked over in front of them. "Peca is the man who chased Billie," she said.

"What?" Ned stared at Quinta. "When? Why?"

"When she left the Comanche. Peca wanted her for his wife, and she ran away. She took one of the horses he left outside the tepee."

Ned looked at Billie. "Is this true?"

Billie nodded.

"I don't understand," Ned said. "She didn't say anything about this Peca fellow when I brought Cat Thompson here."

"Did you ask her?" Quinta's expression made Ned feel like a witless schoolboy.

"No, I guess we didn't. We talked about when she was captured, but not much about when she left them. She did say she took a horse and ran away from them. What else do you know, Quinta?"

"Billie is afraid of Peca. That's why we have the whistles and the hiding place. If Peca comes, she'll get in the hole."

"What hole are we talking about?" Patrillo came over to stand beside her.

Quinta looked up at him. "I'm not supposed to tell."

"Well, the sisters already showed me," Ned said. "And your father won't blab about it."

"Of course not," Tree said. "What's this about a hole and a whistle?"

Quickly Quinta explained the nuns' defense system.

Tree gazed down at her for a long moment. At last he pointed his finger at her. "You be careful, young lady."

"I will, Papa."

Tree stepped closer to Ned. "That place where Cat Thompson told you the Indians take their captives to hide them—the Valle de las Lagrimas—I wonder . . ." He turned to Billie. "Do you think you could lead a detachment of soldiers to the place where the Comanche hid you?"

Billie stared at him.

"Tree," Ned said, "I don't think this is the time to consider that. She probably has no idea what you're talking about, anyway."

"They would not come out alive," Billie said.

"That's right. It would be foolish to try." Ned jerked his head around and stared at her, then smiled. "You understood it all, didn't you? I'm so proud of you." He longed to ask her more about her life with the Numinu, but perhaps it was better to wait until Morgan arrived. He didn't want to add to her distress during this period of waiting, but clearly there were many things he didn't know.

Sister Natalie returned carrying a tray with coffee for the men, a glass of milk for Quinta, and a plate of small frosted cakes.

"Mr. and Mrs. Stein are keeping our cow until spring," the sister said, "but they send out milk quite often. They have one cow of their own that hasn't gone dry yet. It is such a blessing, to have milk for the girls."

"Thank you." Ned accepted a cup of coffee. "I told Herr Stein I'll bring it twice a week when I bring the stagecoach east."

"It's wonderful that so many people are helping us," Sister Natalie said. "Even those who are not Catholic treat us with kindness. I confess I was prepared for some opposition when we came."

Patrillo also took coffee. "Thank you, Sister. You should know there are new stories reaching us of Indian raids to the north. You must be very cautious."

"Thank you for telling me. We are always careful, but we'll keep the students and Taabe—Billie—even closer now. You mustn't worry. God will protect us."

Ned glanced at Tree. He looked as uneasy as Ned felt. Whenever the Comanche or the Apache started marauding, the settlers looked to their arms.

"We could get you some guns," he said.

Sister Natalie shook her head. "That is not our way."

"What is your way?" Tree asked. "I know you believe God will watch over you, but please reassure me so far as my daughter is concerned."

Sister Natalie bowed her head for a moment, then met his gaze. "This house is strong. We are prepared to barricade it for a siege if need be. We keep enough water for several days in the house, and we have a good food supply."

"Increase your water," Tree said. "I will give you two more barrels. Do you have a place inside the house for them?"

"Yes, we could do that." Sister Natalie smiled. "No matter how much we prepare for catastrophe, Señor Garza, things happen that we do not expect."

Tree nodded. "That is so."

"We will take each day as it comes to us from the Lord."

"Be that as it may, you must go to Fort Chadbourne if the raiding comes closer. Please. I want my daughter to be safe."

Quinta wriggled back onto her father's lap, holding one of the little cakes. "Papa, you mustn't worry so."

He wrapped an arm around her. "Are you sure you don't want to come home for a while, *chica?*"

She gazed into his eyes. "In some ways, yes. In others, no. Those new girls—Kate and Minnie and Laura—they need me."

"They do?" Tree's eyes widened.

"Yes. I drill them in arithmetic, and I let them think they are teaching me the catechism, but really I am teaching it to them by repeating it so often."

Tree laughed.

"And Billie and I are teaching them beadwork." Quinta popped the little cake into her mouth.

"Yes, Taabe—that is, Billie—is very popular with the girls," Sister Natalie said. "They were a bit awed by her at first, but now they've begun to converse with her." She smiled at Billie, and Billie returned the smile.

"At first they were rude," Quinta said.

Tree stared at her then looked at Sister Natalie. "How is this?"

"She is correct," the sister said. "I had to admonish them a few times for their remarks about the Indians and . . . and whites who sympathize with them. I explained to the girls that Billie never intentionally aided the Comanche, and that it certainly wasn't her choice to live with them for so long. Sometimes young people don't realize how hurtful their remarks can be."

"They were jealous when they saw my beadwork." Quinta held up her cuff and smiled as she surveyed the red, black, and white design.

Billie touched Ned's sleeve. "Sisters get more beads."

"Really?" Ned asked.

Sister Natalie nodded. "I asked Mr. Stein if he could get us more, so Billie could teach all of the students this skill. Sister Adele and Sister Riva are becoming quite adept at it as well."

"Yes, and I'm going to make beaded moccasins like Billie's if I can get the leather," Quinta said. "Papa, can you get me a hide?"

Tree laughed. "Yes, I will get you some nice, soft leather."

"Not too soft," Quinta said. "It needs to be tough for the soles."

They continued their visit for another half hour, but after they took their leave, Patrillo brooded. During the long ride back to the ranch, he recounted again to Ned the dangers of leaving the women and girls alone at the mission.

"You could have told Quinta she had to come home," Ned said.

"No, she is happy with the sisters now. It is good for her. You saw how much calmer she is. And I think she loves the captive girl now."

"Yes, she's become quite attached to Billie, hasn't she?"

Tree nodded. "It is best. I think."

Ned smiled. "Then we'd better do as the nuns are doing—trust God more."

He tried to remember his own advice over the next few days. The stagecoach had passengers on his next run to Fort Chadbourne, so he and Brownie stopped at the mission only long enough to make sure the sisters and their students were all right and tell Billie no word had come yet from the Morgans. On the way home the next day, they delivered several letters, a large can of milk, and two crates of supplies to Sister Natalie and again reported there was no news.

One of the lead mules strained a tendon on the final stretch of their route, and Ned had to walk the team the last mile. By the time they drove into the barnyard, he and Brownie were both tired and grumpy.

"You shoulda let me take the other leader and ride ahead," Brownie muttered.

"That would leave two wheelers and a lame leader to pull the stage," Ned said. "I couldn't do that."

When he could see the ridgepole of the barn, he blew the horn. Everyone must be worried—he'd never before brought the stage in this late. As he drove the weary team into the yard of the home station, Tree's third son, Esteban, ran out to meet them.

"You all right?" Esteban called.

Ned nodded. "Got a lame mule."

Esteban eyed the leaders. "Want us to bring the new team out here?"

"We're almost in now," Ned said.

"There's a man here."

"A passenger?"

"No. He's here to see you. Says he's been riding for days and days. He wants to see the captive girl. We gave him some dinner."

"What man?" Ned asked. Anyone who wanted to see Billie should have gone to Captain Tapley.

Esteban switched his gaze to Ned. "His name is Morgan."

CHAPTER EIGHTEEN

Mr. Morgan. I didn't expect you for another week." Ned shook the tall, sandy-haired man's hand and looked him over.

"I was going to go to the fort," Morgan said, "but it was quicker to come straight here. The things you told us in your letter—well, my mother and sister and I all felt it was conclusive. I didn't see any reason to wait longer."

"Did you even get my second letter?"

"I guess not. Have things changed? She's still here, isn't she?"

"Yes, but she's not here at the ranch—she's about fifty miles away. In fact, I just came from there."

"I see."

He looked disappointed, and Ned didn't blame him. But he didn't feel like turning around and riding back to the mission.

"It's only an hour until sundown," Ned said. "Stay here with us tonight. I don't drive the stagecoach again for a couple of days. In the morning, I'll take you to the mission to see her."

"Thank you," Morgan said. "I brought an extra horse for Billie. The boys turned them out in one of the corrals."

Ned nodded. "She will be very pleased. But we'd better make sure they're put inside the barn tonight. We've heard rumors of raids, and I'd hate to have you lose your horses while you're our guest."

"The Comanche are at it again?"

"They never stop," Ned said. "Come in and sit down, Mr. Morgan. Let's talk about your sister. I've learned a little more today, and I know she'll have much to tell you."

Morgan paced the length of the dining room and peered out a window. Ned pushed the kitchen door open. Marcos was cutting up a piece of beef.

"Making supper?" Ned asked.

"*Si*. Beef stew. I'm a little late getting started. Is he staying?"

"Yes. I'll take him in the morning. You got any coffee?"

Ned wasn't sure what it was about coffee, but men always seemed to calm down when they had some in front of them. Morgan was no exception. He sank into a chair at the long table where the family took its meals and accepted the mug Marcos brought him. Ned took a piece of cornbread from the mounded plate Marcos set down and reached for the butter dish.

"The boys make good johnnycake. Have some. It'll be an hour or so until supper's ready."

"Thanks." Morgan took a slab and used the knife Ned passed him to smear it with butter.

Ned studied him as he sipped the brew. Morgan was a hardworking rancher with a weather-hardened face. Lines etched the corners of his watchful hazel eyes.

"You said your mother is still alive," Ned said.

"Yes. You can imagine her excitement. She wanted to make the journey with me, but I told her I could travel much faster if she waited at home. I imagine she and my wife are sewing and baking up a storm."

"You must be exhausted, sir," Ned said.

"Please, call me Jud. And yes, I admit I'm tired. But I was ready to keep riding. To be so close to her—well, it's hard to wait even one more night, but I'll probably sleep hard."

Ned smiled. "She's eager to meet you."

"Tell me about her. What is she like now? I know you said she'd forgotten most of her English and her old life, but she seems to have come up with some details. The cat, of all things." Morgan shook his head.

"Yes, that was God's doing, I think." Ned chuckled. "A couple of months ago, I'd have said it was luck, but the nuns keep reminding me that everything comes from God. And I certainly think He placed those kittens in the store at Fort Chadbourne that day. She saw the little orange one and yelled, 'Fluffy!' I couldn't have been more stunned if lightning had struck me."

"She loved that kitten. It disappeared a few months after Billie did. We still have one of the litter mates, though. She thought the world of Fluffy." Jud sighed. "These nuns . . ."

"They've cared for her selflessly. I would go so far as to say they've saved her life."

"But you found her."

"Yes, I believe I saw her first." Ned leaned back in his chair, remembering the day. "Brownie and I didn't know what it was at first, lying in the road, so I stopped the team. Didn't want to run into an ambush. Sister Natalie and Sister Adele were passengers. Sister Natalie hopped out and walked right up to your sister, heedless of the danger." Ned smiled at the memory of the nun's courage and bossiness. "She's fearless, that one. Wouldn't let me take your sister to the fort. At first I thought that was a mistake, but living at the mission has done wonders for Billie.

Of course, her own attitude accounts for much of her adjustment. She *wanted* to come back to the white world. They don't always. But Billie did. Through the years, she kept alive some seed of hope and memory."

"I just hope she can trust me. I want her to know how much we love her. It must have seemed as though we'd forgotten her and didn't try to get her back. But we did." The pain in Jud's voice spoke to Ned more than his words—of dozens of letters written, hundreds of miles ridden, and thousands of prayers that seemed to bring no result.

"I just want to caution you that it's possible you'll be disappointed when you meet her."

"You still think there's a possibility she's not my sister?"

"Well . . ." Ned stared off toward the window. "My heart says no, but my head says be prepared."

"Let's just get there," Jud said.

Ned nodded. "We will. First thing in the morning."

Jud Morgan's eyes had taken on a wistful determination that mirrored what Ned had seen in Billie's. "I can't believe we can finally bring her home. We've prayed for so long. There were times when I just about gave up. But Ma wouldn't let me. She refused to think that Billie was dead, or that she wouldn't want to come back. And she wouldn't abide with anyone saying it, either. And now it's true. We owe you a great debt."

"Not me. Billie got herself away from the Comanche." Ned shrugged. "I wish I knew more about what she endured in her captivity and could give you all the details, but I can't. We're still putting it together piece by piece. But I can tell you this: it was her determination that brought her back."

They ate breakfast in the gray light before dawn and saddled their horses. Tree had decided to leave the boys in charge and go with them. It wasn't a stagecoach day, and none of his freight trains were due in. He listed off a string of chores for his sons to accomplish and warned Benito several times to stay alert.

As Ned led his saddle horse, Champ, out of the barn, Reece Jones galloped into the yard on his old pinto.

"Ned! The station this side of Phantom Hill was hit last night. Where's Tree?"

Brownie, Tree, and Jud Morgan came from the barn, and two of Tree's boys joined them.

"What happened?" Tree demanded.

"Injuns hit the swing station up the line," Reece said. "Drove off a dozen head of mules and horses."

"Anybody hurt?"

"No. The tenders all got in the house in time and barricaded it. A couple of people from the town got in, too, and forted up with them. The Injuns did some yelling and shot a few arrows at the windows, but they didn't waste much effort on that. They just wanted the horses. And they set fire to the barn where all the feed was."

Brownie swore.

"Should we bring in all the stock?" Diego asked. "We put the extra mules out to pasture this morning, Papa."

"Bring them in closer," Tree said.

"Better watch out tonight." Reece shot a stream of tobacco juice to one side. "They might head home for a while, since they got a pretty good haul. But you never know."

Tree nodded grimly. "Does the station agent have a team left for the next stage up there?"

"Had two mules left. Sam Tunney told me they'd check around and see if they could borrow two more."

"I can send a couple up there tonight if they need them." Tree looked at Ned. "You still want to go to the mission?"

"I sure do. But you don't have to go, Tree. If you want to stay here with the boys . . ."

"Go, Papa," Esteban said. "We need to know Quinta is safe."

Tree turned to Ned. "I think we should take the sisters and the girls to Fort Chadbourne."

"Maybe. Let's see how things look between here and there. If the Indians didn't raid any farther west than Phantom Hill, they may be all right."

"I hate to leave the boys." Tree glanced around. Benito had come from the house and heard much of the conversation.

"I'll stay with 'em," Brownie said.

"Me too." Reece pulled his rifle from its scabbard and swung down from his horse.

"All right." Tree nodded at Benito. "Bring all the stock in now. But stay together. Don't any of you ride out alone to get stragglers."

"*Si*, Papa."

"Give Reece some grub when you're done," Ned said. He checked his cinch strap. "It takes the stage about five hours to get to the mission, but we should be able to make it in three. Jud, you ready?"

"Sure am."

Brownie stared at Jud's horse and the one he led on a long cotton rope. "They sure are purty," he said. "So, those are Morgan horses?"

"That's right. Our family has always raised them. I'm not a direct descendant of Justin Morgan, but there is a connection if you go way back."

"He looks stout," Reece said, eyeing Jud's gelding.

"He's a terrific stock horse. I brought the other one for Billie to ride home if she wants. It's not the same horse she loved to ride as a girl—that one disappeared with her. But he's a lot like that one."

"She'll be tickled," Ned said. "And so will Quinta—Tree's little girl."

Tree led his big black gelding over and prepared to mount.

"You know, Morgan," Brownie said, "some captives have trouble learning their own culture again when they return. Now, this one's made great progress, living with the nuns, but she'll still need some time to adjust."

Jud swallowed hard and nodded. "I appreciate that, and what you were saying before, Ned. I also know there have been some captured children recovered who didn't want to return to their families."

"You won't have that problem," Ned said. "Billie nearly died trying to get home. She craves her family. And she made an effort all this time to preserve her identity. She . . . she grieved when she knew she was forgetting, if you take my meaning."

Jud nodded. "I think I do."

Tree hit the saddle and gathered his reins. "Let's go."

Ned raised a hand in farewell to the boys, Brownie, and Reece, and trotted Champ out to the road. Tree caught up to him and pushed his black into a gallop. Ned let Champ run too and looked back. Jud Morgan rode along behind, his jaw set. Ned had no doubt he would keep up, even with the extra horse in tow.

Billie helped Sister Marie in the kitchen most of the morning while the four students had their lessons with Sisters Adele and Natalie. She washed the breakfast dishes and swept the floor, after which she made a large pan of cornbread. Sister Marie had shown her several times how to do it just right, the way the sisters liked it, and Billie now felt competent to make this dish by herself.

Sister Riva brought in an armload of firewood from the woodshed behind the kitchen.

"It looks as though your water reservoir is low," she said to Sister Marie.

Billie kept stirring her batter as Sister Riva hefted a pail and poured it into the tank on the side of the stove. When they kept the reservoir full, they had plenty of warm water for washing.

"I'd better refill the barrels too. Mr. Garza will ask if we've kept them full." Sister Riva took the empty bucket and picked up another near the back door.

Billie longed to be outside—to go even so far as the well with Sister Riva. Perhaps later, when the cooking was finished, one of the sisters or Quinta could go out with her for a short while. She would have to put on the long black robe, but it was worth the inconvenience. Her times outside seemed to come less frequently now. She hoped that when she went to the Morgans' home she wouldn't be kept inside all day.

A moment later, running footsteps heralded Sister Riva's return. She charged through the doorway without the buckets, whirled, and threw the bar in place.

"Sister Riva?" said Sister Marie.

Billie stared at Riva's hands. The sister gave her what she had been clutching—a Comanche arrow with green markings and distinctive feathers—two black and one white.

CHAPTER NINETEEN

"Quickly!" Sister Marie said. "Check the front door!"

Billie dashed into the corridor and around to the entrance. The door was already barred on the inside, as usual. She hurried back toward the kitchen but paused in the dining room doorway. Sister Marie had interrupted the lessons there.

"She came tearing in with an arrow, Sister. What does it mean? What shall we do?"

The pupils let out some muffled squeals—not Quinta, Billie was sure.

"Girls, silence!" Sister Natalie's calm voice held the authority they all needed. When they had quieted, she said, "You will go at once to the kitchen with Sister Marie and get into the hiding place."

"Come." Sister Marie, her face as white as the band of cloth on her forehead, beckoned to the four pupils. They filed out the door after her, with Sister Adele bringing up the rear.

Sister Natalie's gaze fell on Billie.

"Is Sister Riva all right?"

"Yes."

"You were not outside with her?"

"No."

"Where is the arrow?"

"I have it here."

Sister Natalie held out her hand and Billie placed the arrow in it.

"A Comanche shot this at Sister Riva?"

Billie hesitated. If he'd wanted to hit the sister as she hauled the bucket from the well, he wouldn't have missed. "He shoot it near her," she said.

"Where is Sister Riva?"

Billie glanced over her shoulder. "I think still in the kitchen."

Sister Natalie started to walk away, but Billie tugged her sleeve.

"Sister, this not just anyone's arrow."

The nun stopped and peered at her. "Can you explain, Billie?"

"This is Peca's arrow."

"Peca? The man who wished to marry you?"

Billie nodded, feeling her cheeks flame. She had brought danger to the sisters, and now they had the young girls to consider as well. She should not have stayed here.

"You must get into the hiding place at once," Sister Natalie said.

"No. Girls go. I help."

Sister Natalie gazed into her eyes. "All right. We must barricade the doors and cover the windows so they can't see in. The girls will need their blankets and pillows."

Sister Riva came from the kitchen.

"Are the girls in the cellar?" Sister Natalie asked.

"They are going down. Sister Marie is giving them some food and water."

"Good. Are you all right, my dear?"

"Yes, Sister. I was very frightened."

"Not so frightened that you didn't have the presence of mind to grab this and bring it with you." Sister Natalie held out the arrow.

Sister Riva grimaced. "It plunked into the earth beside my foot. I dropped my water buckets and looked all about, but I couldn't see anyone. So I grabbed it and ran for the door."

"They let you go," Billie said. Peca and his friends were probably out there laughing about it.

Sister Riva smiled faintly. "And I thought God protected me."

"He did," Sister Natalie said, "though I'm inclined to agree with Billie. He protected you by letting them not want to kill you, rather than by skewing their aim. Go to the girls' rooms. Take them their blankets and pillows. And try not to stand near the windows. When the hiding place is closed, come to the chapel."

"Yes, Sister." Sister Riva hurried toward the bedrooms.

"Both doors are barred," Billie said.

"Come. We will drag heavy cupboards in front of them."

Although the adobe walls were thick, Billie wasn't sure they would stop Peca.

Two miles from the mission, Ned spotted a rancher working on his fence line near the road. He reined in Champ and called to him.

"Hey, Spence, you heard about any Indian trouble around here?"

"Nope."

"We heard they hit the stage station at Phantom Hill last night."

"That right?"

Ned nodded. Tree and Jud had halted near him and waited.

"You think they'll come down here?" Spence asked.

"I don't know, but I'd lock my stock up tonight if I were you."

Spence gritted his teeth. "Can't do that with all the cattle. Guess I'd better have my boys take a nap today and stay out with 'em tonight. Man, I hate those dirty, raidin' Injuns."

"Take care." Ned tipped his hat. Tree had already resumed riding at a quick trot.

"How far now?" Jud asked.

"Couple of miles. At least no one's seen any sign of the Comanche down this way."

"That we know of," Jud said.

They trotted along, not pushing the horses too hard. Most of the land around them was open range. Most ranchers fenced only their corrals and holding pens. In the distance, bunches of cattle grazed.

They crossed a creek, splashing through the shallow water. Tree had talked to the division agent about building a bridge here—in the spring this creek would be high for a few weeks, and the stage would take a long detour to get across safely. If they put in a bridge this winter, it would save them money and a lot of headaches later.

"Did you see that?" Jud called.

Ned reined in and turned in the saddle. Jud had stopped several yards behind him and was staring off over the rolling grassland.

"What?"

"A flock of blackbirds flew up all of a sudden over there—like something startled them."

Ned peered in the direction Jud was facing and saw a small flock flying away, almost out of sight.

"Not us?"

"No."

Ned looked ahead. Tree hadn't stopped.

"Let's catch up."

"Right," Jud said. They cantered until Champ was on the black's tail again.

"Everything all right?" Tree called over his shoulder.

"Not sure."

They kept up their swift trot, all of them scanning the terrain.

"I saw something," Tree said. "Pretty sure there's a horse down over that rise."

"Where?" Ned asked.

"Southwest."

Ned looked to his left, then back at Jud. "Stay close. We'll be there soon."

Jud nodded and urged his horse forward.

While the other nuns went into the chapel to pray, Sister Adele stood with Billie at the window slits in the front sitting room. With one of them at each opening, they could observe most of the yard. So far, they'd seen nothing out of the ordinary.

Sister Adele had brought a length of dark cloth that they hung over the windows. Billie pushed one corner aside and peered out.

"He is out there."

"I know." Sister Adele glanced at her. "He must be a patient man."

"Yes. He has waited a long time to find me. I thought maybe he gave up, but no. That is not like him, to give up."

The room was dim and cold. They had let all the fires go out, and they didn't light the lamps.

"Tell me about the arrow," Sister Adele said.

"It is his . . . his sign. Each man has his own. Peca has the green and black paint. I don't know how to say it, but when we draw, we make marks."

"Yes. A design, you mean."

Billie shrugged. "Maybe. Always the same."

"Yes. That would help them to identify their own arrows."

Billie nodded. "Like they paint their faces and their horses. It means something—how many raids, how many captives. And the feathers—one white, two black. It is him. No one else would have these."

"What else can we do to defend ourselves against him?"

Slowly Billie shook her head. If Peca was determined to take her back, they could not stop him. Maybe she should just walk out there—it would be easier for the sisters that way, and for the girls. Much easier. She felt a heavy weight on her heart at the thought of Quinta and the others going through what she had.

Sister Adele let her curtain fall over the window. "Billie, you said this man, Peca, left six horses for your family. Is that a marriage ritual for the Comanche?"

"He want to marry."

Sister Adele frowned. "I am surprised you hadn't married earlier. I mean, we believe you are past twenty years old." She turned back to the window. "I'm sorry. That's rude of me, but it does seem odd."

"Not odd," Billie said. She stood for a long minute, staring outward, wondering what the man who wished to claim her would do next—and whether she should tell Sister Adele the things she hadn't told anyone else. Would it matter? If she rode off with Peca today, would it help her and the other sisters to understand?

"Taabe have husband."

Sister Adele stared at her. "Peca?"

"No. Before." Billie sighed. "Maybe is better you don't know."

Adele walked over to stand beside her and touched her shoulder. "Billie, you can tell me anything. But you don't have to. We are friends."

She nodded, tears misting her eyes. "Yes. Good friend." She wiped her eyes and looked out the window. "That happen to Taabe. Now I am not her. I am Billie."

"Yes. You have a new life now."

Billie stood in silence, looking out the crack between the curtain and the wall. She could see only a small slice of the dooryard unless she moved. Slowly she leaned toward the other side of the opening.

"When they take me, I am a girl. I have a new mother and a sister, Pia."

"Your Comanche family?"

"Yes. They are good to me. Not like here, but for the way the people live, very good."

"I'm glad."

Billie hauled in a deep breath. "Then a man wants to marry. I say yes. I don't think I can say no."

"Oh, my dear Billie." Adele slipped her arm around her. "I am so sorry."

Billie let Adele hug her for a moment. Then she pulled away, wiping fresh tears away. "Taabe have little son."

Sister Adele gasped. "You—you had a baby?"

Billie nodded. "I love him. And . . . I know I cannot leave him."

"Of course not. You couldn't leave your child. But . . ."

"Husband die on raid," Billie said.

"When was this?"

Billie held up two fingers. "Two years. And now Peca want to marry."

"But . . . where is your baby now?"

Billie's shoulders drooped, and her chin lowered. "Husband die, and we were alone. My mother and sister take me into their lodge. Baby too. I want to come back to white world."

"Why didn't you?"

"Numinu not let captives leave."

"They still thought of you as a captive? Even though you'd been part of a family for years?"

Billie nodded. "Can't go. And can't leave baby. I love him."

"Of course."

"And mother die." She sobbed. "Little baby die."

Sister Adele enfolded her in her arms once more. "You poor, poor thing. What happened to them?"

"Sick. Spots and fever."

"That sounds like smallpox. Or measles."

"Very sick. Many die. In the spring."

"Last spring?"

"Yes. I was not sick, but . . . I try to help, but they die." Billie wanted to weep until she had no more tears, but she couldn't. Not now. She straightened and lifted the edge of the curtain. "You look. I cannot see."

Sister Adele handed her a handkerchief and peeked out while Billie wiped her face. "I don't see anything. Why doesn't he just come up to the door and ask to see you?"

Billie shook her head. "I ran away. He would not ask. He comes to take me back."

"I'm so sorry."

Billie shrugged. Peca and the other Numinu men saw this as normal—raiding, stealing, killing when it was expedient. She moved to the other window and peeked out. Nothing. Just the same ripple of wind over the grass.

"You were a widow," Sister Adele said. "They wouldn't let you stay unmarried if you wanted to?"

"The chiefs . . . they think . . ." Billie frowned, struggling for words. "It was time for me to have a new husband. Peca wanted me, so he brought horses to the tepee where I lived. My sister, Pia, and her husband, they were my family."

"So that's what the six horses Quinta talked about were for. A bride price."

Billie nodded.

"And he just tethered them outside?"

"Yes. If you take care of them right away, you want to marry soon. Most women make them wait. But if you wait too long, it means you don't care."

"About the horses?"

"And the man."

"What did you do?"

"I wait until night. Pia's husband say wait three days, then take them to water and he will know you marry him. But I don't want to marry. When I tell Pia and Chano this, they get angry. Chano say they can't feed me forever."

"How cruel."

"I think now he wanted to . . . to push me. Make me take the horses and marry Peca. But I work hard, and I help Pia much with her baby. Not right to say they won't feed me. So I wait until night, and I take the best horse. And I run."

"That's when you came here?"

Billie nodded, but realized her friend probably couldn't see that from several paces away. "Yes. But the horse . . . he fall. Fell. We go down."

"I understand. And yes, you would say he fell. Today he falls, yesterday he fell."

Billie smiled. Even in a crisis, the teacher came out in Adele. "I was hurt. When I wake, horse is gone. So I walk and Ned Bright find . . . found me. You and Sister Natalie and Ned Bright."

"Yes."

A faint sound from outside the adobe walls reached Billie through the narrow window. She nudged the curtain aside and turned her ear to the slit through the thick wall.

"Horses. Someone comes."

A flicker of movement and the sound of hoofbeats drew Ned's attention. As he turned to look south, Jud yelled.

"Rider to your left!"

The Comanche warrior galloped his horse at an angle that would allow him to intercept them where the road curved.

Ned reached for his rifle. Tree had his out already. Ned glanced to the other side. Two more horsemen were coming up on their right flank. Champ and their other mounts were tired. The Indians had probably been resting their horses while they lay in wait. Ned gauged the distance to the mission. They were within half a mile. He worried about Jud, slightly behind him and leading the extra horse.

"Let go of Billie's horse."

"No!"

Ned gritted his teeth and hoped the animal wouldn't cost Jud his life. To his surprise, Jud pulled Billie's horse beside his and leaped from his own saddle to the one on the other horse. He leaned back toward his horse and yanked his rifle from the scabbard attached to the saddle. All the while, he kept hold of his own mount's reins. Ned wondered if Jud could outrun the Comanche and keep both horses, but he certainly had a better chance on the back of the horse that had carried only a saddle's weight all morning.

Jud spoke to the horse he now rode, low and urgent. Both Morgan horses surged forward, coming even with Ned.

"Go!" Ned yelled. He turned to his left as Jud swept past

him. The first Comanche was closer—within range if Ned could hold a rifle steady, but he doubted he could. And several more warriors were coming on strong in his wake. One let out a chilling yell, and Champ poured on a burst of new speed. The Comanche were closer, and there were half a dozen of them now.

As they rode into the turn, Ned saw that some scrub trees would obscure the view of those behind him for a few precious seconds. He only had one chance and wouldn't be able to reload. He swiveled in his saddle, took the best aim he could, and let off a shot. He didn't think he hit anyone, but prayed it would give the pursuers pause. He faced front and dug his heels into Champ's sides.

Seconds later, Tree galloped into the short lane leading to the mission's dooryard with Jud close behind him. They stopped so fast in front of the house that Tree's black horse nearly sat on its haunches. Champ barreled up alongside Jud's horse, and Ned jumped down, his empty rifle in one hand. Tree was already pounding on the mission door. Ned drew his Colt revolver and turned to face the lane.

CHAPTER TWENTY

It's Quinta's papa!" Billie ran out of the sitting room. By the time she reached the front door, Adele was beside her. They tugged away the heavy chest they'd dragged in to block the door. A gun went off outside. Billie flung the bar off, and Adele yanked the door open.

Patrillo Garza almost fell in on them, his rifle clutched in his hands.

"Comanche!"

"Come in," Adele said. Another man behind Mr. Garza crowded close, holding the reins of two horses. Ned Bright stood beyond him near his mount, facing the road and holding a pistol.

"The horses," the tall stranger called.

"Put them in the barn," Sister Adele said.

"No, they've burned a barn up the line."

"They'd steal them anyway." Garza glanced at his magnificent black. "I hate to just give them to the raiders."

"Sister Adele, what is it?"

Billie whirled around. Sister Natalie had come from the chapel, and Sister Marie and Sister Riva hovered behind her.

"Friends," Sister Adele said. "Ned and Mr. Garza and one more, with—four horses. But the Comanche are just beyond the wall."

"Bring them in," Sister Natalie said.

"Yes, but the horses?" Sister Adele's face pleaded. She, too, loved animals.

"The chapel," Sister Natalie said. "They won't hurt the stone floor."

Ned fired his revolver, and the tall man aimed his rifle toward the road. Hoofbeats thundered past the house.

"Get in," Ned yelled. "Go!"

The women scrambled back and Mr. Garza entered the dim hall, pulling his horse by the reins. The black snuffled and stepped in timidly. Billie hovered in the sitting room doorway and watched as Garza held the horse's head low and urged him quietly to follow. To her amazement, the black meekly walked the short distance to the chapel doorway. Sister Natalie held aside the curtain in the doorway to the larger room.

Now the tall man was in the front doorway. "Can someone help me?" he called. "I have an extra horse."

Billie stepped forward. "I help."

He eyed her sharply, squinting at her face, but said nothing as he placed the horse's reins in her hand. Outside she heard more gunshots and a wild Comanche yell.

She stroked the horse's sweet face and clucked to him. He calmly stepped over the threshold and walked with her to the chapel. A moment later the man appeared, leading the third horse.

"Ned?" she asked.

"He's coming."

"Taabe, squeeze that horse over here," Mr. Garza called. "It's going to be a tight fit with four of them in here."

Billie nudged the horse's shoulder and flank, and it stepped obligingly sideways toward Garza's black gelding. She dropped the reins and hurried to help Sister Natalie who was stacking the benches against the far wall.

"We'll have to take these out," Sister Natalie said. "Billie, snuff the candles."

Billie wasn't sure what "snuff" meant, but she knew the word "candles."

"Dark," she said.

"It's all right. I'll bring a lantern, but I don't want the horses around open flames. If they knock them over, they could burn the house down."

Billie understood. Though the outer walls were made of thick adobe, the inner walls, ceilings, roof, and furnishings would burn quickly.

She edged around the horses' heads to the shelf that held a dozen small jars containing candles. Four were burning in front of the small statues on the wall. Billie blew them out, grabbed a basket from the floor beneath the shelf, and shoved the jars into it. They had better get all the glass out of this room while the horses occupied it.

She could barely edge past the horses to reach the door and realized the fourth horse was in. That meant Ned was safe, she hoped. She felt her way past the nickering, shifting horses, toward the light that spilled in through the hall doorway.

Sister Riva was hanging a lantern on a peg across from the chapel door. "Best not to put the light in there, I think."

Billie nodded and looked down the hall toward the front door. Ned was helping Sister Adele push a heavy trunk in front of the door.

"Where is Sister Marie?" she asked.

"She and Sister Natalie went to check on the girls."

"Good." Billie could only imagine the girls' fear as they huddled in the root cellar and heard the commotion overhead.

Ned came toward them. "Are all the other doors blocked?"

"There is only that one and the kitchen door," Sister Riva said. "We put a big cupboard in front of it."

Ned nodded. "These windows make it hard to see out, but at least the Indians can't come in that way. We need someone keeping watch on each side of the house, but you need to be extremely careful."

Billie nodded. "Quiet now."

"Yes. I think they've backed off and are deciding what to do next. We surprised them by bringing the horses in. I'm grateful for that—but sorry for you ladies. They'll make a mess of the chapel."

"We will clean it up," Sister Adele said.

Mr. Garza came out of the chapel carrying a tooled stock saddle. "Where can we stash our gear, Sister?"

"I will show you," Sister Riva said. She led him toward the dining room.

Garza paused and called back toward the chapel, "Hey, Morgan! Bring your saddles."

Billie stared at him. Garza hurried away, and she turned to Ned.

"Morgan?"

Ned nodded and smiled, reaching to pat her shoulder. "The man with us is Jud Morgan. Your brother."

Jud returned from leaving his saddle in the dining room. As he came toward them, Ned's gaze was riveted on Billie. She let out a little gasp.

Ned touched her sleeve gently and stepped forward.

"Jud, I know this isn't a good time, but there may not be a better one. This is the woman we believe is your sister."

"Billie." Jud stared at her. The wonder on his face gave Ned no doubt that he saw similarities in her features to the little sister he'd lost so long ago.

Her lips quivered as she returned Jud's scrutiny. He was so tall, he loomed over her. Both seemed overcome for a moment, then he held out his hand.

"I'm Jud. Do you remember me?"

"I . . ." She tore her gaze from his face and looked at Ned.

Ned laid a light hand on her shoulder. "Later you will have time to talk."

Billie nodded.

An onslaught of hoofbeats, yelling, and gunfire made them all turn toward the entrance. Something thudded against the sturdy oak door.

"They come now," Billie said.

"Yes." Ned looked at Jud. "We need to load every gun we've got and take up positions at the windows."

"I'll bring my weapons and get Garza." Jud ran toward the chapel.

Sister Adele dashed past Ned into the front sitting room. "In here, Mr. Bright. There are two windows. I can shoot if you have an extra weapon."

Ned picked up his rifle where he'd leaned it against the wall and followed her. "I need to reload my rifle, but my revolver still has at least four rounds in it." He handed her the pistol. Hanging from its leather strap around his neck was the bag of reloading supplies he'd taken from his saddlebag. He pulled the strap over his head. "Don't show yourself at the window if you can help it."

Sister Adele eyed the rifle. "You can trust me to reload that if you'd rather stand watch at a window."

"All right. That's a good trade." Sister Natalie would probably prefer it if the nuns didn't do any shooting unless necessary. Ned swapped weapons with Sister Adele and gave her the bag. He walked to the nearest window slit. "How many of these openings are there in the house?"

"Ten or twelve. The chapel is the only room without any. This room and the dining room have two. The ones in some of the bedrooms are even smaller than these."

The mounted warriors tore around the front of the house, yelling at the top of their lungs. Ned ducked against the edge of the window. Looking through the slit in the thick wall, he didn't know if the revolver would do him much good against the galloping targets. But if they came in close, he might do well with it.

"They're having to ride way out around the garden wall when they circle behind the house," he said.

"Good!" Sister Adele brought the rifle over. "You have caps and balls for that revolver in here. Shall I fill the empty chambers for you?"

Ned handed it over. "Thank you. You're a nun with unexpected talents."

She grinned. "My father taught me. He wanted a boy, and he got four girls."

Sister Marie came in with a rustle of her habit. "Do you need anything?"

"We're fine," Ned said. "Can you ladies join the girls in the hiding place?"

"It's too small, but that's all right. We'll help you any way we can."

"What about Billie?" Sister Adele asked.

"She is with the horses. She seems very good at calming them. And she told Mr. Morgan she wouldn't hide again. Now that you men are here, she wants to fight."

The noise increased outside, and Ned peered out the window. "We'd better douse the lantern as soon as you're done reloading, Sister."

"It's what they call a dark lantern," Sister Adele said. "I can cover the light when we're not using it, without blowing it out." She handed the Colt to Ned.

He holstered it, still watching out the window. "They're in the dooryard now. I can't see what they're doing."

Sister Marie went to the other window.

"Don't let them see you," Ned told her.

"They're near the barn," Sister Marie said. "I count four—no five."

"Looking for livestock?" Sister Adele asked.

"No. They are going to fire the roof."

CHAPTER TWENTY-ONE

"Are they burning our barn?" Sister Adele asked.

Ned walked to the other window. Sister Marie stepped back so he could look out. "Sure looks that way. They just put a torch to some straw, and they're holding it up to the edge of the roof."

"God be thanked you didn't put your horses in there." Sister Adele crossed herself.

"What's to keep them from doing the same to the house?" Sister Marie asked.

Ned gritted his teeth, but he had no answer. "Pray, ladies. Where is Sister Natalie?"

"I don't know," Sister Adele said. "In the chapel praying, perhaps."

"No, the horses are in there," Sister Marie said. "She is in one of the bedchambers. Señor Garza gave her his pistol and told her to use it if one of the Indians came close to the house on that side. He is in the kitchen with his rifle."

"What about the girls?" Ned asked.

"They are still in the cellar. Quinta wanted to get out and see her papa, but we made them stay down there. I showed him where it is and he talked to her for a minute. They are frightened. Some of the girls are crying—not Quinta. She told him to give her a kiss and the two kittens."

Ned laughed. "That sounds like Quinta."

"She would get out and help with the horses if her father would let her."

A shout came from outside the window. Ned peered out, keeping to the edge. The warrior in the yard called out again, not the bloodcurdling scream he'd heard before. This was a demanding shout.

"Get Billie," Ned said grimly. "They want something." He could see flames along the edge of the barn roof. A single warrior sat on his mustang in the middle of the dooryard, fearlessly facing the house.

Billie left the chapel at Sister Marie's summons, squeezing between two of the horses.

"In the parlor," Sister Marie said. "Quickly."

Only a faint ray of light escaped the covered lantern. That and the sliver of sunlight streaming through the window slit gave enough illumination for her to make out one of the nuns and a man in the room.

"Billie," Ned called. "Come over here, but stay to this side of the window. There's a man on horseback outside shouting at us."

She took her place beside him, and Ned put his hand, warm and firm, on her shoulder. She peeked out, then gasped and drew back. "Fire."

"Yes," Ned said. "They've touched off the barn roof. But what about the rider in the dooryard? Did you see him?"

She leaned forward a tiny bit at a time until she saw the

horseman. He raised a lance high and shouted something in Comanche. Over the wind and the crackling flames, she could make out only a few words, but she recognized the voice and the silhouette.

"Peca. He wants to talk."

"Can you ask what they want? No, wait." Ned squeezed her shoulder gently. "We don't want to let them know for sure that you're here. Can you tell me the words to say?"

Billie leaned slowly until she could see Peca again. He still sat on his mustang, exposed in the dooryard. She wondered if Ned could shoot him from here. If one of them didn't stop Peca, the warrior would not rest until he had her in his grasp.

She was about to draw back when a second horseman trotted over beside him.

"Another man with him now," she told Ned. "White man."

"What? Let me see." Ned pulled her back, and she let him take over the post at the window. After a long moment he drew back and reached for her. He found her hand and held it. "That's Trainer out there. The buffalo hunter."

Billie swallowed hard. "He bring Peca."

"Probably. He went and found Peca's band is my guess. That's why it was quiet the last few weeks. He went to sell information to the Comanche and bring them here."

"Peca burn house too," she said.

Ned's jaw tensed. "This house has a sod roof, doesn't it?"

Sister Adele came to stand closer. "Most of it. But it has a wooden frame, like the barn roof. And the part where the kitchen sticks out is shingled. Part of that side—mostly over the woodshed and the chapel—has shingles."

"Not good." Ned looked out again.

Billie stood quietly, waiting for him to make a decision. Did Ned understand the Numinu way of thinking? She doubted he would credit Peca with the ruthlessness and determination she'd seen in him.

Another shout came to them through the window slit.

"The barn roof is smoldering," Ned said. "Trainer says to come out and parley."

"You mustn't," Sister Adele said.

Billie clutched Ned's wrist. "Don't go. They would kill you. Do not trust them."

Ned nodded. "Thought maybe I could talk through this window."

"Be careful," Billie said. "They might shoot in window."

"All right, get over to one side."

She flattened herself against the wall, and Ned kept hold of her hand as he put his face to the edge of the opening. Billie knew she couldn't take what he did in this time of crisis as a sign of what he would do in the future, but the fact that he continued to hold on to her was something she would think about many times when this was over. She only hoped she would not be riding north with the Comanche as she mourned for Ned.

"Trainer!" Ned pulled away from the window as soon as he'd yelled the man's name.

"That you, Bright?"

"What do you want?" Ned shouted.

"You know what we want. The girl." The wind snatched Trainer's words, but Billie heard them, spooky and faded. She shivered.

"Her family came to get her," Ned yelled.

Billie stared at him in the darkness. Was he trying to bluff Peca and the buffalo hunter into thinking she'd already gone?

"Come on," Trainer answered. "We've torched the barn. We can burn you out of the house too."

Sister Marie fell to her knees and clasped her hands. Sister Adele went to her side and knelt too.

"There's no need for things to get grimmer," Ned shouted. "The Comanche don't really want to hurt the sisters, do they?"

"They don't want to hurt anyone, Bright. They just want the woman called Taabe Waipu back. She's one of them."

"She left the Comanche by her own choice."

"And she can return. They want her back. Send her out and we'll all leave."

"No," Ned yelled.

Trainer wheeled his horse and galloped toward the road. He was soon out of Ned's line of vision.

"Now what?" Sister Adele had left off her prayers, and she stood and walked toward them.

"I don't know," Ned said. "Can you go around to the other rooms and see if anyone has seen activity outside besides the barn roof? That will burn slowly with the sod on top, but it will probably be ruined just the same. I just hope they don't try the same thing on this building."

"I'll ask the others," Sister Adele said.

"You could also put buckets of water in every room," Ned said.

Sister Marie stood. "I will help. We have barrels."

The two nuns scurried out of the room.

"Billie," Ned said softly. He moved closer to her in the darkness until she could feel his warmth. "I won't let them take you."

She reached for him, and Ned pulled her in with his left arm, keeping the rifle clear with the other hand. She leaned against him, her head resting over his heart.

"They will burn the mission," she whispered. "Hurt the sisters. And the girls. They will take them. Quinta. She will fight, so they might kill her."

"No. We won't let that happen."

"Peca will do it. We should tell them don't scream, don't

cry, don't fight. Obey and they will keep you alive."

"No. We can't give up hope." Ned moved back to the window. "They're taking their time. The adobe is on our side. But if we could get word to the fort . . ."

"Too far," Billie said.

"I'm afraid so. But there are ranchers nearby . . ."

"If they come, Numinu will kill them."

"But they might hear the gunfire and ride to the fort and tell Captain Tapley."

"Maybe so," Billie said. The racing hoofbeats returned, and Ned leaned from one side to the other to see as much as possible.

"Ned?"

Billie and Ned turned toward the doorway, where Tree Garza stood.

"Yeah?"

"What's going on? I can't see a thing from the kitchen window. Figured I'd be better off in here helping you. They tell me that part of the house has a shingled roof—I can't say I'm happy that the girls are right under it."

"I know," Ned said. "They've torched the barn roof, but it's slow to catch."

Tree shook his head. "It will smolder for hours."

Yells and hoofbeats, pounding close to the house, reached them, and thunks against the wall made Billie duck back and pull Ned farther from the window.

"They shoot," she said.

Tree dived low against the outside wall. "They're shooting arrows. Wonder how many guns they have."

"Peca have rifle," Billie said. "Maybe a few more. But they shoot arrows in window."

More missiles thudded against the oak door in the hall and the adobe wall close to them. One shaft zipped through the window slit and plunked into the opposite wall.

"Now they're getting close," Ned said.

Tree raised his head and eyed the windows. "That wall out back keeps them from making a tight circle around the house."

"You're right," Ned said, "and they know the front entrance is the most vulnerable. If we're ready when they come around again, we might be able to pick off one or two of them."

"All right," Tree said. He inched up the wall beside the farther window. "Can't see anyone now, but we'll go for the chief."

"Peca," Billie said. "His horse have red stripes on . . . on the front legs. Black and white horse. Peca have two feathers. He carry . . ." She paused in frustration.

"He had a lance," Ned said.

"Yes. With feathers," Billie said.

"Right, I saw it. A bunch of feathers near the point. But, Tree, there's one other thing."

"What's that?"

Ned looked at his friend. "Trainer's with them. The man I brought down from Phantom Hill."

Tree gazed at him in silence. The yelling and pounding of hooves increased in volume. "You take Peca. I'll go for Trainer."

"Got it." Ned stuck the barrel of his rifle into the window slit and maneuvered for the best view.

Billie ran down the hallway and burst into the dining room. Jud Morgan's large form blocked one window, but light streamed in the other, and she circled the dining table to where he stood.

"Ned Bright say everyone come to front room. Need to talk."

Jud turned slowly. "All right. I don't seem to be doing

much good here." He picked up his saddlebag and followed her into the hallway. "Billie, I hope we have a chance to sit down later and get reacquainted."

"I hope too." She led him into the sitting room. Ned and Tree still stood at the windows. The noise outside was much louder here than at the back of the house. The Comanche shrieks penetrated the sturdy walls, and the horsemen took turns riding in and letting off an arrow or a gunshot toward the door or one of the windows.

Sister Adele and Sister Riva stood against the far wall, and the other two nuns came in behind Billie and Jud.

"We're all here now, Ned," Sister Adele said.

"Hold on." He fired his rifle. Sister Marie clapped her hands to her ears too late. "Sister Adele?" Ned turned and held out the rifle.

Sister Adele hurried toward him, ducking low. She took the rifle and sat down near his feet to reload. Ned drew his Colt and looked out the window again. Meanwhile, Tree sighted along his rifle barrel and fired. The yelling stopped, and the hoofbeats retreated.

"All right." Ned turned and stood with his back against the wall beside his window. "They'll be back soon. This seems to be their pattern—swoop in, everyone shoot off a volley, ride out, circle the buildings, ride back in. Did anyone see anything from the other windows?"

"Only the Indians riding past," Jud said, "but the angle was bad from the dining room and I couldn't get a clear shot. If they'd held still maybe I could have."

Sister Natalie said, "I could see riders once in a while, and once they shot arrows toward my window. That was all."

"Pretty much the same from the kitchen," Tree said. "It's not a good vantage point, and no one approached the back door while I was in there."

"I think we need to keep somebody out there for three reasons," Ned said. "The roof there is shingled, so it's more vulnerable. They could rush the back door, especially since we don't have a good view of it, and the girls are under the kitchen."

"I'll go back there," Tree said. "Those are all good reasons to defend it well."

"Make sure you've got containers of water," Ned said.

"We have plenty in the kitchen," Sister Marie said. "We also put a wash boiler of water just outside the chapel door and buckets in the dining room and two of the bedchambers. We can bring a tub in here and fill it."

"Probably a good idea," Ned said. "Morgan, anything else you can think of?"

"Some blankets, maybe. Put them close to hand, and we can soak them if the need arises. And ladies—" He looked at the nuns. "Other liquids can help if fire does break out."

"We have a large can of milk," Sister Marie said, "and a keg of vinegar."

"Good," Jud said. "In a pinch, we can use those."

"I will get the blankets," Sister Riva said.

"I'll help with the water when I go back to the kitchen," Tree said. "Anything else?"

"Jud, stay here with me," Ned said. "Sister Adele is a proficient reloader, and Billie can run to the different stations to keep us all up to date on what's happening in other parts of the house. Agreed?"

They all assured him they would follow his instructions.

"The girls need to stay in the cellar," Tree said.

"I think—" Sister Marie stopped and looked at the floor. "They may need to get out to . . ."

"Bring them one at a time to my room," Sister Natalie said. "They can use the chamber pot."

The nuns and Tree hurried to carry out their tasks. Sister Adele and Billie stayed with Jud and Ned in the sitting room. Already the Comanche were back, whooping and shooting at the house.

"What took 'em so long?" Jud yelled.

Ned poked his rifle into the window slot, then removed it and leaned in for a better look. "I see two with torches. Sister Adele, make sure the girls are in the cellar. Keep them there until we have another lull."

"Billie, can you check the horses?" Jud said.

"Yes." She ran toward the chapel.

Someone had tied a rope across the doorway at waist height. The horses snuffled when she pushed the curtain aside, and Señor Garza's horse whinnied. Billie ducked under the rope and stepped in. She rubbed the big black's neck, crooning softly to him. The noise of the battle barely reached them, but the horses seemed restless. She wondered if Sister Marie had any carrots or dried apples she could spare. Circling carefully in the near darkness, Billie patted each horse and spoke to them in turn. Then she edged her way among them to the doorway and slipped out. She lowered the curtain, checked the rope barrier, and dashed to the kitchen.

Tree Garza glanced over his shoulder from his post by the one window. "You should be with the girls."

"No. I can't hide."

"Why not?"

She went to stand close beside him so the girls would have no chance of hearing. "It is because of me that this happens. If I hide with them, Peca will search until he finds me. Then he find them too. Is better if he find me but not girls."

Tree eyed her keenly. "We will protect you, Taabe."

"Please. I am not Taabe any longer. I am Billie Morgan. I want to live and be Billie Morgan."

Tree frowned. "That's what we all want."

She nodded. "Señor Garza, you love Quinta."

"Of course."

"I love her too."

"I'm glad," he said.

"I would do anything to save her. And the others, all of you. I would go with Peca."

"But . . ." His dark eyes bored into her. "But then you'd be Taabe Waipu again, not Billie Morgan."

She nodded. "Is better than all being killed. The sisters . . . the little girls. Even you and Ned Bright and my brother."

"No," Tree said. "That's not going to happen."

"It's certainly not." They swung toward the doorway. Sister Marie had come in as they talked, bringing Minnie, the newest of the pupils, back from her trip to Sister Natalie's room. She stood just inside the doorway with her hands on the girl's shoulders.

Minnie's gaze was riveted on Billie and her expression was filled with awe. Billie glanced at Tree.

"Let's get her back in the hole," he said. "Come on, *chica*." He lifted the trapdoor.

"Papa!" Quinta cried. "When can we come out?"

"Not yet."

"I have to go."

"You can wait," Tree said. Minnie crawled under the table and down the ladder. Tree lowered the trapdoor and slid the rug over it.

He stood and looked at Billie. "If you won't get in the cellar, take this." He pulled a hunting knife with a five-inch blade from his belt and held the hilt toward her. "If the worst happens, you can use it."

Billie put it in the deep pocket of her skirt.

Sister Marie strode to the shelves near the washstand and

picked up a butcher knife. "We don't want to fight, Mr. Garza, but we would rather fight than give up the girls—and that includes Billie."

A loud neigh came from the hallway, followed by the squeal of another horse. Billie's skin prickled. She lifted her skirt and ran for the chapel.

Ned reached the doorway before she did and thrust the curtain aside.

"The roof's on fire," he said. "The horses are going crazy."

He dodged aside, and a hoof thudded against the wall.

CHAPTER TWENTY-TWO

Billie seized the bucket of water near the doorway and stepped cautiously into the dark room. In one corner, an orange glow illuminated the ceiling, and she could hear crackling over the horses' shifting and snorting.

A horse brushed against her. Lurching back, she sloshed water over her skirt and moccasins. She spoke firmly in Comanche and reached out to touch the horse's flank and push him aside.

"Ned! Water here."

She could see him now, standing beneath the burning rafters, gazing up at the place where the blaze had eaten through the roofing. The stench of smoke was strong now.

"Bring it here and fetch me a blanket."

She advanced cautiously toward him, speaking to the horses. When she reached him, she looked up. She could see daylight beyond the burning ceiling.

"Quick," Ned said. "More water and blankets. Maybe get

a pole or something that I can knock stuff down with, and something I can stand on."

Billie moved back toward the doorway as fast as she could without further agitating the horses.

Sister Marie met her in the hallway, carrying a large stew-pot full of water. Tree was hefting the copper wash boiler.

"Can I get in there?" Tree asked.

"I will go first and move horses," Billie said. She grabbed the folded blanket they'd left on the hall floor and went back inside. Fighting the urge to yell and slap the horses out of the way, she spoke calmly and pushed them away with gentle hands.

They reached Ned, and Tree set the boiler down. Billie shook out the blanket and dropped it into the water.

"I will get a stick," she said and turned away.

Sister Marie stood just inside the doorway with her bucket. "Can you . . . ?"

Billie took it from her. "Get more blankets and a long stick for Ned."

Sister Marie dashed into the hall, and Billie turned back toward the fire. She heard gunfire outside, amid fiendish yells, and one shot fired from within the house. Her brother, in the sitting room, must have gotten a clear shot at one of the Comanche.

By the time she got back to the corner, the hole in the ceiling gaped as big as a washtub. Ned stood on an upturned bucket. He and Tree swatted at the smoldering rafters with wet blankets.

"Pour that right into the tub," Tree said.

She dumped the water into the wash boiler and went back to the door. Sister Marie waited with another blanket and a broom.

"It's the longest stick I could find."

"It is good," Billie said. "Do not let horses out. Stand in door."

She made her way back to the corner. The horses milled about, whinnying, nipping at each other, and occasionally kicking or squealing. The smoke stung her eyes.

Ned and Tree both stood on buckets. She handed Ned the broom and soaked the second blanket for Tree. The men worked feverishly, dropping the blankets occasionally for her to wet again. Ned used the broom handle to hit at the burned shingles and knock them off the edge of the roof outside.

"Look out!"

A flaming clump of wood tumbled onto the chapel floor. Billy scooped water from the wash boiler onto it with her hands.

"Move away," Tree said.

She stepped back, jostling one of the horses. It leaped away, and the others shuffled and whinnied. Tree threw his damp blanket down on the burning debris. Billie lifted the edge of the blanket and beat the bright embers until they no longer glowed.

"Good work," Ned called.

She soaked the blanket, wrung it out, and passed it up to Tree. The horses still moved about, bumping one another and snorting. She reached for the nearest one's halter and stroked his neck, speaking quietly to him.

Ned said, "Tree, give me a boost."

"They'll shoot you."

"No, it's quiet out there now. I want to get a good look."

Tree left his bucket and went to Ned. A moment later, Ned climbed onto Tree's shoulders. Billie watched, holding her breath. Ned grabbed the edge of the adobe wall and cautiously stood. Tree held his feet, and Ned struck his head through the gap in the ceiling. A few seconds later he ducked back down and hopped to the floor.

"The sun's going down. It'll be dark in an hour. The barn roof is still burning. The sod's smoldering."

"What about this roof?" Tree asked.

"I think we put it out," Ned said.

"And the Comanche?"

Billie edged closer to hear his response.

"They galloped off, away from the road."

"You don't think they gave up?" Tree asked.

Ned peered at Billie. "What do you think?"

She shook her head. "Peca not give up. He rest and watch to see if house burn. He come back."

"After dark?" Ned asked.

"Maybe."

"He won't wait until tomorrow, I'm guessing."

Billie shrugged. "No, I don't think he wait that long. Too close to fort. Someone come along and see, tell soldiers."

"That's what I'm hoping," Ned said.

Tree pushed the buckets and wash boiler against the wall. "I hope so too. We don't have feed for these horses, or enough water to spare them much of a drink."

"Someone may have heard the commotion already," Ned said. "Or seen the smoke."

"Let's hope we get some help soon." Tree turned toward the doorway as Sister Adele moved the curtain aside.

"Everyone all right in here?" she called.

"Yes," Ned said. "They threw a torch on the roof and it caught, but we've put the fire out."

"Mr. Morgan says they've fallen back. He thinks he wounded one of them. We thought this might be a good time for everyone to eat."

"Great," Tree said. "Hadn't thought about it, but I am hungry."

"Me too," Ned said.

"Come to the kitchen when you can," Sister Adele said. "The others are fixing a light meal and letting the girls out for a few minutes."

Billie waited until the men were gone, then spent a few more minutes calming the horses. When she stepped into the hall, she noticed the temperature was much cooler away from the warmth of the horses. The nuns hadn't kept their fires going since the attack began. Passing the dining room, she saw Jud and Tree eating while standing near the windows. Ned must have taken his food to the front room so he could keep watch there.

She watched Jud, and a certainty settled over her. This was the tall man from her memories. Though he seemed a bit stern, the circumstances could account for much of that. There had been no time for her to talk to him or observe him closely, but an unmistakable affinity drew her to him.

He turned and caught sight of her. She waved, and he nodded with a half-smile. She moved on to the kitchen.

Quinta and another girl sat on the floor against the wall eating bread, apples, and cold chicken. Billie knelt beside them.

"You all right?" she asked, forcing a smile.

"Billie, we were so scared!" Kate said. "We thought those natives would get you."

"No, I am still here."

Quinta rolled her eyes. "*I* didn't think so. I told them you were too smart to let them get you, and you'd fight if they tried."

"That's right," Billie said.

"Do we have to go back in the cellar?" Kate's eyes brimmed with tears. "I hate it down there, and we can't have the candle lit when they shut us in. It's awful."

"We held hands and sang," Quinta said, looking at Billie.

"Songs are good," Billie said. "Stories too, and praying. You help each other."

"Here's your food, Billie."

She stood and took the plate Sister Marie offered her.

Billie ate quickly while the nuns brought the other two girls their meal. She gave her empty plate to Sister Riva, who stacked the dirty dishes.

"We're saving what water we have," Sister Riva said.

Billie was glad they weren't using any of their precious supply to wash dishes. "Horses hungry. You have carrots? Apples?"

"That's a good thought." Sister Riva put several of each into a basket for her.

Billie walked quickly back to the chapel. The horses were once more jostling and nipping at each other. She spoke firmly and ducked under the rope barrier. She whistled and stroked the nose of the first to approach her—one of Jud's horses. Billie took a carrot and held it to his nostril while tucking the basket behind her back.

The horse sniffed at the carrot then took it with his lips and crunched it. Tree's big black nosed her arm, and she gave him one. She tried to make sure all four horses received equal treatment, but the black gelding snapped at the others to keep them away. He nipped her sleeve, and she slapped his nose.

"You stop. Greedy horse!"

She couldn't blame him—he was a big boy and hadn't eaten all day. But that didn't mean Ned's pinto and the others shouldn't get their share. She made sure Jud's horses got equal consideration. They looked like the horse she had ridden the day the Numinu took her, and she stroked their faces and necks. They didn't jump around as much as Ned and Tree's horses, and they seemed content to wait for the humans to change their situation.

Billie leaned against one of the dark brown horses and

entangled her fingers in his mane. Carefully she formed English sentences in her mind.

Father God, thank You for bringing my brother. Help us to live. Do not let Peca hurt anyone here.

All of those within the mission were dear to her—the sisters, who had treated her with compassion; Señor Garza, who had been kind to her; Jud, who had loved her and tried to find her for many years; the innocent little girls crouching in the dark cellar; and Ned. He filled her heart now, and she left it to God to understand how much Ned meant to her.

None of these people deserved to be shot or scalped, or to have the house burned over their heads.

If I walk out of here, Peca will leave them alone.

Did she believe that? Señor Garza had forbidden her to offer herself to save them. But why should all these people die because of her?

Father God, show me wisdom. Give me a gift now. I do not ask for myself, but for them.

The horses' treats were gone, and she placed the basket outside and edged around the wall to stand beneath the hole in the roof. The horses lost interest in her and milled about, somewhat calmer now. She looked at the ceiling, where the light flowed in. It had the late afternoon slant that would soon haze into twilight.

All was quiet outside. How long before Peca and his followers returned? She, better than any of the others, knew he would be back. He would have promised his friends rewards if they helped recapture her. The horses, no doubt, and captives. Scalps of the men. But the Comanche's greatest honor in battle was not scalps. It was counting coup, touching the enemy during the battle while he was still alive. These adobe walls prevented the warriors from doing that. Peca must be extremely frustrated. No wonder he had resorted to fire. He wanted not so much to kill them as to drive them into the open, where they could count coup on the white men and rip her from their grasp.

Perhaps those inside the mission could gain an advantage if they could see where the enemy lay. The hole in the chapel ceiling extended almost a third of the way along the wall, but was mostly confined to the area near the edge.

The upturned bucket wasn't high enough. Billie stretched, but she couldn't even touch the top of the wall. She got down and put the bucket in the hall to refill later. She caught the halter on Ned's horse and led him over to stand beneath the gap. The pinto stayed steady as she swung up on his back. Her moccasins slid on his smooth hair, but she found purchase and stood straight on his back until she grabbed the edge of the wall.

She tested her weight on a crossbeam to see if the fire had weakened it. The rafter felt solid. She drew in a breath and leaped upward, pulling with her arms. She rose through the gap and flopped onto the charred roof. Her tired arms felt useless. For a minute she lay panting and longing for the strength she'd had before her flight across the plains. But that would do no good. She raised her head and looked toward the barn. Smoke rose along the roofline—lazy wisps blending with the gray sky. The ridgepole had collapsed and fallen into the barn, leaving a black gulf.

Below her, the horses shifted about and huffed out their breath. Poor, hungry horses. They would have to wait at least until morning for food.

Probably her dress would be stained beyond repair from the charred wood. At least she was wearing the dark blue, not the lavender dress Señor Garza had sent. Later she would think about whether she could salvage it—if they made it through the coming night.

She lay still, watching a sliver of moon rise in the east. That was the direction where Ned and Señor Garza lived—the direction from which the stagecoach came on Tuesdays and Fridays. Tomorrow was a stagecoach day. She gritted her teeth. Would the stagecoach come with another driver on the box? What would Tree Garza's sons do when he failed to come home tonight? She hoped the boys wouldn't ride into a Numinu ambush. And what of the sisters and their pupils? Would they still be under siege tomorrow morning, or would she be riding northward with Peca toward the Valle de las Lagrimas? If she thought for one moment that Peca would ride away without harming the others, she would go to him, despite Señor Garza's words.

She jerked her head up to listen. Hoofbeats. Not from the road—from the plain. Peca was coming back.

CHAPTER TWENTY-THREE

Ned leaned against the wall, his ear to one of the window slits in the sitting room.

"I hear them."

From the other window, Jud said, "Me too. They're galloping in, I think from the north."

"Is everyone ready?" Ned asked.

Sister Riva stood. "I'll go and make sure the trap door is closed and everyone knows they are coming back." She hurried from the room. Sister Adele stayed, ready to reload for the men.

The Comanche swooped in, looped about the yard, fired a volley of arrows toward the mission, and headed out the lane. Ned ducked back as a couple of arrows bounced off the wall outside. He peeked out and got off a shot at a fleeing warrior, but the man concealed most of his body by dropping down along the far side of the horse. Ned was sure he'd missed.

"I don't want to shoot their horses out from under them," Jud yelled, "but they hang so low on the off side, that may be the only way to get them."

Sister Riva returned. "All the sisters and the girls are safe."

"What about Billie?" Ned asked.

Sister Riva hesitated. "I did not see her. I'll check her room."

Sister Adele stood. "She may be in with the horses. I'll look there. Do you want me to reload for you first?"

Ned clenched his teeth and handed her his rifle. "Yes. No. Oh, I don't know. Go on, and I'll use my revolver when they come around again. Jud's right—we can barely get a shot at them anyway."

When she'd left, he said to Jud, "I thought there was one less horse this time. Maybe you did get one of them."

"The white man," Jud said. "I thought I got him, but he didn't fall."

"You're right. He wasn't in the pack this time." Ned leaned heavily on the narrow window ledge, his heart still pounding. Had Trainer been wounded, or had he simply had enough?

"How you doing on ammunition?" Jud asked.

"I've got another thirty rounds or so for the rifle."

"I'm down to a dozen." They looked at each other bleakly.

"Wonder how Tree's doing," Ned said.

"The good thing is, they seem to be low on lead too," Jud said. "They only fired arrows that time."

"Billie! Billie, are you in here?"

Sister Adele's call wafted up to where Billie lay flat against the blackened shingles. She inched toward the edge of the burned-out section and stuck her head over the gap.

"I am up here."

Sister Adele gasped and pushed past Tree's horse to stare up at her. "What are you doing? The Comanche will see you."

"I came up to see if I could tell where they were, and then

they came back. But it is getting dark, and my clothes are dark. They didn't see me."

A yell in the distance made her gasp.

"They come again."

Billie turned her face away from the sound of galloping horses and lay as flat as she could. *Father God, don't let them see me.* She suspected she was so much higher than the horsemen that she couldn't be seen unless they spotted her from a distance, and the growing darkness and the position of the barn and the garden wall favored her.

"Come down," Adele pleaded.

Billie lay still until the horses thundered past and surged toward the front of the building. She stuck her head through the hole. Sister Adele was staring up at her, cradling a rifle in her arms.

"How in the world did you get up there?"

"I stood on one of the horses."

"Well, come down! You're scaring me to death."

A yell in the dusk sounded closer than before. Billie looked over her shoulder. A pinto horse leaped over the garden wall and pounded toward the side of the house. The warrior on it waved a blazing torch.

Billie's heart hammered as she lay down and willed her body to be still. The horse thundered closer, closer. She heard the torch hit the shingled roof over the kitchen. She ducked her head as the painted warrior passed below her.

When he'd ridden away, she raised her head and looked toward the torch. She gasped then called into the hole, "Adele! Fire on the kitchen roof!"

Without waiting for a reply, she rose on her knees. Perhaps she could creep along the edge of the chapel roof to the place where the kitchen jutted out at the back. She would make a fine target in the light of the torch. As she watched, the flames licked at the edges of the dry shingles. On her hands and knees, she scrambled across the low pitch of the roof. She seized the end of the torch and flung it to the ground, then used her skirt to smother the flames. When she was certain the shingles wouldn't flame up again, she sat back to catch her breath.

Thank You, Father God.

She started back toward the break in the chapel roof.

Across the barnyard, another horse leaped the low adobe wall of the garden. This warrior also wielded a torch. By its flickering light, she recognized the hideously painted face of Peca.

As the horse careened closer, Billie sent up a wordless prayer. One of the pole rafters, stripped of its burnt shingles, extended a foot or so past the edge of the roof. The eaves near her had burned away, but the pole might still hold her weight. She reached for it. No time to test its strength.

The horse galloped toward her. Peca swung his arm back and then forward. As he released the torch, his eyes widened. He had seen her. Billie swung down on the rafter as he wheeled his horse in a tight turn.

She pushed out as far as she could before letting go. Her feet hit Peca's flesh with a satisfying thud. She fell to the ground and lay gasping for breath. A confusion of shouting and hoofbeats surrounded her.

Her arm throbbed. Billie rose on her knees clutching it. Ten yards away, the dismounted warrior struggled to his feet. She managed to stand and face Peca, with his garish red-and-black mask of paint. He had no weapon in his hand, and his horse ran loose toward the front of the house. Billie's heart thudded as she met his furious gaze. With her injured arm, she fumbled for her pocket. Through the fabric she felt the hilt of Tree's knife.

Out of the shadows came another horse. It stopped beside

Billie, pawing and snorting. She looked up, expecting to be trampled.

A man with his eyes outlined in streaks of red-and-black paint stared down at her. He looked at Peca and shouted in Comanche, "Your horse get away."

Peca eyed him stonily, then turned and slunk into the shadows.

"Taabe Waipu."

Billie gasped as she recognized the voice and form of the horseman—Pia's husband, Chano.

"You counted coup on Peca," he said.

Billie clenched her teeth. What would he do to her? She set her jaw and met his stare.

"Well done, Sun Woman." Chano urged his horse a step closer and held out his hand. "Come. I will help you if you wish to go back up there." He looked to the roof. "Or I will take you to the Numinu village if you wish, but . . . I do not think you want that."

Taabe stood still for a moment. Would Chano go back on his word? Would he turn his horse toward the north as soon as he had her on it?

"You will not take me back against my will?"

He smiled. "I would not so dishonor a woman who has counted coup on a chief and shamed him."

"Billie!"

She turned and looked up at the roof. Sister Adele's head and shoulders stuck up through the hole in the chapel ceiling. A chill struck Billie as she realized Adele held a rifle and was aiming at Chano.

"Don't—"

Adele pulled the trigger.

The shot was surprisingly loud amid the other sounds. The startled horse leaped to one side. Chano clutched a hand to his chest and tumbled to the grass. Billie ran to him, and he stared up at her.

"Chano! I am so sorry. They didn't know—"

He grasped her wrist. "Let them take me." He slumped on the ground.

Billie's head whirled. Her position was more dangerous than ever.

"Billie!"

She looked up at Adele.

"Billie, hurry! You've got to come back in."

Chano's skittish horse danced close to the barn wall. Billie dashed across the open expanse, seized his bridle, and led him to the spot where she had jumped.

"Hurry," Adele said.

Billie stood between the horse and the wall, looking toward the front of the house and speaking softly to the mustang. The other warriors yelled and thundered about the yard. She swung onto the horse's back and stood precariously on the saddle.

"Help me!" She reached up to grasp the roof, ignoring the pain in her arm. The horse began to move, and she gave a desperate push with her feet. Adele dropped the rifle down the hole and pulled Billie's upper arms until her moccasins gripped something solid and she was able to join Adele on the roof.

Adele embraced her for a moment. "God be praised. Quickly! You must get inside before they come back for you." The sister wriggled down through the hole. The horse no longer stood beneath her in the chapel, and Adele hung for a moment from the exposed rafter, then let go.

Billie thrust her feet into the hole.

"Hurry," Adele called. "I'm afraid I broke Ned's rifle stock when I dropped it on the floor."

The Comanche riders circled the barnyard once more.

Billie lowered her feet and legs, but she couldn't tear away her gaze. Four riders charged around the yard between her and the barn. One caught the reins hanging from Chano's bridle. Another dismounted and lifted the fallen warrior. He laid Chano's body over his saddle and leaped onto his own horse. The four Comanche men rode out of the dooryard, turning behind the barn. Last of all Peca, mounted once more, emerged from the shadows and rode away in their wake.

As their hoofbeats faded, the wind was the only sound competing with Adele's anxious cries.

"Billie, please! Come down!"

"Sister!" Ned shouted. "What's going on?"

Billie lowered herself and hung for a moment by her hands. Strong arms surrounded her waist and hips.

"Let go," Ned said.

She plummeted into his arms. The chapel seemed very dark after the twilit roof. Ned pulled her close and stroked her hair. "What on earth were you doing?"

"I . . ." How could she tell him all that had happened in the last ten minutes?

"The Comanche rode away again," he said, still holding her close. "They may come back. I was worried about you."

"I am not hurt," she said. "Well, not much. But they will not return."

"How do you know?"

"Please," Billie said. "I tell you. Not here."

He looked around at the crowded chapel and the snuffling horses. "All right. We'll go somewhere else."

"Mr. Bright, I'm afraid I damaged your rifle," Sister Adele said. "I have it here."

Ned took it from her. He kept his other arm around Billie and drew her toward the doorway.

When they reached the hall, he said to Sister Adele, "Please tell me what happened."

"Perhaps we should go out to the front room and let everyone hear."

"Go ahead." Ned held the rifle out to her. "We'll come right along."

Sister Adele took the rifle and walked toward the sitting room.

By the light of the lantern in the hallway, Ned studied Billie's face. "What happened on the roof?"

She drew in a deep breath. "Numinu come with torch and throw on kitchen. I crawl over and throw torch away."

Ned's jaw dropped.

"Then I see Peca come with torch. I jump . . ." She held her breath and waited for his reaction.

"You jumped? What do you mean?"

"I kick Peca hard. Horse not . . . not on all feet."

"Off balance?"

"Yes. He turn, he off balance. Peca fall off horse. Chano come. He say, 'Taabe Waipu, you count coup.' And Peca go to catch his horse."

"What?" Ned grinned and shook his head. "You counted coup on the leader?"

Hesitantly, Billie nodded. "Not my thinking—I just want to stop him burning mission roof."

"Oh, you amazing woman." Ned hauled her back into his arms. "I wish I'd been there to see it, but in some ways I'm very glad I wasn't."

She pulled away from him and put her hand to his cheek. "Ned."

"Yes?"

"Sister Adele have your gun. She kill Chano."

Ned sobered. "Oh, no."

Billie nodded. "I not tell her."

"She didn't know?"

"She knows she shoot him, but she did not know he help me. Not know it was Chano—my sister husband."

"Slow down," Ned said. "This Comanche that Sister Adele shot—it wasn't Peca?"

"No. Peca . . . disgrace. Woman count coup on him."

"I understand that part."

She nodded. "Chano tell me he help me get back into mission. But Sister Adele not know. She think he kill me, so she shoot."

Ned let out a deep breath. "What should we do?"

"I think . . . nothing. They take him away."

"Yes," Ned said. "Comanche always take their dead if they can."

"I not tell her who she shoot."

"But he was a friend?"

Billie shrugged. "Taabe love sister Pia. She marry Chano. He treat me well. But . . . he tell me to marry Peca." She looked up into his brown eyes. "How can friend help Peca chase me and raid mission?"

Ned stroked her cheek gently with his thumb. "Billie, sweet Billie. I'm afraid there will always be difficult times for you. I'm very sorry."

"You tell brother?" she asked.

"Do you want me to?"

Billie nodded. "When sisters not there. You tell him Chano help me. And we not tell sisters what he did. Sister Adele is my friend. I don't want her to . . ." She shrugged.

"You don't want her to feel guilty."

Billie nodded.

"All right. Did you see the buffalo hunter when the Comanche rode in close?"

She shook her head. "Not see buffalo man."

"We think he may be out of it, but we're not sure. Are you ready now?"

"Yes. They not come back."

"You're sure?"

"Yes."

Ned walked with her, keeping his arm about her. It felt warm and safe to walk next to him. Billie felt more secure than she had in twelve years.

As they entered the sitting room, Sister Adele was telling Jud Morgan, ". . . and the next thing I knew, she wasn't there. She'd jumped down off the roof. I climbed up to where I could see the barnyard, and she was on the ground below me. An Indian was reaching to take her up on his horse. I shot the savage right out of the saddle."

Jud looked toward the doorway and saw Billie. He strode forward.

"Are you all right?" He took hold of her shoulders and looked deep into her eyes.

"Yes." Billie glanced at Ned. "Comanche gone."

"That's right," Ned said. "She assures me they won't come back."

"But why?" Sister Natalie asked.

Ned sighed. "Can someone get Tree, please? And I think we can let the girls out of the cellar."

"They should stay in there," Jud said. "We'd better keep watch until morning at least."

Sister Natalie eyed Ned and Billie. "I think we'll let them out for a while, Mr. Morgan. Let's all hear what Billie has to say, and then we can decide what to do."

Sister Marie hurried to the kitchen, returning with Tree and the four girls. Quinta settled in the armchair with her father, and the other girls sat on the floor.

When all of them had gathered, Billie told her halting story, with embellishments by Sister Adele. She left out the words Chano had spoken to her and his offer of help, ending the story with her recovery of his horse and Adele's aid in getting back on the roof.

"She was so brave," Sister Adele said. "I couldn't believe she'd done what she did."

"We must thank God for her safety," Sister Natalie said. "Shall we pray?"

They all bowed their heads, and Sister Natalie said, "Dear Father in heaven, we thank Thee for Thy goodness to us. We beseech Thee for wisdom now."

After the "amens," Quinta, from the comfort of her father's lap, gazed at Billie with huge brown eyes. "I wish I'd been there."

"Be thankful you weren't, little one." Tree squeezed her.

Jud, who had insisted on keeping watch at one of the windows, called out, "A big section of the barn roof caved in. I'm afraid the fire's done its job, even though the sod slowed it down."

"At least the house roof is intact," Sister Natalie said.

"Maybe we can get the horses out of the chapel now," Ned said. "It's quite a mess in there."

"We can't put them outside tonight." Jud turned from the window and stared at him.

"They not come back," Billie said. She didn't want to sound defiant, but she knew Peca would not return.

"We could at least venture out and cut some grass for the horses," Sister Riva said.

"Tree and I could do that." Ned looked at Patrillo. "What do you think?"

"In a while. Let's wait a little longer to be sure."

"Yes," Jud said. "Let's not get overconfident."

Billie longed to assure him the crisis was over, but she kept still. Knocking Peca from his saddle was one thing. Lives were at stake then. But there was no need to belittle her brother's thoughts in front of the others. And if she explained that Peca's shame and the death of his friend had driven Peca away for good, the others would realize she knew the warrior Sister Adele had shot.

"If you think it's safe, I'd like to use a little water and light the stove now, so I can prepare a hot meal," Sister Marie said.

"I will help you." Billie rose.

Quinta squirmed around to see Sister Marie. "Can we make a cake?"

The sister smiled at her. "Perhaps tomorrow, my dear."

When Sister Marie called them all to the dining room to eat a belated supper, Ned touched Jud Morgan on the shoulder.

"I'd like to speak to you."

Jud hung back as the women and girls, along with Tree, left the room.

"What is it?" Jud's face was set in hard lines, as though he expected bad news.

"Your sister. She's a courageous woman."

"I gathered that."

Ned nodded. "Sit down for a minute."

Jud sat gingerly on the edge of the sofa, still holding his rifle. "You got something to say?"

"Yes. The Comanche the nun shot—he was trying to help Billie."

"What?"

Ned ran a hand over his stubbly chin. "She told me he was her brother-in-law. I mean, the husband of her Comanche sister. He spoke kind words to her and offered to help her get back inside. But Sister Adele saw him, and she thought he was threatening Billie, so she shot him."

Jud stared at him. "Are you sure that's what happened?"

"What do you mean?"

"Billie wasn't planning to go back with them, was she?"

Ned eyed him keenly. "No. If she'd wanted to go back, she'd have left here long ago."

"Garza told me she offered to surrender to them to save the rest of us."

Ned sighed. "That's like her. But she didn't do it. She kicked the leader off his horse. That was the worst shame for him—having a woman count coup on him. If Billie were going to surrender and marry the man, she certainly wouldn't have humiliated him first."

Jud leaned back and stared at the opposite wall. "I suppose you're right." He rubbed his eyes with the back of his hand. "I'm so tired. I just want to take Billie home."

"I know. But there's something else I should tell you."

"What's that?"

"I love your sister."

Jud let out a short laugh. "Tell me something I don't know."

Ned smiled. The relief of saying the words astonished him. "All right, then. Let's get something to eat. You should sleep after that. We can take turns keeping watch, at least until the sun is well up."

"Right. Just in case." Jud rose.

A sound Ned had come to dread came faintly from outside. "I hear horses."

"I knew it!" Jud ran to the nearest window and poked his rifle's muzzle into the opening.

Pulling his Colt, Ned hurried to the other one and peered out. Several horses galloped into the yard and stopped.

"What are they up to now?" Jud asked.

"Wait! Whatever you do, don't shoot." Ned squinted into the starlit dooryard. Voices reached him, calling softly to each other in Spanish.

He turned to Jud and grinned. "It's Tree's boys. I guess they were worried when Papa didn't come home." He holstered his gun and strode to the hall. "Come on, Morgan, help me move this chest."

CHAPTER TWENTY-FOUR

During the boisterous reunion of the Garza family, while Quinta delighted in introducing her four brothers and Brownie Fale to all the nuns and students, Billie slipped around the edge of the room and stood beside Jud.

He looked down at her with thoughtful eyes. "Is there someplace quiet where we can talk?"

She nodded and walked out into the hall. At the far end, she opened the door to her chamber.

"My room," she said. She went to the small table and lit the lantern, then placed the stool for Jud and sat down on her bed.

He sat opposite her and looked long into her face. "I'm so happy to be here with you." Tears glinted in his eyes. "I can't tell you how much we've prayed for this day."

"I pray too." She reached out both hands. Jud took them and held them gently, rubbing her knuckles with his thumbs.

"Billie, I'm so sorry for what happened to you."

She ducked her head so he wouldn't see her tears. "Not your fault," she said.

"I've felt as though it was. Ma said she let you ride out to find me and show me something you'd brought from school. But I wasn't where I'd told her I'd be that day. I'd gone farther than I'd planned, looking for a few strays."

Billie bit her lower lip as the memories cascaded in her mind. Something from school. She reached for her parfleche and dipped her hand into it.

With a shaky laugh, she held the tattered paper out to Jud. "Here. I bring this."

Slowly, Jud unfolded it. The ink had faded and the creases nearly obliterated some parts. He stared at it for several seconds. A bittersweet smile touched his lips.

"Dear Mrs. Morgan, I wanted to inform you that Billie is the top scholar in our school. She will receive a special honor at the Christmas assembly. I hope you and your family can attend. Sincerely, Miss Thurston."

He looked at Billie. "Your teacher sent this. Do you remember Miss Thurston?"

Billie frowned. She put a hand to her eyes. "Not see. Spectacles?"

Jud laughed, and the care slipped away from his face. For the first time, he looked to Billie as he had twelve years earlier.

"Yes, she's short-sighted. Wears eyeglasses all the time. Oh, Billie." He reached for her hands again. "I need you to know how much we all love you. How much *I* love you. Will you please come home to the ranch? Ma and Marion are so excited. They're getting ready for your return. I do hope you want to come."

Billie nodded, and her tears spilled over. "I come."

Jud let out a deep sigh and nodded. "What about Ned Bright?"

Billie blinked. "Ned?"

"Yes. He loves you. Surely you know that."

Billie sat very still. Inside she felt warm and eager, hoping Jud's words were true.

He leaned toward her. "I . . . wasn't sure you'd want to go so far from him."

"I go home," she said firmly.

Jud smiled. "Good. And if you want to see Ned later, we'll arrange that."

Billie withdrew her hands and tried to marshal her thoughts and the words to express them.

"What is it?" Jud asked.

"Ned . . . he not know."

"What doesn't he know?"

Her throat tightened. "I . . . I have husband. Comanche husband. Not my choice."

Jud stared at her. "You are married? I thought this savage who attacked us wanted to marry you. Don't tell me it's already done!"

"No, no." Billie patted his arm. "Not Peca. Husband dead now. He . . ." She needed to be sure she spoke correctly, that there was no misunderstanding. "He *went* raiding."

"Yes?" Jud studied her closely. "He went raiding."

She nodded. "He die on raid. Chiefs give his bow to his little son."

Jud inhaled sharply. "You have a child?"

Billie shook her head, tears flowing freely. "He die too. Sick. But Ned not . . . he *does* not know."

"Oh, Billie." Jud slid off the stool and sat beside her. She curled into his arms, weeping against his shoulder.

For a long time he held her, letting her cry. At last she sat straighter and sniffed. If this knowledge drove Ned away, she would still have her family. Jud wouldn't hold her if her news repelled him.

"I should have a handkerchief." His voice cracked.

Billie patted his cheek. "You good brother." She rose and went to the table. A wash cloth hung on the side, near the pitcher of water. She took it and wiped her face.

"Billie . . ." Jud rose and stood close to her. "I want you to know that if you had been able to bring the child back with you, we would have loved him too."

A new wave of tears streamed from her eyes, and she caught them with the cloth. She choked out a muffled, "Thank you."

In the hallway, a horse whinnied. Billie stepped to the doorway and looked out. The front door was open, and one of the black-haired Garza boys was leading his father's horse outside. Behind him, Ned came from the chapel leading his paint.

Billie turned to face Jud. "They take horses out."

"They might as well. The Garzas' horses are out there anyway. I expect the boys will stand watch while they graze."

She nodded. "I help clean chapel."

"You don't have to do that."

"I want to help. Sisters do much for me."

"I meant that we men would do it."

She smiled. "Not the way Comanche men do."

"No, I'll bet it's not. In this culture, women are spared the hard work. You let us clean it out."

She nodded. "I bring basket and hot water."

"Good." Jud put his arm around her. "Little sister, don't you worry about Ned. He's a good, stout man. I don't think what you told me will matter to him."

Billie gazed up at him. "I hope . . ." She stopped. That was all—she hoped now, with a new assurance that she had a place in the white world, whether on the Morgan ranch with her family or someplace else. She didn't dare think too far into the future so far as Ned was concerned. She only knew that she wanted to go with Jud and spend some time with him and her mother and sister. That thought brought a new question. "Sister?" she asked.

Jud's smile changed his face, erasing the worry lines. "Marion."

"Marion. Hair like mine."

"Yes." His eyes lit in surprise. "Perhaps a little lighter than yours. And she will be so happy to have you home." He squeezed her shoulders. "Come on, Billie. Let's go muck out a chapel."

As they walked down the hallway, the front door flew open and the youngest of the Garza boys tore in yelling, "Papa! Papa!"

Tree came out of the chapel. "What is it, Diego?"

The boy spouted an agitated string of Spanish, and Tree hurried out the door with him.

Billie looked up at Jud. "Did you understand?"

Jud nodded. "They found a man lying dead near the lane. I expect it's the white man who helped the raiders."

Billie pulled in a shaky breath. "They leave him behind—the buffalo man. He not one of them."

Ned and Tree entered the dining room, where the nuns waited with the girls.

"We think it's safe now," Ned said to Sister Natalie.

She rose. "Come girls. Get your things."

"Should we take all our clothes?" Laura asked as the nuns shepherded the pupils toward their bedrooms.

"I think not," Sister Adele said. "Just take what you will need for a couple of days."

"That's right," Tree said. "The captain will find you a place to sleep at the fort until his men have patrolled the area and made sure the Comanche are gone."

"Papa," Quinta said, "can't I go home with you until the others come back to the mission?"

His reply was lost as they followed Billie and the others into the hall.

Ned glanced at Sister Marie, who had lingered in the dining room.

"Would you gentlemen like more coffee?" she asked.

Ned held up his cup. "Thank you, Sister. I've been hankering for hot coffee all day."

She smiled and refilled Jud's cup too, then left the room.

Jud took a sip and looked at Ned over the rim of his cup. "Billie and I talked. She's ready to go home."

Ned pressed his lips together and nodded. "I'll miss her."

"Yes." Jud set his cup down. "Look, Ned, I'm sure she has feelings for you, but we need a little time. Time to rejoice and to . . . well, just to get used to having her with us again."

"I understand."

Jud nodded. "That doesn't mean we expect her to stay with us forever."

Ned raised his eyebrows. "You wouldn't object?"

"Not in the least, so long as everything's done properly. Will you go with the sisters to the fort?"

"I don't need to. Tree and Brownie and the boys can escort them. Two of the boys are riding ahead to get a wagon from the Steins at the home station."

"They're taking the dead man?" Jud asked.

Ned grimaced. "Yes. Sister Natalie said we could bury him here, but I think we'd better take him to Captain Tapley, just to be sure everything's done properly. He may have family somewhere. I hate to have the little girls see it. We wrapped the body in blankets, and they can take him in the wagon.

Unless the captain will send a detail out for him."

"I hope he'll do that."

Ned sipped his coffee and set the cup down. "Tree and I discussed arranging for some men to come and repair the roof. He'll ask around. And I need to look the barn over before we go and see what can be done about that."

Jud nodded. "I thought you might want some private time with Billie before we go."

"You could both ride to the ranch with me and spend tonight there."

"That sounds like a good plan. Wouldn't want to ride much farther than that today."

"It's a good, long ride," Ned said. He could hardly wait to see Billie's face when she mounted her new horse.

"You have been so good to me." Billie hugged Sister Adele fiercely. "You are in truth another sister for me."

"Thank you, dear Billie. That means so much." Adele pulled away, blinking back tears. "You will write to us?"

"Of course." Billie smiled. "I will keep learning to write better, and I will tell you all about my family and the Morgan ranch. And you will tell me how the school goes?"

"Yes. I wish you happiness, and we shall all pray for your safe journey."

"Thank you." Billie said a briefer good-bye to the other nuns, ending with Sister Natalie. She wasn't sure whether to offer her hand or an embrace, but the older woman put her arms around Billie.

"My dear, you shall be sadly missed. You have brought much to the mission, and we've learned many lessons through having you here."

Billie ducked her head. "I shall always remember your

kindness and the things you have taught me."

"May God watch over you and bless you."

Quinta was next, wanting a hug and a kiss and promises of letters. "I'll send you a drawing of the new wall we're going to have built," she said.

"I will like to see it," Billie said. "You will be safer with a wall all around the house and barn."

"We'll take good care of Fluffy."

"I know you will, *chica*." Billie kissed her again and moved away.

Tree and Brownie shook her hand and wished her Godspeed. The Garza boys formed a row of handsome young men with sparkling brown eyes and bright smiles. "*Adios*, Señorita Morgan," they repeated down the line. She laughed and waved at them as she turned to join Ned and her brother.

They mounted the horses, with Billie wearing her leather Comanche dress and high moccasins. Her few other possessions were tied behind the saddle. She reveled in the smooth trot of the dark Morgan horse Jud had brought for her.

A mile down the road, Jud rode close beside her. "What do you think of him?"

Billie grinned and patted the horse's withers. "He is wonderful."

"He can go like that all day," Jud said. "We'll stop to rest them and eat something in a couple of hours, though."

"He rides like the horse they stole from me." Billie frowned. "I cannot remember her name."

Jud laughed. "You called her Velvet."

Billie smiled in delight. "Yes! Yes, I did."

She rode along savoring that memory and anticipating the reunion with the rest of her family.

They'd traveled less than an hour when they met the stagecoach, coming down from Fort Phantom Hill.

The driver pulled up in astonishment when he saw Ned.

"Bright," Sam Tunney called from the box. "Where on earth have you been? We found your ranch station abandoned and a note on the barn door that said, 'Driver didn't return home last night—gone to look for him. Team in barn if Comanche haven't been here.' We thought you'd been ambushed and were lying somewhere without your scalp!"

Ned gritted his teeth and looked over at Billie. "Not quite that bad, Sam, but the Ursuline mission *was* attacked yesterday."

"You're joking. Anyone killed?"

"One Comanche, so far as we know, and the buffalo hunter, Isaac Trainer. But the sisters and their students are fine, and we're fine. Glad we're out of it."

Sam eyed Billie and Jud. "Who you got here?"

"This is Miss Morgan and her brother, from down Victoria way. Miss Morgan was staying at the mission."

"Aha." Sam nodded knowingly. "Pleased to meet you, miss." He lifted his hat to her and nodded to Jud. "Mr. Morgan."

Billie wasn't sure how to respond, but Ned gave her a reassuring smile.

"Sam and Henry are friends," he said.

Billie nodded.

Sam looked over at the shotgun rider. "Well, me and Henry are tuckered out, doing the extra miles, but I guess we can make it to the fort. No point in having you take over out here."

"I appreciate that," Ned said. "I'm taking these folks back to the ranch. Tree and his boys and Brownie have gone to take the nuns and their students to Fort Chadbourne. They'll stay there a few days until they're sure things have calmed down, but we think the band of raiders that attacked them has gone home."

"Glad to hear that. Well, we'd best move along." Sam

called to his team and flicked his whip near the wheelers' flanks. He and Henry lifted their hats, and the stagecoach rolled off westward.

Billie was suddenly weary. Her eagerness to see Ned's home was overshadowed by the desire to sleep through a full night without listening for hoofbeats or war cries.

They ate breakfast before dawn. Ned wasn't much of a hand in the kitchen, but Jud and Billie pitched in, and they sat down to eggs, bacon, fried potatoes, coffee, and applesauce. After they finished, Jud picked up his and Billie's bundles.

"I'll come get you when I've got the horses saddled." He headed out to the barn.

Ned and Billie sat in silence. The moment Ned dreaded had arrived, and his throat seemed paralyzed.

"Thank you for everything you have done for me," Billie said softly.

Ned leaned across the table and took her hand. "Billie, I don't want you to go, but I know you need to. Is it . . ." He cleared his throat. "Could I maybe ride down to Victoria and see you? After the holidays and the first of the year, maybe?"

Billie blinked at him with an expression of slight confusion.

"In a couple of moons," Ned said.

"Two moons? Months on calendar?"

"Well . . . yes." He chuckled. The nuns had done their work well in the short time they'd had. "If everything's all right here and they can get another driver for a short while."

She nodded. "I would like that. Jud said you could come if I wished it."

"I talked to him a little more last night, and he said whenever you're ready. Do you want to leave it that you'll write and tell me when you want me to come?"

"No," she said.

His heart plummeted. "No?"

"You come. One moon."

That was better. He laughed and squeezed her hand. "I probably won't be able to make it that soon. Billie, listen." She sobered, and Ned said carefully, "Jud told me some things . . . things you'd told him. About . . ." He glanced at her and then away. "About your Comanche family."

She sat very still.

"He was supposed to tell me, wasn't he?"

For a moment, he thought she would burst into tears. Her face twitched. She pulled in a deep breath. "You know."

"I do. At least, I think he told me everything. About . . . well, the baby and everything."

"You still come?"

"Yes. I want to."

She nodded, meeting his gaze. "I did not want to marry, but . . . I loved my baby."

"Aw, Billie, I'm sure you did."

A single tear trickled down her cheek. "But Peca . . . when he want me to marry again, I say no, I will not. Not again, not here, not this man. I cannot love him."

Ned nodded, his heart aching for her sadness. "Billie," he whispered, "do you think you could love me?"

She smiled, in spite of the tears glistening in her eyes. "Oh, yes. I love you."

Ned got up and walked around the table. She put her hands in his, and he drew her into his arms. "Billie, I love you. I want you to have time with your family, but I will come to you. Soon."

"Two moons," she said, smiling.

Ned bent his head and kissed her. She responded with a warmth that solidified his hopes. The next two months would fly. While he drove the stagecoach he would think about how he could bring her back and where they could live. But now, all he could comprehend was Billie, in his arms, wanting a future with him.

EPILOGUE

Business and weather had delayed Ned. Tree had an unexpected spurt of freighting, and extra drivers were hard to come by. Heavy rains had bogged down both freight teams and stagecoaches. At last, in mid-February, Ned was able to get away for a few weeks, leaving Brownie to drive his mail route with Benito Garza riding shotgun.

For the first couple of days, Ned rode with his head down against the driving rain. At last the clouds broke and the rain stopped. He dismounted and rolled up his waterproof coat. The ranch outside Victoria drew him, and he rode on with a light heart.

Billie's letters over the past three months had developed from short notes describing her joy at meeting her family and learning the Morgans' everyday routines into longer, thoughtful missives that moved him to his core. Billie pondered her place in life, her relationship to God, and the proper way to deal with her past. Each letter also included questions about life at the stagecoach station and the mission, and a touching admission of her eagerness to see Ned again.

He cherished these letters and responded to each with a compilation of all the news he knew she longed to hear: The mission's chapel roof was repaired, and Sister Adele had drawn plans for the addition they wanted built that summer. The nuns had their cow, and the kittens had grown fat on the milk and were keeping the mice out of Sister Marie's kitchen. Quinta had come home for three weeks at Christmas, and while she had reverted to wearing overalls and riding breakneck around the ranch with her brothers, she'd also organized the preparation of a huge Christmas dinner. Quinta had happily received her father's gifts of feminine clothing and Ned's of tooled leather boots. Benito was courting a girl whose family lived near Phantom Hill. Cat Thompson had taken supper with Ned at the fort and reported the recovery of a captive child—a boy who had spent six months with the Apache.

At last Ned would be with Billie again. In a letter from Jud he'd received detailed directions and reassurance of his welcome. He hurried Champ along past ranches and greening fields.

As he rode farther south, he began to pass large farms where dark-skinned workers were planting cotton. Slaves. Ned gazed at them with uneasiness in his heart. In her letters, Billie had told him more about the slaves kept by the Comanche or sold to the Comancheros. It didn't matter to them what color skin the person had—whites, blacks, Mexicans, and Indians from other tribes all could be forced into slavery. Ned loathed the cruelty of it, and he couldn't fathom how white farmers justified owning these people. But Texas had come into the Union as a slave state. He hadn't seen much of it up where he and Tree had their ranch, but they'd heard of the unrest the issue brought to the entire nation. Ned didn't like it, and was relieved that Billie reported the Morgans had only free workers on the Running M ranch.

On February twenty-second, he trotted under the gate to the ranch and up the lane toward the Morgan house. On either side were pastures and holding pens. A sizable herd of beef cattle grazed off to his right. Ahead sat a substantial, two-story house and large barn. In the corrals near the barn and the pasture beyond them, horses grazed or dozed. Colts ran about, nipping and chasing one another, kicking up their heels for sheer joy. Ned had never seen so many horses—and all of them looked like healthy, sturdy mounts, with sweet faces and well-muscled, compact bodies. He stopped his pinto and gazed at them before he rode on to the dooryard.

Was he out of his mind to ask Billie to leave all this? And would she be afraid living up north, closer to the Comanche lands? They raided everywhere, especially in summer, but Victoria seemed quite civilized now, and she'd have more people around her here. Would she agree to leave the family she'd just found so soon?

The barn door stood wide open, and a couple of men worked inside, so Ned rode up close and swung out of the saddle. It felt good to stand on solid ground. He let the pinto's reins fall and stepped inside, pulling his gloves off.

Jud Morgan turned toward him and grinned.

"Ned! Glad to see you!" He clasped Ned's hand. "This is Ricardo Estanza, one of my ranch hands. We're just cleaning things out a bit and making plans for our spring roundup."

Ned shook hands with Ricardo and chatted for a few minutes about cattle and the weather.

"I know you want to see Billie," Jud said. "Let me take you inside. Ricardo, could you put Ned's horse up, please?"

Ned retrieved his bundle of clothing and saddlebags and followed Jud to the house. They went in through the kitchen door. A lovely blonde woman wearing an overall apron stood at a work table cutting biscuits. She looked up and gave them a dazzling smile.

"You must be Ned."

"This is my wife, Wande," Jud said.

Beyond her, Billie whirled and met his eyes.

"I'm pleased to meet you, Mrs. Morgan," Ned said, but his gaze slid back to Billie—more beautiful than he'd ever seen her. She wore a bright red calico dress that suited her coloring, and her hair fell in glossy waves over her shoulders.

She came and held out her hands, her face slightly flushed and her blue eyes sparkling. "I am so glad you got here safely."

Ned dropped his bundle and took both her hands in his. He wanted to draw her into an embrace, but that wouldn't be proper. He blushed as he stammered a thank-you. "You look wonderful."

"Doesn't she?" Wande asked.

"We've put a lot of effort into fattening her up," Jud said.

Wande's mouth opened wide as if she was horrified at his remark. "Really, Jud, that is not the way to speak of a lady's health."

Jud laughed. "One thing about Billie, she knows when I'm teasing."

She really did look healthy, not emaciated as she had in October. No sign remained of her injuries.

Wande laid a hand on Billie's sleeve. "Why don't you take Ned into the parlor? You know Ma is longing to meet him, and I think Marion is in there too."

In a whirl, Ned was introduced to Billie's mother, sister, nephews, and niece. He noticed a piano against one wall, and he had to ask.

"Billie, did you find that you could still play the piano?"

An impish smile curved her lips. "You will see later."

"All right." She hadn't mentioned it in her letters, and he sensed a surprise was in store.

"She picked it up again very quickly," her mother said, "but then, it runs in the Morgan family, just like the penchant for raising horses."

"And the flute?" Ned asked.

Mrs. Morgan smiled. "It was as if she'd never laid it down. Of course, she had her Comanche flute, though it's not the same. I was astonished at how much she remembered. In only a few weeks, she was reading music."

"It is another language," Billie said.

Marion laughed. "Yes, we've decided you are very good at languages. She's even picked up a smattering of German from Wande and my husband, Peter."

An image flashed through Ned's mind of Billie, sought after and much respected as a translator of fine literature into other languages. Perhaps people would ask her to lecture on linguistics—or music or—

He looked at her, slightly troubled by his thoughts. It had never occurred to him, but Billie had such an engaging personality, people would flock to hear her speak about her experiences. How could he ask her to go back up north and be the wife of a stagecoach driver?

While Ned was upstairs settling in, Billie headed back to the kitchen.

"Oh, no you don't!" Wande shoved her back out into the next room. "You are done working for tonight. Marion and Ma will help me finish getting supper ready."

"But—"

"No buts," Marion said from behind her. "Peter will be here soon to eat supper with us. We'll call you when it's time."

"Take Ned out and show him around the place," her mother suggested.

Ned appeared at the top of the stairs, and Billie smiled at him, feeling a bit shy. "I am supposed to show you . . . I'm not sure what."

He laughed. "I'd love to see it."

She threw on a shawl and took him out to the barn. They found Ned's horse contentedly stabled and eating hay. Jud joined them as they walked around the corrals, explaining to Ned some of the finer points of breeding Morgans.

After fifteen minutes, he went off to help Ricardo. Ned walked slowly along the rail fence with Billie.

"Ma said she would call us when Pastor Bader gets here. He's Marion's husband. When he comes, we will eat together."

"Your family's terrific," Ned said. "I can see that they love you very much."

"Yes. This time with them has been a blessing—one of those gifts God gives us."

Ned nodded, remembering their broken conversation about "Amazing Grace" back at the Ursuline mission. "I'm very happy for you. I can't believe all of this is happening, and I'm finally here with you."

"I know. It has been wonderful to be here these past few months, but all the time I was waiting—waiting for you." She lowered her head and focused on the ground. Ned here beside her—the reality she'd waited for so long almost took her breath away. Every anxiety she'd had over the past few months slipped away. Ned hadn't forgotten her or tired of her—silly notions, those. Over the winter there had been no more Comanche raids along the stagecoach route. He had come through the season in good health, and he'd made the long journey safely. Ned was here—the answer to a thousand earnest prayers.

He stopped walking and snaked his arm around her. "Billie, I love you."

Her heart swelled with contentment, and she smiled up at him. "This is what I have wished for."

He squeezed her gently then let go of her and leaned on the top rail of the fence. "I never saw horses like these. There's not a sorry nag in the bunch."

"That is true." She stood beside him in silence. What had caused this sudden change of mood and topic? The last rays of sun tinged the sky orange and pink as they watched the horses.

"I can't imagine you'd ever want to leave this place," Ned said at last. "It's so beautiful here, and your family loves you so much."

"I feel safe," she said. "But . . ."

Ned straightened and looked at her somber face. "But what?"

"But I love you, and I want to . . ."

He waited.

She glanced up at him then looked away, afraid she had been too bold.

"Please say it, Billie. Do you want to be with me? Would you marry me and come back to the ranch?"

The blazing colors seemed to leap from the sky to her heart. "Yes. Oh, yes, Ned."

He engulfed her in his arms, and she held on to him.

"I love you," he said. "I'd marry you tomorrow, or next week, or I'll come back again in the summer if you want."

"Will we live in the ranch house with Señor Garza and his children?"

"We could build a house of our own if you wanted. That might be better. We could stay with Tree's family until it's built. Or I could go home and build it first." He kissed her, and she knew she didn't want to wait. She wouldn't insist on a perfect house. She'd lived in a tepee for years, and she could adapt to nearly anything, so long as she was with Ned.

"I think maybe tomorrow is too soon," she whispered, "but next week . . . Hmm."

Ned drew back and studied her face. "Really?"

"I think my mother will insist on at least that long. The Morgans are big on celebrating properly. There will be baking and cleaning and sewing. Maybe even two weeks. Were you going to stay that long?"

For a moment, Ned seemed speechless, then he let out a whoop. "I expect I'd better go talk to your brother again. Whatever you and your Ma decide on for time, I'll abide by."

"Thank you," Billie said. She wasn't going to let him get away so easily, though. "You can talk to Jud after supper."

"All right."

She felt very daring as she slid her hands around his neck and drew him down to meet her. Ned pulled her back into his embrace without protest.

EXCERPT FROM *The Long Trail Home*

PROLOGUE

WACO, TEXAS, 1858

"That one right there—he's your mark."

Annie Sheffield slipped past her daddy and peeked around the corner of the building. A handsome youth with wheat-colored hair stood in the dirt road in front of the mercantile, a shiny pocket watch dangling from his fingers on a silver chain. Annie squinted when a shaft of light reflected off the watch, and she blinked several times, refocusing on her prey. A much younger boy with the same color hair reached for the watch, but the older boy lifted the treasure higher to safety.

The older boy's look was stern but gentle. "No, Timothy. Remember this watch was Grandpa's. It's very old, and we must be careful with it."

The younger boy's face scrunched up but he nodded. Then the comely youth bent down and allowed Timothy to hold the shiny watch for a moment before he closed it and put it back in a small bag, a proud smile on his handsome face.

Ducking back into the alley, Annie leaned against the wall in the early evening shadows. She glanced at her daddy. "Do I have to?"

"You wanna eat, don'tcha? We need that watch."

"But that boy looks so proud of it."

Her father narrowed his gray eyes. "I'd be proud if'n it was *mine*."

Annie sighed. If her father possessed the watch, he'd just go hock it or gamble it away.

"Go on with ya." He flicked his thin index finger in the air, pointing toward the street. He tugged down on the ugly orange, green, and brown plaid vest that he always wore. "Scat!"

Annie peered around the building again, taking a moment to judge how fast she'd have to run and where she could hide once she'd taken the watch. She'd come to hate being a pickpocket. Ever since she heard that street preacher several months back in Galveston hollering to a small crowd of spectators that stealing was breaking one of God's special laws, it had nagged her worse than a swarm of mosquitoes. But she was hungry, and they had no money.

She studied the boy's long legs. Could she outrun him? And what about his little friend?

Her daddy was an expert pickpocket. He could snitch a wallet and disappear into a crowd like a crow in a flock, but when it came to running away from a target, well, that's where she came in.

The tall cowboy was probably only a few years older than her thirteen years. He motioned to the younger boy, and they hopped up on the boardwalk, and strolled toward her, completely unaware they were being spied on. He held one hand on the younger boy's shoulder, as if wanting to keep him close. Now that they both faced her, she could see their resemblance.

They had to be brothers. The big boy glanced at his watch bag, tucked it in his vest pocket, and gave it a loving pat.

Annie jumped back. "He's coming," she whispered over her shoulder.

Her father scowled. "I want that watch. Go!"

He gave her a shove. She stumbled forward and turned.

The youth's blue eyes widened. "Hey, look—"

They collided—hard. Annie was knocked backwards, arms pumping, and her cap flew off. The youth grabbed her shoulders, and in a quick, smooth move that had taken Annie her whole life to master, she slipped his watch from his pocket and into hers. She ducked her head and stepped back. "Sorry, mister."

Her apology was more for stealing his treasure than crashing into him. She spun around and ran, hating the baggy trousers her father made her wear so she'd look like a boy. Hating the life she was forced to live. Hating that the handsome youth would hate her. She ran past a bank and a dress shop, then ducked down another alley. Behind the building she turned right instead of going left and back toward her daddy. Right now she didn't want to see him.

"Hey! Come back here, you thief!"

Annie's heart lurched, and she switched from trot to gallop. She could no longer see the watch's owner, but she knew it was him hollering. Bumping into that young man had flustered her. She hadn't expected him to be so solid, not for a youth not even full grown yet. Men grew taller and tougher here in Texas than in the other cities of the South where she'd mostly grown up—a different city every few weeks. A thief wasn't welcome in town for long.

Loud footsteps pounded behind her. She ducked under a wagon that sat behind the smithy, rolled, and dove into the open doorway. She crawled into the shadows of the building and curled up behind a barrel that had oats scattered on the ground around it. She took several gasps of air, and listened for footsteps. The watch pressed hard against her hipbone, causing her guilt to mount. A horse in a nearby stall snorted and pawed the ground. Annie's heartbeat thundered in her ears as she listened for her pursuer's footsteps. Would he thrash her if he found her?

She peeked between around the barrel. The tall boy stood in the doorway, looking around. She shrank back into the shadows like a rat—like the vermin she was.

After a moment, he spun around and quick steps took him away. Annie leaned against the wall, hating herself all over. Why couldn't she have been born into a nice family who lived in a big house? She'd even be happy with a small house, if she could have regular meals, wash up every week or so, and wear a dress like other girls.

But, no, she had to be born the daughter of a master pickpocket.

The blacksmith—red-headed, with huge shoulders and chest—plodded over to a shelf directly across from her, pulled something off it, then returned to the front of the building. He pounded his hammer, making a rhythmic *ching*.

What would he do if he found her hiding in his building? Would he pummel her like that he did horseshoe? He'd have to catch her first, and surely a man that muscled couldn't run very fast. And if she was anything at all, she was fast.

Annie yawned and glanced at the door. Was it safe to leave yet?

Nah. She'd better wait until dark. Her stomach gurgled, reminding her that she hadn't eaten since early this morning, when her pa stole a loaf of bread right off someone's table. The family had been out in the barn, doing chores, and he'd walked right in as if he owned the place. He'd laughed when he told her that the only person who saw him was a baby in his cradle—and he wasn't tattling.

The sweet scent of fresh straw and leather blended with the odor of horses and manure. Annie leaned back against the wall, wincing when it creaked, then closed her eyes. She was so tired of her life. Of moving from place to place. If only her daddy could get a real job and they could live in a real house. . . .

Riley Morgan chased the boy, running until his side ached, but the little thief had disappeared. He bent and rested his hands on his knees, breathing hard as he watched the street for any sign of the pickpocket. Few people were on the streets of Waco this late. Most businesses had closed before suppertime, except the saloons. The lively tune of a piano did nothing to dampen his anger. How could he have not noticed that thief had slid his grandpa's watch right out of his pocket?

Movement drew his attention to a couple strolling arm in arm on the far side of Main Street. Maybe he should ask if they had seen the pint-sized robber, but then they only seemed to be looking at each other. Riley glanced toward the boardinghouse where his family's wagon was parked. They'd stay there tonight, then travel to their new ranch, a few miles outside of town, along a river called the South Bosque.

Riley heaved a sigh and shoved his hands into his pockets. He studied the small town that sat all cozied up to the Brazos River. He hadn't wanted to come here in the first place—and neither had his mother. Their old farm had been perfectly fine, but his father said there were new opportunities in Waco and inexpensive land, too. Riley scowled and blew a heavy breath out his nose. He hadn't wanted to leave his friends, especially Adrian Massey, a pretty neighbor girl he planned on courting once he was a few years older. He hoped that she would follow through and write to him as she promised.

His mother's tears hadn't swayed his father, though they made Riley's heart ache. She wanted to go back to Victoria where her family and the rest of the Morgans lived. But not Pa. He loved his siblings, but he had a need to be independent, to play a part in developing Texas—and now they were even farther away.

At least his pa had pacified his ma by taking her for a visit back with her family and then on to the ranch where the Morgans had been raised, so they could see his aunt and attend her wedding. Talking with his aunt Billie about her time as a captive with the Comanche had been the most interesting part of the trip—that, and seeing the beautiful Morgan horses that his uncle Jud raised. At least he could look forward to the delivery of the dozen broodmares and the young stallion his pa bought.

Staring down the street, he watched his pa take a small box off the wagon and hand it to Timothy. Riley winced, as the realization hit that he'd run off and left his little brother. Pa slowly turned in a circle, looking all around. Riley ducked into the alley. He couldn't head back without searching for that thief again. The boy had to be here somewhere, and the town wasn't all that big.

He ran his fingers through his hair, dreading seeing his father's disappointment. Riley had overheard his pa's initial objection to giving him the watch when Uncle Jud had suggested it—said that he wasn't responsible enough to have something so valuable to the family. Riley kicked a rock and sent it rolling. Why didn't his pa have more faith in him? Gritting his teeth, he had to admit he'd been right—at least in this instance. He forked his fingers through his hair and gazed down the alley, realizing that somewhere along the way he'd lost his hat too.

Half an hour later, as the sun ducked behind the horizon and cast a pink glow on the clouds, Riley headed back to the boardinghouse. Maybe if he were lucky, Timothy hadn't tattled about him losing the watch. But as much as he loved his younger brother, he knew the truth. Pa would be waiting, and he would insist on hearing the whole story. And once again, his pa would be disappointed.

A horse's whinny startled Annie and she jerked awake. During the night, she'd huddled up in a ball to stay warm and must have pulled hay over her from the empty stall on her left. She yawned and stretched, her empty belly growling its complaint. Bright shafts of sunlight drifted through the cracks on the eastern wall, and dust motes floated in the air, as thick as snow. The front door creaked open. She jumped, then ducked back behind the barrel and peered over it. Chilly air seeped through the cracks in the walls, making her wish for her blanket. She wrapped her arms tight across her chest.

Her daddy would be so mad that she'd disappeared all night.

At least this town—Waco, he had called it—was small enough she shouldn't have trouble finding him. The blacksmith plodded through the building and opened the back door, letting in a blast of cold air. Annie waited a few minutes while he fed the five horses then grabbed a bucket and headed out the back door. She tiptoed to the opening and peered outside. The large man walked toward the river then bent down, lowering the pail into the water. Annie spun around and raced to the front door, peeked out, then dashed down the street and into the first alley she came to. Would her daddy be upset with her for being gone so long? Would he wallop her? Keeping as close to the buildings as possible, she hurried back to the spot she'd last seen him.

Three long days later, Annie nibbled on the moldy bread crust she'd dug out of someone's trash heap and gazed out over the small town from the tree she had climbed. Her pa had up and left her—as he'd threatened on so many occasions when she hadn't returned to their meeting spot with enough stolen goods.

She watched people coming and going, doing their Saturday shopping. Mamas held the hands of their youngsters and stood chatting with other women or walking between shops. Men compared horses, checking their hooves and sometimes their teeth. And the girls all wore dresses—some prettier than others—but dresses all the same. Her eyes stung. One man swung his daughter up in his arms, and even from so far away, Annie could see her smile. She rubbed her burning eyes. Her daddy wasn't much of a family, but he was better than none at all—most of the time, anyway.

She swung on a nearby branch and dropped to the ground. With so many folks around, she should blend in. Hurrying past the livery and several other buildings, she stopped only to dip her hand in the horse trough for a quick drink, then continued to the far end of Waco. The house she aimed for sat a short ways out of town. She'd been there the past two days, drawn by the delicious aroma of baking bread and the children's happy squeals.

Squatting down next to a sparse shrub, she peered through the wooden fence at the house she'd dreamed about—the one she longed to live in. Two stories, white with a dark roof, half a dozen rocking chairs on the porch, and even a few flowers out front, in spite of the chill that still lingered at night.

The children, all younger than she was, were an oddity, though. They walked around, holding their hands out in front of them, feeling their way along knotted ropes that lined the path. She decided they must be blind, just like some of the beggars she'd seen in New Orleans.

But these children wore nice clothes without ragged hems and torn sleeves, and their cheeks were rosy, and smiles lit the faces of most of them. Annie shook her head. What kind of person was she to be jealous of the blind?

The youngsters felt their way to the far side of the house, and Annie stooped down and ran around back. The odor of something delicious wafted out the back door. Someone inside banged cooking pots.

Annie hunkered down behind a rain barrel. A barn sat a short ways behind the house. Maybe she could sleep there tonight.

The back door opened, and a pretty woman who reminded Annie of her mama glided down the steps in a bright blue dress. Her yellow hair was piled up on the back of her head. Annie tugged at her short, plain brown hair. It had never been long enough to put up like that—not after her pa hacked it away with his knife. Besides, she wouldn't know how to fix it anyway.

Fragrant odors drifted toward Annie. Her stomach moaned a long complaint.

The woman clapped her hands. "Children, time for lunch."

As one, the youngsters turned toward her voice, carefully feeling their way toward her. Would anyone notice if she sneaked inside with them?

She glanced down at her dirty hands and fingernails. Her pants stunk, and her head itched. Maybe those kids couldn't see her, but they sure would be able to smell her.

The idea she'd been chewing on for two days sounded better and better. Those children had everything she wanted—they were clean, had decent clothes, ate regular meals, and lived in the house she wanted.

Come morning, she'd be sitting on the front porch. And if she had to pretend to be a blind orphan in order to be taken in—so be it.

A Morgan Family Series

paperback 978-0-8024-0583-8

eBook 978-0-8024-7873-3

LONE STAR TRAIL

After Wande Fleischer's fiancée marries someone else, the young fraulein determines to make new life for herself in Texas. With the help of Jud's sister Marion, Wande learns English and becomes a trusted friend to the entire Morgan family.

As much as Jud dislikes the German invasion, he can't help admiring Wande. She is sweet and cheerful as she serves the Lord and all those around her. Can the rancher put aside his prejudice to forge a new future? Through Jud and Wande, we learn the powerful lessons of forgiveness and reconciliation among a diverse community of believers.

paperback 978-0-8024-0585-2

eBook 978-0-8024-7876-4

THE LONG TRAIL HOME

When Riley Morgan returns home after fighting in the War Between the States, he is excited to see his parents and fiancée again. But he soon learns that his parents are dead and the woman he loved is married. He takes a job at the Wilcox School for the Blind just to get by. He keeps his heart closed off but a pretty blind woman, Annie, threatens to steal it. When a greedy man tries to close the school, Riley and Annie band together to fight him and fall in love.

But when Riley learns the truth about Annie, he packs and prepares to leave the school that has become his home.

www.RiverNorthFiction.com

www.MoodyPublishers.com